# Pages for her

Sylvia Brownrigg is the author of seven books of fiction, including *Pages for You* and *The Delivery Room*. Her work has been included in the *New York Times* Notable Books and the *LA Times* Best Books of the Year. Her reviews have appeared in the *New York Times*, the *Guardian*, and the *TLS*, and she has taught at the American University in Paris. Her novel for children, *Kepler's Dream* (published under the name Juliet Bell), has been made into an independent feature film. She lives in Berkeley with her family, and continues to spend time in London.

*Also by Sylvia Brownrigg*

Morality Tale
The Delivery Room
Pages for You
The Metaphysical Touch

# Pages for her

Sylvia Brownrigg

PICADOR

First published 2017 by Picador

This paperback edition first published 2018 by Picador
an imprint of Pan Macmillan
20 New Wharf Road, London N1 9RR
Associated companies throughout the world
www.panmacmillan.com

ISBN 978-1-5098-3108-1



1 3 5 7 9 8 6 4 2

A CIP catalogue record for this book is available from the British Library.

Printed and bound by CPI Group (UK) Ltd, Croydon, CR0 4YY

*for a friend who died*
*and for a friend who breathes*

# PART ONE
## September

# 1

There was no fall in California, and this had forever been a problem for Flannery. September was hardly a marker of anything, it just ran doggedly on from August and erupted erratically into stifling heatwaves that, when she was a child, people would call *Indian summers.* (Words were less worried over, then.) The Bay Area's climate baffled even its natives by running cold then hot then cold again; not fickle like a lover so much as grandly indifferent to people's comfort or convenience. Fleece-thick fog gave way at random hours to a sudden burning sun, and winterish layers had to be shed for bare skin to better tolerate the abrupt new warmth.

You might get used to it, but Flannery Jansen never had. She had grown up along the chaparral-covered and forested peninsula of the San Francisco Bay, so had a girlhood to adjust herself before she headed eastwards for university and adulthood. Now thirty-eight years old and the mother of a young child, Flannery had moved back to San Francisco, where the morning cold still bit her bones and she missed the sultry evenings of the east.

She should have acquired a feel for this weather and its patterns; an ease with its ambiguities, an indulgent shrug toward the sibling rivalry between fog and sun. Somehow, though, other difficulties distracted her, and Flannery found herself wrong-footed every summer and into autumn. Six years earlier she had been heavily pregnant in this season, and she had a weighty memory of waddling around in a sweat brought on by the October surprise of a ninety-degree day. Wearing black, and melting.

She had known a different cityscape once. Streets with leaf-shedding trees, faux-gothic buildings, celebrated libraries, and scholars of a hundred stripes and stars. A geography she associated with the opening of her mind and body, and the much philosophized problem between the two. A college campus where broad old elms and maples burst into colour (not flames, or tears) every fall, showering Flannery and her fellows with beauty, and promises of the harsh but stimulating winter to come.

Flannery had loved that place, and she had especially loved the autumns there. It was a climate that communicated with her northern European blood and reminded the ancestors nestled within her of their dark, dense breads, their stark churches, their impending snowfalls. Since then fall rituals, even simple ones, the kind you keep without recourse to calendars, trusting the clock within, seemed sacred to Flannery – from the buying of new notebooks and pens for the start of school, to the putting away of summer's vacation gear, and the sobriety of starting to learn again.

One September morning, Flannery left her home on Ashbury, a sloped, once hippied street in San Francisco. The fog clung cold, like an unshakeable regret, and Flannery found yet again that she had miscalculated. Rushing out the door to get her daughter to school, Flannery had donned only a light cotton top, leaving her chilled and exposed. She dropped off Willa – who waved back at her, happy and jacketed, from the sidewalk, because somehow as a mother you are smarter about your child's clothing than you are about your own – then drove to a nearby coffee shop to warm up. Flannery took her laptop in to revivify herself with more caffeine, and the morning's first hit of email.

As rituals go, opening email wasn't much, but waiting for Flannery in the unfathomable pixels of her machine was a message from someone at that distant university, on the other side of the country, in New Haven. Yale. The same one she had attended as an undergraduate.

The note was an invitation. And Flannery, who had become heavy-blooded with an unnamed despondency these recent years, felt for the first time in a long while the quickening of her pulse, and a looking forward to something, a possibility in the future.

# 2

Dear Ms Jansen

– the email began in its bland, black on grey tones.

It was the kind of missive you should read walking slowly up from the mailbox to your home (if your home weren't so fraught), shaking the letter free from its envelope, which drifted down to the stone steps without your even noticing. The city's distinctive mist would lend its drama to the occasion as you inhaled sharply, aware that your life was about to take an important turn.

Instead, here was Flannery at the bustling brown coffee shop with the punning name (Bean There, Done That, though it could as easily have been Common Grounds, or Café Olé), where entitled customers broadcast their coffee requests with precise specifications, and selected the worthiest scone from a windowed display of candidates. Seated at a counter, a suited professional spoke angrily into her cell phone, castigating someone about the delay in her insurance reimbursements; at a table near Flannery a young white man sat, styled in the studied casual of tech workers, his hands folded in the supplicant position, as he awaited an older Indian man for what looked like a job interview.

> I'm writing from the Alumni Association. Recently we've been organizing more events on campus focused on women graduates, to inspire current students. I apologize for the late notice here but we have been putting together a three-day conference in October (19–21) called 'Women Write the World' and we are hoping you might be able to join us. Professor Margaret Carter of the English Department will be chairing the conference. We've got a great line-up of participants already, including . . .

A woman in her twenties who had recently had a hot flush of success with a sexually adventurous novel set in Thailand. (Li Mayer.) The well-heeled Bostonian who produced exquisite sentences and had won honours and plaudits. (Bishop. Flannery had worked hard not to envy her.) A television comedy writer (Chatterjee); the nation's Poet Laureate (Jefferson); one brainy journalist who had produced the definitive work on Stalin's gulags, and another who wrote a weekly political column for the *New York Times*. (Kessler, Green.) Yes, yes, yes. Flannery knew this roster, the gist if not every particular. It had been that kind of university. The great and the good attended it – winners of races, climbers of ladders, tappers up against the glass ceiling. Yes, those too. Women undergraduates had been permitted through Yale's gates since 1969, though still struggled to have the faculty representation and fat slices of power that the institution's men had. Hence, of course, this conference. *Here we are: us girls! See how we've done!*

Such politics were not central to Flannery these days. As an agitating twenty-something she had carried placards along the National Mall, protesting about women's rights and freedom of choice, but lately the collective she poured her time into was made up of just three – and was mixed, in age and gender. From where she sat now, in Bean There, Done That, Flannery saw her younger activist self through a backward telescope, tiny and out of scale. The idea of appearing professionally, in a guise other than as the driver attached to her daughter or a softening embellishment to her husband, appealed to Flannery, and she was flattered to be asked, but her first reaction on reading the dates and location focused on logistics: how could she get there? Who would look after Willa? And what kind of resistance should Flannery expect from Charles to the prospect of her flying across the country for a gathering called *Women Write the World*? ('Do they?' she could imagine her husband challenging, with mock solemnity. 'It's a big world. That's a lot to write.')

Such were the dreary cogs that started turning in her mind, before another item stopped all the machinery cold. Then warm.

At the last name she saw on the list.

Moderating the proceedings . . .

There followed a name so vibrant to Flannery that it appeared to pulse in some foreign colour on her screen, pomegranate red or a sleek jade green, not the black on grey of the others.

Professor Anne Arden.

A woman she once knew.

# 3

A hand touched her elbow. Flannery startled.

'Hi!'

A short, busty figure whose shape was mauvely emphasized by clingy yoga clothes, her hair pulled back in a neon hair tie and her skin simultaneously freckled and tan, stood next to Flannery, panting slightly, though in an amiable way.

'Flannery, right? How *are* you?' She gestured to her own shoulder. 'It's Wendy – from the moms' group.' She grinned in encouragement, then added forgivingly, 'It's been a couple of years.'

'Oh, right!' Flannery returned the smile and pulled her laptop screen half down, modestly, as if it were a revealing garment, then tried to wipe from her face the heat brought on by Anne Arden's name. 'Gosh. How are you? How's –' Flannery felt a surge of satisfaction that she could retrieve the child's name, though she wasn't sure she could have picked him out of a toddler line-up – 'Eli?'

'He's terrific. We're at the Franklin School now, and we're really loving it.'

'That's great.'

'Yeah. Where are you?'

'We're at Alpine.' It was like the *we* of pregnancy: collective pronouns were how you referred to familial situations. Parenting, Flannery learned early, was spoken of as a team sport.

'How do you like Alpine? We looked at it for Eli.'

'Did you? It's a nice school. You know . . .' Flannery nodded. Willa's education was a matter of essential interest to Flannery, whose love for her daughter was fierce and sustaining and for whom she would have lain down under a train, if it would help her, or married a man she shouldn't have, or attended a weekly 'moms' group' meeting in the early years. Still, she seemed suddenly empty of scholastic adjectives. 'They're good people.'

'We were a little worried.' Wendy winced awkwardly. 'That it might not be academic enough.'

As if to make up for this remark, Wendy launched into an ostensibly modest account of an elaborate art project her first grader was hard at work on, which she eye-rollingly called *crazy ambitious* – that kind of maternal boast masquerading as complaint Flannery recognized. The assignment had something to do with Frida Kahlo, and self-portraits that included the children and their favourite animal. 'Of course, Eli had to choose his *tree frog*, which is cute but incredibly hard to draw . . .'

Flannery yawned.

Widely, inadvertently. It was a genuine yawn, not staged, but the rudeness of it disturbed her and she immediately shook her head and laugh-apologized. 'I'm so sorry!' she said, making a vague excusatory gesture at the laptop, as if her boredom were due to the computer. Through no fault of the friendly Wendy, Flannery had found instantly exhausting this exchange about their children and their schools and their teachers and their classes. All Flannery wanted to do that minute was travel her willing memory back to the territory of her own former school, former teacher, former class. She wanted to focus on the invitation to visit her old university, and the chance to meet Professor Arden.

Her Anne.

'Gosh, I didn't mean to interrupt your work.' Wendy's smile was a little thinner, as she cast a slightly jealous glance at the machine. Flannery doubted whether Wendy had much idea of Flannery's work, as one of the dislocating elements of the moms' group had always been that its members were stripped of their previous clothing as lawyers, educators, designers, writers. They were all just *moms*. That Flannery had authored two books was of less import to her fellow moms than the fact that at the age of three Willa had liked to eat olives and mushrooms, which was thought to be extraordinary and precocious.

'No, not at all,' Flannery lied, but she did lift the laptop lid back up purposefully. Then, in that way of confessions made impulsively to near strangers, Flannery added, 'I've just been asked to go to a writers' conference on the East Coast next month. It would be really good to go, but I'm trying to figure out if I can manage it. You know. Spousal relations. Childcare . . .'

'Getting away is hard, isn't it?' Wendy sympathized, and Flannery glimpsed the possibility that this well-adjusted-seeming mother might have yearnings and frustrations of her own.

'It is,' Flannery agreed. 'Getting away is hard.'

# 4

Charles would object.

Flannery saw this from the first moment in Bean There, Done That, the knowledge hitting her almost simultaneously to her reading the email invitation.

Flannery's husband – and that too seemed an improbable word to attach to herself, 'husband', something Flannery Jansen had never expected to have, or to hold – was an artist. Charles Marshall. His work was widely known, out in the world and close to home, too, where an installation of his enlivened a recently revamped terminal at the San Francisco airport. Charles Marshall (never Charlie or Chuck, unless you wanted to irritate him) was a big man: big appetites, and the girth that went with them; big creations, and big emotions, not all of them positive. When tall, broad, goateed Charles was in a benevolent mood, he was loud, funny, warm, and generous, a showman, a story-teller, a circus master. When he was angry, the windows rattled and the lights flickered, and small animals retreated to their warrens until the rage had spent itself, and the city's workers had cleared the debris from the streets.

Charles Marshall did not, Flannery knew, think of himself as a man who would object to his wife's travelling to the East Coast for a writers' conference. An *all women* writers' conference. Certainly not. How could he mind? He was an artist too, and progressive, a good husband and a doting father who would delight in having a few days on his own to take care of his sweet little muffin, his six-year-old daughter. He was not any sort of ogre. He was a good-natured, cooperative, supportive man.

'That's a bad time for me.' Charles shook his head, though his words were somewhat garbled by a mouthful of spanakopita. Flannery had decided to run the travel idea by Charles right away, and, as a mood enhancer, she had cooked something interesting. Occasionally, Flannery took to kitchen consolations. Making spanakopita was a kind of inside joke (for a party of one), having had the Greek salad days of her college years so vividly in mind since that morning cafe correspondence. Willa asked for more water as she tried to make the fork do its work on the salty feta and filo dough. Charles swallowed, then repeated more clearly, 'October's going to be a bad time.'

More than usual? Flannery wondered, as she got up to refill her daughter's water glass. Charles could sit still through half a dozen such requests without apparently hearing them. 'Why?' Flannery asked levelly.

'*One.*' Charles stuck a blunt thumb up in front of him, like a maverick politician. 'I've got to finish that piece that's going to Detroit. They want it by Thanksgiving, and the woman I'm dealing with there is a pain in the ass. *Two.*' Up went the index finger, and he tilted his hand, making an L. 'That kid Lowell, Michael's son, is coming to start "helping" me in the studio in a few weeks, but you know what that means, there are bound to be fuck-ups at the beginning. He'll probably set the place on fire or gouge someone's eye out. *Three . . .*'

But Flannery chose not to look at her husband's middle finger as it prepared to help him enumerate a third difficulty.

Instead, she half turned in her chair to face her daughter across the table, and smiled with a seizure of love into that dear, concentrating, squirrel-cheeked face.

# 5

Flannery was thirty when she met Charles Marshall at an opening in San Francisco. It was a milling around, wine-drinking, opinion-scattering affair set on several floors of Geary Street galleries – neon acrylic smears hanging in one room, surreal porcelain masks displayed in another – that her roommate had taken Flannery to in order to force her out of a motionless glummery.

'Come *on*, Jansen.' Susan Kim had known Flannery since they were in their late, matriculating teens, and had been drawn to each other because they both sensed something tough and fibrous in the other under the mass of freshman mush. 'We've got to get you out of here.'

Flannery had gone so far already, these recent years; she was not sure she could go a single step further.

She had left home at seventeen, flown over many flyover states to attend a famous and foreign university. Once there, she had waded far and wide and deep into love. (The furthest she had ever gone. *Her Anne.*) After graduating, she had gotten a job in publishing and moved to New York, in order to prove to a woman she was no longer even in touch with that she could take on that never-sleeping city. A couple of years later she made the decision to adventure across Mexico for a year with a girlfriend, a trip which culminated in an encounter with a garrulous, ageing American hippie in San Miguel de Allende who happened to be Flannery's father Len, a parent she had never previously met. She had returned to New York and, at twenty-five, gone so far as to do what she had always meant to do: write. She produced a wry, racy memoir of the girls' circuitous odyssey and that fraught paternal meeting. *A Visit to Don Lennart*, a book of wit and raunch and many-pixelled vividness, spent months on the bestseller list and handed Flannery her quarter hour of fame. Under duress, she had pushed herself to appear on television and radio to talk about herself and her story, a degree of exposure that Flannery had foolishly not anticipated, and which led to a strange interior dislocation. She began to find herself hard to find. Still in motion, Flannery carried on to write a second book, because everyone told her to while she was still *hot* – as if her name were a potato, or a pizza – but this second was a novel with subdued characters set in a remote and not quite real California, pulled from some mournful place within her and in which she deliberately chose to avoid any autobiographical elements. After Flannery finally clawed her way back from the dark dream of its composition she learned that the book had gone largely unread, consigned to the death heap of fictions deemed to be *quiet*. By this point fairly unmoored, Flannery went a little crazy and cheated on her girlfriend Adele, who had been her companion in Mexico and had anyway never recovered from the shock of being turned into a character in her lover's pages. Flannery drifted into the deserved, expected, but nonetheless distressing breaking apart of that relationship. She had finally, in a combination of resignation and surrender, retreated to San Francisco to recover, the best part of which was that she could live again with her old college roommate Susan Kim, who now worked at a boutique fashion designer's and was as stylish, smart and impatient as she had always been.

'I can't move a millimetre. I'm exhausted,' Flannery protested from the chic second-hand daybed by the window. 'Wake me up when it's time to vote for the president.' But Susan, undeterred, dragged her out anyway, with the authority of a decade-old friendship and to thwart Flannery's desire to stay in watching an entire season of a television show about the mob. Susan made Flannery dress, and dress presentably. 'You're getting some oxygen. Like it or not, lady.'

And there, under gallery lighting, in a room with stark, gorgeous desert photographs Flannery mistakenly thought were his, she met the artist Charles Marshall, a large and charismatic man, who with his stories and attention took her far away from herself – which was precisely where Flannery Jansen wanted to be.

# 6

Charles charmed her, compelled her, pursued her.

His beard was a deep animal brown that matched his warm dark eyes, and his laugh was like a punctuating blast from the orchestra's brass section. He found Flannery amusing, and himself too, as he unspooled practised, theatrical tales of his exotic life in a world Flannery knew little of – galleries, studios, commissions. The humour in his stories came from his sharp eye for surreal detail ('So we open this gargantuan box and under a thousand peppermint-green Styrofoam popcorn nuggets find this exquisite little eagle skull, the size of a walnut') and neat way of puncturing inflated egos, if not always his own ('So the guy's standing there holding his champagne flute talking about the St Kitt's wedding he went to and *flinging* names down, all the pop stars and moguls who were there. It was like celebrity confetti, you couldn't even see the ground around him for all the names he'd dropped'). Flannery could sense the energy and wit in Charles's art mirrored in these performances. The scale on which Charles Marshall created, along with the sheer dimensions of his success – in the nineties he was the American Pavilion's featured artist at the Venice Biennale – reassured Flannery. He was large enough to shelter her after her own overexposure (her skin still felt pink and peeling from the experience with *A Visit to Don Lennart*, as if she'd been irradiated by all the attention) and more than that, to dwarf with his notoriety the very brief period of hers.

'Flannery Jansen?' Charles Marshall laughed, shaking her hand, engulfing hers with his supple and substantial paw. 'The author of the book about Mexico?'

She nodded, oddly surprised that this man knew of it. Hadn't she seen gossip page pictures of him with an indie film star on his arm? And maybe years before that, when she was still in college, a reference somewhere to his lavish wedding to an East Coast heiress?

'Sex in the saguaro patch. Right?'

Flannery nodded again with a practised smile. The saguaro patch always came up. 'The single best-known thing about me,' she said with mock ruefulness, pushing her sandy hair behind her ear. 'It's like my signature tune, that scene – it follows me wherever I go.'

'But you knew it would. Right?' The man had not quite let go of Flannery's hand. 'Two girls going at it, fuelled by tequila – a great steamy scene, and cactus spines to be extracted afterwards, bringing it back to comedy. Come on! It had everything.'

Flannery agreed obligingly, and then Charles issued his brief brass laughter and she, disarmed, found herself joining him. She had had this scene quoted back to her a hundred times, yet somehow in his telling it seemed comical to her again, and better than that – forgivable.

They were standing close enough by then that Flannery could smell him, and something stirred in her. Charles Marshall had the scent of real stuff about him – oil, paint, wood, steel – unlike all the writers she knew who gave off the air of nothing more substantive than neurosis, perhaps the lingering aura of a struggle with language. She was tired of writers, herself included. They did not build. They needed no muscles. Their hands were scrawny, and lacked strength.

Lust travelled between Charles and Flannery in the gallery. It was dense enough that you could almost touch it, and Flannery, young though she still could be, was old enough to recognize that they both intended to satisfy their desire.

# 7

This affair was not, if you had been reading Flannery's life closely, a complete surprise.

As she had recognized in the early days of her adulthood, not long before she introduced Adele to her dear, puzzled mother (who did not want to be *negative*, she just wanted to *understand*), Flannery had known attractions to men as well as to women. Flannery had gone to bed with a few, even. The tall and rangy contractor guy. That notorious poet. Ill-advisedly, her publicist on the paperback of *Don Lennart*. She could be drawn to men; she had just never been drawn in by a man.

Charles Marshall drew Flannery into him, and he did not let go. He almost smothered her, with his size and his personality and his disproportionate gifts. He showered her with offerings, flowers and jewellery and clothing and, even more persuasively for Flannery, small Charles Marshall originals: a tiny ingenious bicycle built of beat-up ballpoint pen casings and two old typewriter ribbon wheels, with a banner that said *love story* across its handlebars; a headband of interwoven shot silk and oxidized silver with a card attached that said *to my Beauty*.

Strangely, Flannery found that she did not mind being smothered, and she did not object to the inundation of splendid gifts. ('The guy's a genius,' said Susan Kim, somewhat awed. 'I may have to steal some of his designs for my boss.') After the artificial public self Flannery had had to create for the promotion of her memoir, it was a relief to disappear into the encompassing embrace of Charles Marshall. ('Charles Marshall, honey?' her mother said, when Flannery eventually confided in her. '*The* Charles Marshall?') Truly grateful, Flannery reciprocated in the way she was best able to at that time: she gave up every inch of her lithe body to him, handing over to Charles all the pleasure he had the hunger and the energy to take.

The lust between them was intense and mutual and all but unquenchable, for a time. Charles was the opposite of all that Flannery had wanted before and perhaps that mirrored inversion generated some of the heat of the attraction, like a magnifying glass focusing solar rays. The man was large, a heavy breather, a snorer, a guffawer. Previously Flannery had loved the petite, the tactful and the elegant – her first great love having embodied those qualities most purely – though anyone Flannery loved had also to have a straight spine, and a strong nerve. When Charles and Flannery made love, the man announced himself like an important guest at a party when on the threshold of climax, and Flannery came to relish those announcements.

There was conversational texture between them, too, their talk a colourful thread along which were strung bright beaded nights of sex. It was when Charles started to share stories of his early New York years, before his success, his scrappy early marriage long before the heiress ('my very first wife,' he called the New Yorker jokingly; 'we were kids, we were pups, we scratched and bit each other because we didn't know any better') that Flannery started to feel the shape of the man beside her, and a tenderness toward him surfaced, which only enhanced her attraction. Flannery noticed, with the surprise you have at finding a new wrinkle or mole on your body, the desire within herself to protect the great Charles Marshall. How crazy was that? That she, Flannery Jansen, author of one hit book and one not, believed she might somehow tend to this famous man who commanded steel and aluminum, men and machines, art critics and dealers? That she did, as a matter of fact, want that job?

People experiment in romance in so many ways. They need to leave themselves behind, or complement themselves, finding substance in the areas where they feel empty. They risk similarity, or difference. They find their twin, or their opposite. They seek loves of different ages or creeds, nationality or skin hue, to rub up against the expectations of their family or culture or simply to create roughness and traction in their own interior. Montagues want Capulets, Janes their Rochesters. Flannery Jansen might once have made sweaty, urgent love under a saguaro cactus with a willowy Nordic girl named Adele, who was frequently mistaken for her sister, but at thirty she was in a rolling, rollicking affair with the heavy, hearty artist Charles Marshall.

Opposites attract? Yes, Charles was Flannery's opposite. A man with arresting charms and pungent faults, loud virtues and quiet failings, just like anyone else; but also, point by point, a person like a study in everything Flannery, in her native self, preferred not to be. On she went, though, taking and acing it, the Charles Marshall course. Swallowing new knowledge. Earning an A.

# 8

The knife-edges of sexuality.

Separations fine and sharp between the two sides.

Flannery was thinking about the issue as she walked up from the arts college on Dolores Street where she taught part-time, to the house Charles owned in the Haight, where she was spending more and more evenings, and mornings, and portions of the day. It was a steep climb, then a cresting of the hill and a saunter back down near Buena Vista Park. There was plenty of opportunity for vertigo.

She imagined an interlocutor, an interviewer, quizzing her.

Off one edge of the blade: your newfound passion for a man requires suppressing your previous yearnings for a woman. Are you in denial? What about Anne, or Adele?

Off the other edge: your engagements with lesbian lovers did always mean not acknowledging your equally real heterosexual feelings. Were you in denial? (Adele had been wary of that drift in Flannery; at points in their travels Flannery had flirted with men with a little too much intention, and Adele had nipped at her afterwards, in jealousy.)

Bisexuality, though – as a word or a label, as a principle, as anything other than a simple, ubiquitous, under-spoken truth about the human heart – satisfied nobody. To Flannery it had always sounded like a science project, and not the prize-winning kind. It confused people. You were better off disavowing it, just as retaliatory parents sometimes disavowed their gay children, or gay friends coolly shook their heads over one of their own who stepped out with the opposite sex. (*Hasbian!*) To describe yourself that way made you seem shifty and indecisive, like an independent voter. *Pick a party! Pick a side! Come on, your allegiance matters.*

Flannery's heart was pounding at this point in her walk, as she neared the top of Seventeenth Street, and the city was spreading out behind her. If she turned around, she could see the Castro melting into the Mission District, whose *taquerías* and *mercados* were losing ground to tech-influenced joints like single-drip coffee purveyors and chic design shops. Past the Mission, looking east, there were still the shipyards, and beyond them the grey and mobile Bay, flecked with vessels.

And what about the guys?

Flannery breathed. Panted, a little. (Really, she ought to be fitter than this.)

What, specifically, about this particular guy, the one she had met?

Was Charles the kind of straight man who hankered after watching two women make love, perhaps so he could enter the fray at some point and helpfully assist – a *Penthouse* letters type? Adele had been certain, rightly or wrongly, that there were plenty of those. Or did Charles nurture an ambition to conquer and convert a nice lesbian, like missionaries in African nations hoping to bring Christ's blessings to the uninitiated? Or was Charles rather – this had to be a possibility – simply a confident person, at home in his ample masculine self, who accepted the complexities of sexuality and was as content to hear about Sapphic love as any other kind?

Flannery was thinking of a conversation the two of them had had the night before, at a bar at the edge of the Castro District, near her apartment. Several gay men drank together, generally muscled and tattooed, while two women leaned toward one another heatedly over bottles of Dos Equis. Charles and Flannery noticed the women at the same time, and each took a sip from their own brews.

'Do you miss . . . that?' Charles asked unexpectedly, tilting his chin in the direction of the women's table.

Flannery blinked. *That?* Having a drink with a girl, or trading jokes with her? Making love to a girl? What precisely was Charles asking? Flannery took a pull of her beer, pondering possible answers, but was relieved of the need to try any of them.

'I mean . . .' Charles continued. 'I get it. You know?' He looked serious, and sympathetic, so Flannery nodded apprehensively. Then a light flickered in Charles's eyes. 'You may not realize this, but . . . I was a lesbian once, too.'

This Flannery had not expected. She laughed with relief. 'You know,' she parried, 'that doesn't surprise me.'

'You felt the vibe, right?'

'I totally did.'

'I figured.' Charles nodded.

'Besides,' Flannery shrugged. 'All the best people were.'

'Apparently!'

'Though . . .' Flannery pushed it further. 'That thinking seems, you know, binary. Straight, gay. Like you have to be one or the other.'

'Ah hah. Kind of virgin/whore, you mean?'

'Well, I didn't really mean that! But . . . sure.' Flannery was enjoying this. 'Right. Are you a prude, or just cautious? In touch with your desire, or a nymphomaniac?'

'Easy . . .' Charles ventured, with a satyr's grin. 'Or hard?'

'Dry or wet?'

'Top or bottom?'

'They want you to choose one,' Flannery said, a little drunkenly, and with a hint of melancholy. She could not have said who *they* were. 'You have to choose.'

It wasn't conventional foreplay, but it got the two of them pretty worked up. They drained their beers and then Charles drove them back up to his house, where they fully explored together the possibilities of the heterosexual option.

# 9

There was a perfectly pleasing place this exciting outlier relationship might have taken in the unfolding narrative of Flannery's life: a round roll of adventure, a brush with art celebrity, a sexual exploration; a lush indulgence of gifts and pleasure and bodies and surprise. From there you would have expected its slowing, and then its probable ceasing, as the personality differences finally made themselves felt.

Charles was older than Flannery by fifteen years, but there was an exoticism in that too. Flannery felt at sea but not unpleasantly so, as if she were on a cruise ship filled with people of some remote English-speaking nationality. Scots, perhaps, or Australians. Charles could enthral a table with the stories he told in his jovial baritone, while Flannery's stories flowed through her fingertips, and on the whole she mumbled. When she joined Charles with his studio assistants out at a favoured Italian joint, she was most comfortable listening to the men laugh; when the gathering was around his own oversized table she found herself *doing what women do*, assembling and serving the food. It gave her a way not to have to talk or perform. Charles's eye for colours and dimensions meant he was great to see the world with, like a chatty camera – 'Look at the way that woman in line is holding her dog, like it's a sweater she's pulling close, to stay warm' – while Flannery was more of an old-fashioned solvent, taking weeks or months to develop what she had observed. Charles marked his environment, mobilizing people and materials to change the landscape, while all Flannery commanded were the creatures of her own imagination, and she sometimes felt her feet left a faint tread.

It was several months after their autumn meeting at the gallery night, and Flannery had decided simply to enjoy herself. Why not? She did not have to overthink everything. She could simply follow this dalliance to its end. Until then she was a tourist of a foreign lifestyle: fancy restaurants, art openings, heterosexuality. *So this is how they live!* It transpired that a man and a woman on the street together were invisible to the world, and for Flannery, who had always hated to be watched or even noticed as two women together tended to be (the familiar stranger's double-take: *Which one is the . . . oh, they* both *are!*), this was an unexpected reprieve. She felt as though she had been permitted into one of those country clubs she had previously considered snooty and boring, but it had turned out to be good fun (they had an air hockey table!) and have great facilities (so many clean towels, and fantastic water pressure in the showers!). This straightness made her feel older. At last she was introduced to the way Regular People coupled. Partnered. Made love. This club had existed for millennia, and finally she was, temporarily at least, a member. As long as she could leave again after, all would – probably – be well.

Then she got pregnant.

Late January, a chill San Francisco winter, all light greys and subdued browns, even the Golden Gate Bridge dulled down to a flat, parochial orange – and inside Charles's house on Ashbury Street in San Francisco, and within his black modernist bathroom, the plastic stick showed two hot pink, unexpected lines.

This happened with straight sex. Flannery had heard of it. Novels, romances, salacious newspaper articles, movies – they all mentioned this. It was a plot device, a soap opera staple, a career changer or reputation smircher; a punishment, or a miracle, or a reward. Women got pregnant after having sex with men, sometimes.

*Right.*

Once, after she and Adele broke up, Flannery had briefly dated an amusing buck-toothed English woman, who used the phrase about someone, 'She fell pregnant.' At the time, Flannery, who loved to hold strange expressions in her fingers like samples of exotic fabric, to test their weave and their texture, commented on the comedy of the words, as she saw them – as if pregnancy were an affliction, like an illness, that you picked up by accident. As if it sent you off in some sort of swoon.

Now, suddenly, fearfully, Flannery was not laughing.

She had fallen.

# 10

How could Flannery be so smart, and simultaneously so stupid?

It was one of her own enduring questions about her character, from the time she was a bright kid in her fifth-grade class and the teacher's pet, yet wrote a sarcastic note about an assignment that got her sent to the principal's office (could she not have foreseen that the joke would misfire?), to her failure to predict, on the elaborately planned Mexico trip, just how rattled and wild it would make her to meet, at last, her father.

What had she imagined – a quick coffee then she and Adele would be on their way? Why would Flannery go to the extensive trouble of finding her unknown father in the first place if she didn't think it would rearrange her interior, as it did? Yet as the two women got ready to encounter Len Jansen at the bohemian hotel bar he had suggested, Adele fretted over what they should wear, and whether they should act like friends or lovers, to which questions Flannery replied with uncharacteristic hardness, 'What does it matter? The guy will be too stoned to notice, probably. And we won't stay long.' Even Flannery could hear how unFlanneryish her voice was, saying that, and she was wrong and wrong, as it turned out. The meeting might not have been a tear-jerker of reconciliation or redemption between father and daughter – Flannery was pretty sure her father understood the relationship between her and Adele, but it seemed not to fluster him – yet there was a connection between this man and herself that Flannery had not conceived of ahead of time. In their physical appearance, yes, but also in some of the turns of their thinking, unnerving enough for her that hours into the surprising conversation of that first meeting, Flannery offered up an abrupt excuse to leave. Soon after that she hit the tequila, and from there the sex by the saguaro story more or less wrote itself.

Flannery was wise yet foolish. She knew so much, and so little. 'The eternal sophomore,' she called herself in *A Visit to Don Lennart*, a book she wrote in part to understand this very contradiction.

Flannery knew she was smart. Others did too, though not instantly, which gave the discovery an element of surprise when they came upon it, like a hit of salt in a caramel dessert. Flannery was soft-voiced in conversation and not inclined to show off, yet she was not timid about making a reference or an analogy that would catch her listener's attention. At the publishing house where she worked after college, her boss, a brisk sardonic New Yorker with limited patience, once skimmed sceptically through some catalogue copy Flannery had handed her. Gradually Eleanor's frown eased, and her eyebrows raised. 'You wrote these?' she asked, as if speaking to a child prodigy. 'With the slant quote from Leonard Cohen? That little quip about mood rings? Nice work, Flannery.' Flannery had pinkened with pleasure. 'You play the sleepy Westerner well, but you've got a brain in there, haven't you?'

Sometimes. And yet: her stupidity, leaning at times into an 'accidental heartlessness' (her own phrase, again). Just as she had settled into her position at the publishing house, Flannery blindly trampled on a friendly colleague's territory by sleeping with the philandering poet the woman edited, offending the editor to the point where Flannery wondered if she ought to leave, and started to plan her Mexican adventure. Or it could be a more basic cluelessness, shown by the number of times (two) that Flannery forged a brilliant route for Adele and her to take through a strange and possibly dangerous territory, only for her to get pickpocketed later in some obvious, open market square in Guadalajara.

The ways Flannery saw and didn't see; looked ahead, yet was blindsided by what came at her.

That was the only way to explain how she could have let herself get pregnant.

It was a teenager's error. Made her feel seventeen again. Had she really thought she had matured?

There was a morning, once, soon after she arrived at Yale, when Flannery travelled what felt like a great distance from the campus (about two blocks) to find breakfast away from the many freshman eyes in the dining hall. She went into a spare, tiny diner called The Yankee Doodle and ordered from its grease-smeared menu a 'jelly omelette'. It seemed part of being in the new place – sampling the local cuisine. These crazy people from Connecticut made jelly omelettes! Why not try one?

The waitress raised a brow and smirked at the order. Flannery had misstepped. And indeed the plate that arrived, a yellow-brown slab of egg oozing sickly purple, was both ridiculous and disgusting. Had Flannery been older, she might have framed the mistake for herself forgivingly – *Oh well. I'm learning!* – but at seventeen she could only dissolve in embarrassment, particularly because the whole fiasco was observed, emerald-eyedly, by an auburn-haired woman who sat a few tables away, drinking coffee and reading.

The bad breakfast at The Yankee Doodle turned into a story of Flannery's. That act of idiocy got someone's attention, and the moment Flannery saw that beautiful reader, she was smitten. She learned that the woman was a graduate student named Anne Arden, and one day a few months later, they would start to discover everything important about each other, relish every taste and surface, savour all art and intelligence together. In the headiness of that pleasure, the jelly omelette tale became a joke and a fondness, a necessary first story in the two women's eventual heated courtship.

So there was that kind of mistake you could make in your life. The silver-lined cloud. The paint spill that tips the canvas into masterpiece. The wrong number you dial, which connects you with a person who becomes one of your most significant.

# 11

Was this pregnancy like that – a wrong number? Was Flannery at thirty-one going to start a nine-month journey to meet someone she had occasionally imagined – a pen-pal, a character – but did not yet know?

Or was this pregnancy the other kind of mistake – the dead-end error that had neither excuse nor benefit, was nothing but a blot, a crash, a rending? Was Flannery about to be torn up?

'It's not a great time for this,' Charles had nakedly said, lying back in bed one cold morning after a shot of slippery, eager intercourse followed by a hit of the blackest coffee. The drama of the situation had ignited lust in them both, but it subsided, once spent, into a chilly realism. They had known each other four months. It was not long enough to have learned how the other handled surprise, or crisis, or responsibility.

Charles frowned as he looked up at the high ceiling of his bedroom, and his goatee frowned along with him. His New York dealer had just finalized the date of a show in the spring of the following year, and his professional mind was racing along its track toward that goal: timetable, works, contacts, ambitions. Flannery's professional mind was a disused carriage on a side track, waiting.

A yellow-grey light stole weakly in through the broad sash

windows, a bashful ghost. Though not icy, San Francisco could nonetheless be bleak in January.

Flannery lay alongside Charles, moving her hand across his broad, silver-tufted torso. Stroking a wiry chest was an exotic sensation to her still; sometimes it felt like one of the most different sensual pleasures of touching a man rather than a woman. She watched the face of this person she had opened herself to again and again, a man she had allowed to come inside her body and change her life – if she chose to pursue that change. She would be altered, certainly, even if she didn't. Either way, Charles had, in the way peculiar to that sexual act, taken possession of Flannery's body. Her physical self would never be hers in the same way again.

Four months! Flannery could not believe her stupidity, nor his, at having so mangled the handling of birth control. Shouldn't he have been adept at that kind of thing? Charles professed to have been out of practice using condoms, having mostly had partners who were on the pill, and certainly Flannery could claim no expertise, but the bungling was, like the sex itself, their shared endeavour. There was a riot of confusion, yearning, and fear within Flannery, along with an incipient sickness that gave Charles's bedroom a nauseating tilt. The cruise ship image came to her mind again, though this time she thought more clearly: *I might just want to get off, next time we dock, and get back to land.*

Flannery palmed Charles's massive shoulder, pale as Venetian marble and as sturdy. She loved the sheer heft of Charles's muscles. He could lift a lot, and it showed. If she were ever trapped under a crashed car, Flannery sometimes thought, or in a collapsed building after the next big earthquake, Charles would be able to extricate her. There was a comfort in that. As she touched him, Flannery was thinking, wondering, picturing. She wanted this man who had so marked her to say the right thing to her now. She was not sure what that might be, in these compromising circumstances, but like a voice in tune she would know it when she heard it.

Charles blinked his deep coffee-brown eyes and turned back to Flannery. 'My Beauty,' he called her, and sometimes 'Venus on the half shell' and, as of a few days ago, 'Lady Madonna'. She could see a new light in his eyes, and it scared and excited her, both.

'Listen, Beauty,' he said, easing himself into Flannery's caressing hand, 'if you want to build this person, if you want to sculpt a human being, whoever it turns out to be –' and his voice was low and nearly breaking, far deeper than his customary register of joke and bluster – 'I want to be right there with you, Flannery Jansen, for the unveiling.'

He kissed her tenderly. Flannery closed her eyes. Tears collected at their corners, as some wordless image moved through her mind of Lenny, that hippie in Mexico she had to travel thousands of miles to meet, in her twenties. This father-to-be was right here. She was in his arms. He was saying he'd stay there.

Flannery opened her eyes and looked at her giant lover, half walrus, half genius, who had with her complicity brought the two of them to this precipitous edge together. It wasn't the metaphor for parenthood Flannery would have chosen – child as art piece – but what mattered was that Charles was, in his way, giving her a yes. *He had said the right thing.* Flannery kissed him back, and pulled him closer to her with a shortsighted and old-fashioned passion, along with the even more old-fashioned belief that it would somehow all work out fine.

# 12

They married, too.

Why not? Flannery was dizzy, excited, seized with a sense that she could change everything about herself in some mad, blurred tumble of adventure. It was like being at some noisy party in an unknown part of town. Do I want another glass? Of *course* I want another glass! (Wait, where are we again? Do we have a way to get home?)

She moved in with Charles, into the smart, Fauvishly shaded Victorian a few blocks up from the famed intersection of Haight and Ashbury, where hippies and itinerants still slouched toward Bethlehem, just as they had when Didion interviewed them forty years before. At the art college where she had been teaching, Flannery was so unable to discuss *maternity leave* with her boss that she simply told him she was going to finish the semester and then needed to 'take time off for some other projects'. She told her mother about the marriage ('Charles Marshall, honey? *The* Charles Marshall?'), though left the baby news for a later, rainy day. Flannery's mother was one of the three people who came to witness what Charles enjoyed calling the couple's 'shotgun wedding' at the San Francisco City Hall on Valentine's morning. Laura Jansen wore a lilac dress and carried a colourful bouquet of gerbera daisies, as if she were Flannery's flower girl. The other two in attendance were Charles's best friends, an architect and his pianist wife, who brought leis to put around the couple's necks after the ceremony. Flannery stood in the grand, gold-domed building where Dan White shot and killed Mayor Moscone and Harvey Milk, a gory fact she could not for some reason get out of her head as she took the vows and promised to do all the things you were supposed to do for your spouse. *Check, check, check. I will, I do, I promise.* (Where had the murders taken place, actually? Who first found the bodies?) The efficient Chinese American officiant was doing a steady business in marriages that day. 'People like to choose the fourteenth,' he told them, with a mild, bureaucratic smile. 'Helps husbands have an easy date to remember, so their wives don't get mad at them.' He winked.

This was the life Flannery was entering: the one where people made jokes that might have seemed fresh in the nineteen fifties, about absent-minded husbands and their nagging wives. *The ball and chain. Take my wife . . . please!*

The experience was like one of those episodic, night-long dreams. It was strange and at points surreal, drawing promiscuously on history and fantasy and odd juxtapositions, yet it had its own internal logic. Flannery was nauseous, she was pregnant, she was married, and she lived in a house – with her husband. She had become a wife and, if all went well, she would, in October, become a mother.

She found herself wondering in quiet moments, on a sloped street, in a slanting light, when she would finally wake up, and how she would feel when she did.

# 13

When she looked back on this period later, Flannery would have difficulty distinguishing between the intense nausea of her pregnancy (constant vomiting, in no way restricted to mornings and often at the most insalubrious places – a Safeway parking lot, a museum bathroom) and the dizzying extremity of her leap of faith into the arms and home of Charles Marshall.

Flannery had studied the concept of the leap of faith at college one semester, during a late adolescent foray into existential philosophy. She had been trying to regain her balance after being abandoned by Anne, and delving into explorations of being and nothingness seemed the right way to go about it. Flannery sat listening to a professor who was the spitting image of Leo Tolstoy and as irascible, who spoke chiefly to himself, it seemed, or to the imagined spirit of Søren Kierkegaard, about the paradox of Abraham's willingness to sacrifice his only son, Isaac, by God's outlandish request; the way Abraham could simultaneously be convinced he would slit his son's throat, and at the same time entrust to God that at the last instant there would be some catch and he would not have to, after all. Sitting in her self-pitying sophomore slump on a shapeless plastic chair under unflattering fluorescent lighting, Flannery was never entirely sure she *got* it, but Tolstoy gave her a good grade for the final paper she wrangled for him, so he must have thought she did. Throughout her life Flannery would find that in writing she had occasional access to wisdom or perceptions that eluded her when she spoke aloud. Or acted.

'Do you worry, though?' Flannery asked Charles one evening at their local Thai garden. They had learned a few hours earlier that the genetic testing had all looked normal, and Flannery was carrying a girl. She had been surprised by Charles's ostentatious relief at the news. 'I mean,' she tried to explain, to translate the roil of thoughts in her mind to an actual question, 'about all the sacrifice?'

Charles frowned. 'Of what?'

'You know . . . time. Freedom.' Flannery waved a forkful of green mango in the general direction of all they might be giving up. 'Independence.' Charles seemed baffled by the question. At the time Flannery found this endearing, a sign of her husband's intention to throw himself wholeheartedly into fatherhood, but later she would come to wonder whether it was simply based on assumptions they did not discuss.

'Nah.' He shook his head.

'Our ability to work. Having to take care of the baby all the time.'

'Art versus parenthood? It's a cliché, we don't need to fall into that.' He slid several morsels of chicken satay off their skewers. 'We can do this differently.'

Flannery admired his certainty. That was very Charles: sure of himself and his ability to organize the world around him in the way he wanted. She had always responded to people, men or women, who had clarity and edge. She appreciated the ability to be definite, something she often lacked. Such characters aided Flannery in her own efforts to focus the large areas of her internal blur.

'Great,' she affirmed, hoping the tasty curries and rice would not make the return journey back up her throat within the hour. 'I like your confidence. We'll do this differently. That's good! Let's do that, then.'

Flannery decided to have faith. It was a leap, yes. But really, she had already taken it.

# 14

For a time, they homesteaded.

Charles fed her, hunted and gathered for her. He provided warm, filling meals that pushed Flannery's belly further and further out. He developed a network of takeout joints from which he collected multiple boxes, and even cooked a few meals himself, eighties-inflected dishes (beef stroganoff, chicken Marbella) that earned Flannery's briefly sated gratitude.

He massaged her feet, was nice about the ugly clothes, and made sure she drank a lot of water, while he knocked back a near cellar's worth of his own preferred Cabernet. This was Charles at his best, this slow-motion lope to their child's arrival. That the man admired himself for doing these uxorious tasks was inseparable from his actually doing them. Flannery did not mind being Charles's gentle, flattering mirror because she did feel cared for, and that fed something that yawned within her. There was no sign that this man would be down in Mexico getting stoned at the time of his daughter's birth, and for that Flannery was deeply, yearningly grateful. 'I feel like I'm in *Little House on the Prairie*, or *The Waltons*,' she told Adele on the phone one day when Charles was at the studio. 'I should be out collecting eggs from the henhouse.' She and her former co-traveller, who lived in Chicago, had a friendly telephone relationship now.

Adele was quiet for a minute, then said, 'Well, you always said you used to love those shows.'

'They're so cheesy,' Flannery agreed. 'But I really did.'

For Flannery, the house was expansive after the years of apartment living, and gradually she came to feel it was less of a movie set and more her actual home. On the main floor, raised above the sloping ground level, was a broad bay window that looked out over the row of painted Victorians facing, and in the window was a long, electric-blue couch that became one of her favourite comforts.

'My first wife, Miriam, wanted us to have a baby,' Charles informed Flannery one sleepy May afternoon, when they lounged together on that couch. 'We were way too young. It would have been a disaster.' Flannery's legs stretched across Charles's lap, her puffy feet encased by his ample hands. 'Then there was this very athletic woman I dated, Rebecca. She wanted to us to have a kid together, too – I've told you about her?'

Flannery shook her head. *And you don't have to now*, she added silently, but she had learned the futility of trying to stop Charles when he had a story to tell. He fondled his beard affectionately as he recalled these waystations in his life, temporarily pausing in his attentions toward Flannery's swollen ankles.

'She was an amazon, black hair, very into yoga, before anyone else had heard of yoga except for hippies. I mean, before there were spandex outlets on every corner. Bec was *amazingly* flexible.' The memory caused Charles to pause. 'Anyway. She thought she was pregnant briefly, then miscarried. She bled, heavily. It was alarming.' Flannery felt a sharp pang of sympathy for this remote, unknown woman who had lost her potential child. 'And after that she went into this crazy pregnancy overdrive – she *had* to get pregnant, we had to have a kid together, it was a sign from the universe . . .' He shook his head, and sighed. 'I wouldn't do it. Not like that, under that kind of pressure. It was the wrong time.' Flannery marvelled at how certain he had been, and how the cold clarity of his thinking had not, she guessed, felt to him like coldness.

'Not until you, Beauty,' Charles said. His brown intelligent eyes returned to her. He had made their own story one of predestination, inevitability; which made it very close to being, actually, planned. It was up to Flannery to hold on to the small kernel of truth that it had not been. 'And the Peppercorn, of course,' the future father added, touching Flannery's swelling belly. 'Peppercorn' had been Charles's name for the creature growing within Flannery since she had early on found a chart that illustrated foetal growth by food items: peppercorn at week five, blueberry at seven, kumquat at ten. At week twelve, Flannery encouraged Charles to change his nickname to Passion Fruit, but it hadn't caught on. 'I was waiting for the two of you.'

'We're flattered,' Charles's third wife joked, placing her hands over the bump, too. She was still astonished by what was happening beneath it. 'Flattered.'

At the word *flattered* a flirtatious joke Flannery and Anne used to share surfaced suddenly in Flannery's memory. 'Flannery will get you nowhere', Anne used to say to her with mock sternness, standing half clothed, her deep red hair giving the white walls a fiery glow, as if the apartment were a den of delicious iniquity; Anne said the phrase with a slight admonishing shake of the head when she felt their affair was taking too much valuable time away from her efforts to work on her doctoral thesis or prepare for the job market. 'Oh, on the contrary,' the eighteen-year-old Flannery would reply, with the verbal swagger love makes possible, 'Flannery will get you *everywhere*.'

She smiled inadvertently at the recollection. Charles, caught up in his own reflections, did not notice, and Flannery chose not to share the memory with him. Past romances: was it always a good idea to discuss them? Not necessarily. Sometime Flannery might tell Charles about Anne (if he proved interested). But not now. For the moment that long-gone passion could stay deep within Flannery, not far from the little Passion Fruit herself – who jumped or kicked slightly just then, the first of many occasions on which the growing girl would seek to weigh in on her parents' spoken and unspoken conversations.

# 15

Before the child's arrival there was an eruption – not in itself significant, and certainly not as bad as others that followed, but it gave Flannery a preview of scenes that would one day mar her future, like ruptures in a canvas.

It was the day of Flannery's last class. She bade farewell on a fog-shrouded morning to a group of mid-twenty-year-olds of varying talents, including the multiply pierced boy who had written a smutty but smart piece about a blonde art teacher named Eudora, whom, Flannery realized only after she had graded and returned it, was probably based on herself. (Wise, yet foolish: there it was again.) Most of the young adults had shuffled out of class with muttered expressions of thanks, and Flannery was sitting at the formica desk gathering up her papers. She felt sick, as always, and fat, and brainless – she had been reading an early Iris Murdoch novel a colleague had pressed on her, which obscurely contributed to her sense of imprisonment. Had Flannery ever written, actually? Had there been any point to it, if she had?

A tall, freckled student with the awkward long neck of a giraffe approached her, his bulky grey backpack giving him an ominous stoop. Flannery looked up at him and felt a sentimental pang – *her last student.* Pregnancy made her sappy, all the time.

'Hi, Ms Jansen,' he said. 'Do you mind if I ask you something? Before you go?'

Flannery hoped it was a simple question, answerable in a few minutes. She could stretch to so little at this point. She just wanted to lie down. 'Sure,' she encouraged him, faintly.

'What's it like to have a book on the bestseller list?'

'What's it like?' The question disarmed her, though she knew that *A Visit to Don Lennart* was largely the reason people signed up for her class. She stared into the young man's face. He had bright, eager eyes, a smattering of colour on either cheek, rubbery lips slightly open with curiosity. He had written, she thought she recalled, an oddly affecting piece about a barber.

'It's . . .' she started, her muddied mind searching for the right adjective, because she wanted neither to mislead nor condescend to her student. *Surreal?* (Too easy.) *Fun?* (Only somewhat true, and lazy.) *Unexpected?* (Accurate, but it didn't tell you anything.) 'It's . . . um . . .'

A slap on the door. It swung wide open.

'*Flannery!* There you are. Jesus. Come on, we've got to go.'

Flannery and the freckled student startled. 'Sorry,' Flannery said, her face flushing, but she stood up. Was this really happening in her classroom? Being ordered out like a dawdling child?

'No problem,' the boy shrugged. 'I just—'

'I need you to come *now.*' Charles snatched Flannery's jacket from the back of the chair, and made an impatient sweeping gesture to get his wife out of the room. 'I'm not even legally parked. I don't want those fuckers to give me a ticket.'

Charles glared at the young man, as if he represented the parking authority. Flannery apologized again to her student but allowed herself to be ushered out so that as little as possible of this would be witnessed by someone else.

'It's disorienting,' Flannery threw over her shoulder hurriedly. 'In a word!' She tried to laugh, as if this were a joke, but she was too embarrassed to look the kid in the face, and see whether he had heard her.

# 16

In the car, free from eyes – not that eyes bothered Charles much, anyway; when he wanted an audience he imagined everyone seeing him, and when he didn't he believed he was invisible – Charles continued, his voice quavering with impatience. He was behind the wheel in congealing city traffic, and everyone was his enemy.

'Jeffrey's coming today. Remember? And Baer is out of town.' Jeffrey was Charles's New York dealer, Baer his studio assistant.

'Okay . . .' Flannery said slowly.

'No. It's *not* "okay" because he wants me to have come up with a line on my new work. I need you to help me with the language. You're a writer.'

'Well, I can do that, but I was teaching. You can't just—'

'Class was over. You were done. He's coming *today*, Flannery.'

'I understand. But—'

'You don't understand. You're not listening to me.' He shook his head in frustration. His teeth were gritted.

'I am listening! I just—'

'No. You're not. Because if you *were*, you'd stop nitpicking here, and realize this is *important*.'

'OK, sweetheart, but teaching is important too. It's embarrassing—'

'Oh, I embarrass you? Really?' The contempt in Charles's tone hung in the air like an industrial fume. Flannery's heart was thudding now.

'Please don't raise your voice.'

'I'm not raising my VOICE.'

'You're shouting.'

'This is such *bullshit*!' He slammed his hands down on the steering wheel, after a sudden jerking brake to avoid rear-ending the Prius in front of him. 'I'm a *man*, Flannery. This is what we sound like.'

Flannery turned her head away from her husband then, and watched San Francisco's dingy streets blur, through her wet eyes. She hated crying. It was so weak. She did not want Charles to see it (though of course she did, too).

The drive to Charles's studio continued without further conversation. If Flannery expected a softening from Charles, she would be disappointed, though at least the object of his anger shifted, to the other *jackass drivers*, one slow dog-walking pedestrian in a crosswalk (*Can you move along, Grandma?)* and the traffic engineers of this *stupid backward city*.

Flannery made herself think of something else, clear this episode from her mind. She travelled back to her appearance on the TV morning show, when she was interviewed for *Don Lennart*. The interview had been a short, confusing badminton match between herself and the two hosts, a sparkly black woman and a powder-cheeked grey-haired white guy, each feeding her easy questions that she was supposed to bat back, entertainingly. In the segment's last seconds, Flannery thought of a funny story she had forgotten to tell about Adele, one that cast her in a warm, heroic light, rather than as the comic side-kick.

'That reminds me of a time right at the beginning of our trip,' Flannery began, gathering the practised sentence in her mind. In that infinitesimal pause, though, the mascaraed hostess talked over Flannery. The seconds drained away, her cheerful summary of Flannery's book built inexorably to the commercial break, and eventually Flannery had to smile, purse her lips, and know that she had come to the end of her time on the air. Adele had been nice about it afterwards, said she had done great, but Flannery regretted not managing to get out that detail.

When they finally reached Charles's studio, Charles frayed and damp with exasperation, they sat at his broad work table together, and Flannery calmly helped write a few good paragraphs that framed and contextualized Charles's new work. She sculpted some language on his behalf.

There would be no apology for Charles's outburst. Over time, Flannery eventually learned the pattern. Much later her husband might make some other compensatory gesture – that night, he picked up ice cream for her on the way home – and he would turn the story around, neatly, so that it was Flannery who had to be absolved.

'Listen,' Charles said understandingly, as he donned his grey silk pyjamas. This was hours later, almost midnight, after Jeffrey's visit to the studio, which had gone very well, and the dinner afterwards, from which Flannery had excused herself. She had been dozing already for an hour or two when Charles came in. 'I realize the pregnancy makes you emotional. I get that.'

Flannery, lying plumply in bed, nodded, only half awake. She was a writer, yes, or had been once, and sometimes she could still be beautifully articulate.

Other times she simply could not find the right thing, or anything at all, to say.

# 17

With Willa was born light.

That was all Flannery saw in the first few minutes. She did not see or feel the infant, properly, before people masked like thieves whisked her away to be weighed and measured and deemed to have the appropriate biometrics to join the human race. For Flannery, of course, there was no question about her daughter's perfection. How else could anyone account for all this light?

It was inside and outside of Flannery, both. The illumination. The point was, the source must have been Willa, and yet it was not as though that tiny baby, just emerged, was emitting bright beams of gratitude that she had escaped her dim cave and gotten her life rolling. (What she primarily emitted were the loud cat cries of any newborn's arrival.) It seemed rather, to Flannery's drugged mind – they had tanked her up with pain-killers and then anaesthetic, when it eventually transpired that the doctors had to slice Flannery open to get Willa out safely – as though on Willa's joining everyone else in the room, all the darkness went out of the place, out of every corner, leaving only this light.

She could not speak this. She could not say anything at all. Flannery was simply mute and smiling and bewildered. She took in the sequence of events: Charles joking with the nurses, though his eyes blinked with tears; the extreme contrast between his hefty self and the scarcely substantial creature he was cradling, like an image from some cartoon, a bear with a diminutive kitten in its paws; the swaddling of Willa and some helpful nurse's holding the child before the mother's eyes. *Look at her! Isn't she beautiful?* The images lodged deep within Flannery's memory, concealed under other immediate realities, and they would stay there always. Her daughter's arrival.

She had Willa now, and Willa had her, and Flannery's heart was ripped open into a new, great, terrifying capacity for love. (And, simultaneously, grief, because for some old, indelible reason Flannery felt the fear right alongside the joy – they were inextricable.) She had never known she would be capable of this love, and the feeling left her absolutely exposed to the world and its elements, like driving down the freeway at a hundred miles an hour with the top down and the windows open. Anything could get in.

What shape her fears had, what could happen once you became a mother – all of that would come later. For that day, that timeless hour, Flannery simply allowed herself to bathe in Willa's light.

# 18

Once, a long time before, Flannery had felt vulnerable in this way. She had loved deeply and she had lost, and though the experience broke and rearranged her (like a shattered and reset limb), it did not really surprise her. Woven deeply into this calm and melancholy woman was the conviction that all love ended in loss, that abandonment was the norm, that ecstasy was fleeting. It was the order of things.

A self-protective reflex came naturally to Flannery, and after Anne she always simply, somewhere in her, held back. It just made sense. Flannery could be, and was, kind and funny and attentive and hardworking and patient with those she loved; but she never offered that most private self to another person again. It was not worth the risk. She had learned that once, right at the start of adulthood.

If you asked her, Flannery would never have said she was scarred by her relationship with Anne. On the contrary. She had grown, learned, thrived, revelled. She had been touched and moved, and she had touched and moved Anne, too. It was Flannery's early life's greatest, if mostly interior, adventure, and next to it the colourful, wild, extraordinary year in Mexico with Adele seemed a movie set, an epic, as opposed to the sharp, true lyric that had been Anne. Though at acute points of self-reflection, Flannery understood that her determination to find her father was triggered by the way loving Anne had opened and changed her.

Now, she was with Charles. Flannery loved her husband, relished him, yes, but she would not say (if anyone asked her; luckily, no one did) that she had fallen headlong for the complicated man. Her passion was not on that order. Americans tended to shake their heads over countries with traditions of *arranged marriages* but Flannery wondered, once inside one herself and trying to adjust to the odd, boxy shape of it, how different their Western ritual was, really. Weren't all marriages arrangements? It was like trying to fit your body into a rectangular wooden drawer, as Flannery was told by one of her mother's friends she could do with her newborn infant if she didn't want to 'throw away good money on bassinets and such'.

Flannery managed it – marriage, that is, not cost-cutting measures for Willa, who slept happily in her raised, padded bassinet for the first six weeks of her life – with a combination of effort and determination. At points, she liked to hope, with grace. Flannery cooked dinners and prepared breakfasts, she attended to laundry and wrote holiday cards to their friends and buyers, she sought and gave back rubs in front of the TV; she organized cans in the pantry and towels in the cupboard and baby bottles, sanitized in boiling water, on the counter. She was competent with the new range of tasks, and kept a cheerful face toward it all, animated as she was by the shock of new life. Of new love.

In the grey flavourless hospital room where she recovered for the first few days, Charles reading or dozing in the corner chair, flowers and treats left by visitors bringing colour to the place, Flannery held this warm, small life, wrapped in a nurse-folded blanket or pressed nakedly against her skin and nursing, her new eyes closed and her sweet hungry mouth learning how to feed – and she toppled helplessly into love with her. *Willa*, Flannery murmured to their girl, in the hospital; back at home, in the small bedroom upstairs where Flannery slept for the first months, near the bassinet, so she could rise at any hour to tend to the beloved creature. *Willa, Willa*. The name itself was a lullaby, easy to sing.

This tiny treasured child stirred something within Flannery that she had not known to expect. How blind, again, not to have foreseen this! What had she imagined about motherhood? Love, of course, exhaustion, responsibility – and joy, and pride. She had read of all that. Flannery had not suspected, though, that this altering passion for another person would have all the same symptoms as the other kind. Everything you saw reminded you of her; you thought about her all the time; the world's other shades faded next to the implacable brightness of the one you loved. Her name was always on your tongue, the sound of her breath and her noises were tunes that played on a loop in your inner ear, her scents and textures were so familiar to your senses they were the fundamental atmosphere. You held her in your arms, even when you didn't.

Now it was Willa. Once, it had been Anne.

# 19

Flannery, siblingless, counted her friends as her family and her mother as her only actual parent. Lenny, though at least a person she knew existed, remained most vivid on the pages of Flannery's book. She received periodic emails from him, generally with links to animal videos or occasional rambling political reflections. A week after she had sent out a brief general email about Willa's birth, she received a one-line note back from Len: *YOWZAH!!!!*

Most who could expressed their congratulations in person. People trooped through the house on Ashbury Street after Willa was born, offering their advice and admiration, their snacks and their blankets. Flannery didn't know this ritual. Few of her friends had had children yet, she hadn't grown up in a community with many babies in it, and she felt as though she were visiting a country whose religion she had only read of, a place more vibrant and lively than she had expected.

Flannery's cousin Rachel came to the door with her ringletted three-year-old Claudia, who stiff-armed a soft cotton-candy-pink bunny in Flannery's direction though it looked from her pout as though she would rather have kept it herself. In Rachel's cashmere arms was an aluminum dish of lasagne, and though Flannery had never been much of a lasagne eater before, she found now that she was an everything eater and accepted the dish gratefully, along with Rachel's lengthy tips on getting the baby to sleep through the night. Charles's nice architect and pianist friends, whose children were teenagers (an unimaginable age, and dimension), brought pumpkin scones and a soft grey cap with mouse ears; Susan Kim had bags of fragrant Korean barbecued beef and a teething ring in the design of a shark. 'Other people can do the teddy bears,' she announced. A colleague of Flannery's from the art school brought wine for the parents and rusks for the baby, saying, with a little chuck under Willa's chin, 'This is how it goes, kid: the grown-ups get all the good stuff. You might as well know that now.'

By the time Flannery's college friend Nick showed up with his sleek-skinned Greek boyfriend, a felt ball that played a musical jingle, and a spread of delicious meze, Flannery was almost overwhelmed.

'More swag! Thank you,' she stage-whispered, as Willa had just gone down for a nap. Flannery ushered the men into the living room, where Charles's Roche Bobois looked on disapprovingly at the collecting pool of pastel and polyester objects scattered on the Turkish carpet. 'I wasn't expecting all this. When you publish a book, people don't bring you stuff. They congratulate you, but they don't feed you.'

'No,' Nick said. 'They just come to your launch party and drink.'

'And nobody asks to hold the book. You don't pass it around.'

'Which is why it feels really overlooked, and has to go to therapy later, when it grows up. Where's Charles?'

'At the studio.'

Nick tilted his ashy blond head and raised a questioning brow at her, as only an old friend can.

'No, it's fine.' Flannery answered his wordless question. 'I don't mind having some time to myself with Willa. Charles has a lot of work to do.' In response to the continued look, Flannery said more firmly: 'He does the meet-and-greet in the morning with whoever is here. But afternoons he has to go to the studio.'

Nick nodded, looked around the home, took in the shape of Flannery's life. Possibly swallowing some other thought, the boy she once thought had a crush on her said simply: 'I can't believe you got to parenthood before I did, Jansen. You always were secretly competitive.' He gave Stavros a sideways embrace after he said it, and the two men exchanged a tender moment that did not require her.

When Willa woke up a little later with a rhythmic cry, Nick did indeed ask to hold her. Flannery cooed a moment in private over Willa, lifted her from the bassinet, then handed her baby to her old friend, who received the bundle with the appropriate solemnity – and humour. He chuckled and chatted over her.

'Everyone's a winner, Nico,' Flannery said as she watched Nick's gentle, fathering hands. 'And anyway, you'll catch up.'

# 20

Flannery's mother came frequently, of course, driving up from her modest home on the Peninsula. Charles's mother had died of lung cancer several years before he and Flannery met, and he was in scarce contact with his father in Ohio, so Willa was a girl with a single present grandparent.

Now in her sixties, unmarried, a few years away from retiring from the high school, Laura Jansen's face gently sagged but was still pretty, her weathered skin creased mostly by kindness, her undyed hair the shade of sandy driftwood, streaked off-white with the tracings of sea creatures, or years. Laura was perplexed by but tolerant of her daughter's shifting choices, and had a formal respect for the man Flannery had married, without necessarily understanding either his work or his attraction. She had never been a baby person, Flannery recalled noticing at a family gathering after Rachel's child was born, but Laura was interested in people and their stories, and as her granddaughter grew older, she happily read picture books to her, listened to the girl's tales and opinions, and wandered hand in hand with her to story hour at the local library.

For the moment, Laura nestled Willa gingerly until she started crying, then handed her back with visible relief. Charles, trying perhaps to establish his paternal standing with his mother-in-law, took Willa and walked with her, rocking her. This did not happen altogether often, Flannery quietly knew, but she saw her mother registering Charles's thick, loving arms holding the tiny girl. A complex cloud moved over her mother's face that had in it memory and wistfulness, both.

'I've told you about the trip I took with you to Italy, haven't I?' Laura said to Flannery, though the question was really aimed at Charles.

'Tell it again,' her daughter said.

'Well. You were ten months old, and a girlfriend of mine was living for a term in Florence.' That *Don Lennart*, as Flannery ironically named him, had deserted Laura shortly before Flannery was born was a fact the single mother skipped over. 'Jennifer said I had to come visit, though I'm not sure her husband was completely thrilled to have a baby wailing in their tiny apartment. You were quite a loud little thing!' Laura watched Charles holding Willa, whose cries had turned to hiccups and were subsiding. The part of this story Flannery had always least enjoyed was how piercing her own scream had been as an infant. It was a bit late to apologize for it now.

'I'll never forget,' her mother laughed ruefully, 'taking the train from Florence to Rome. I realized I needed to give Jennifer and David a break so I thought I could manage an overnight in Rome, alone. With you.' Laura winced at her own naive determination. She had been brave then. In 1975. 'But I had left the bag of diapers on the train, when I got off. So there I was in the Rome train station, your lovely yellow onesie was soiled and you were crying, and I sat on a bench trying to clean you up – to fashion a cloth diaper from one of your little sleepers, sweetie – and making a godawful mess of it.' As she rolled her eyes up to the high living room ceiling, Laura's face was the young mother's again. 'A Roman conductor came up to me, waving his hands, in more despair than I was, saying, "*È un disastro! È un disastro!*"' Laura did the big Italian hand gestures, which fascinated little Willa. 'Of course, seeing that I was without a man, he then tried to pick me up.'

Charles laughed obligingly, though Flannery could see from her husband's face that his thoughts were elsewhere. She could read him well by now, see from the interior focus of his eyes that his mind was travelling over a problem from his work. He disguised it well enough that Flannery's mother felt merely flattered by the loud barked laugh of his response. She glowed.

'That must have been tough, doing all that alone.' Flannery was wearied by midnight feedings, but made herself smile at the familiar story.

'Oh, it was!' Laura said, almost gaily. 'Luckily I was still young, and didn't know any better. You can be braver, really, when you don't know what you're doing.'

Flannery leaned across and hugged her mother from a mixture of impulses, among them sympathy and apology (she was sorry to have caused her such trouble, thirty plus years before); though also, given recent argumentative outbursts at the Ashbury Street house, another feeling was folded in there too.

How hard it must have been, to do all this alone; yet on the other hand, there might have been moments when it was simpler, and purely sweet.

# 21

Flannery's daughter had a father.

This was a novelty.

Flannery saw, even drained as she was by her paradigm-shifting exhaustion – when a new mother believes she has sunk so far into sleep debt that it would require a government bail-out, or intervention by the World Bank, to extract her – that her daughter had a father. Daily, that small miracle nourished Flannery. Charles held Willa and he cherished her, and Flannery had not in her own childhood known a man's holding or his cherishing. How else could *A Visit to Don Lennart* have moved so many, and sold so well? The ache at the heart of that story, her fatherless melancholy, gave Flannery's otherwise wry, jaunty tale of adventure and pilgrimage its salt and its truth.

A doer, an actor, Charles liked taking Willa places, even when she was tiny. He left the hands-on tasks – feeding, bathing, dressing – mostly to Flannery. This division was more unexpectedly lopsided than Flannery felt comfortable admitting to her friends, or sometimes even to herself, since when she did bring it up with Charles he responded to her perceptions with caustic disbelief. ('Is that a line from the feminist playbook?' he asked her once during a tart exchange about the unequal share of diaper changing. It proved an effective silencer.) But he did get their daughter out into the world, proudly pushing the sleek navy stroller that contained her, and enjoying the way strangers admired and smiled at a baby in a stroller, as well as the parent accompanying her. He liked taking her places not specifically separated out for children, so avoided playgrounds and toddler pools, but happily walked with Willa past the tattoo parlours and used-clothing stores of Haight Street, the exotic botanical gardens at Golden Gate Park, or art museums, galleries, art shops, hardware stores. By the time Willa was three, the hardware store was one of her favourite outings with Daddy, who indulgently let her pick up objects in the carpentry aisle, encouraging her to feel the texture of sandpaper, or even the heft of a hammer.

*Daddy*: hearing her daughter speak those two syllables rearranged something within Flannery, fixed one of her inner workings, got some fundamental emotional mechanism to run more smoothly. She was forever grateful to Charles for that, and when her husband aggravated or disappointed her, demeaned her even, she reminded herself of this shift, and how permanent it was.

'You won't have the same material as me, sweetheart,' Flannery whispered into her daughter's perfect mollusc ear, as she splashed and cleaned her in the evenings in the large and elegant claw-foot tub. There, too, Charles's previously tasteful arrangement of soapstone dishes on a weathered wooden cabinet had been brought downmarket by Willa's brightly coloured frog sponge, her waterproof Dr Seuss books, and the bubble bath that smelled of fake strawberries. 'You already have a very different story from mine.'

Willa might have nodded had she been older, but at that tender age she simply grew, as children do, into herself, as the particular braid of nurture and nature came together to form her.

From her father Willa inherited an infectious laugh, an urge to build, and a knack for playing with Lego that set her apart from her princessed peers. (She was focused, careful, and inventive as she wove imaginative tales in and out of her constructions.) Her dark eyes; her dimples; her square feet. From her mother she received thick fair hair; the ability to sit still, to observe and remember; a will not to do the done thing; strong teeth, and a smile that brought abrupt light to an otherwise serious, worry-tending face.

From both her parents, or more precisely how they were together, Willa acquired an innate uneasiness, borne of the unarticulated reality that neither father nor mother, given their own angled histories, knew properly what it was to be a family. They were attempting roles for themselves and the others in their triangle, as if posing constantly for hidden cameras. Husband and wife, father and mother – parts that Charles and Flannery had, after a few months of sex and camaraderie, pledged to play, in the presence of a dutiful bureaucrat one Valentine's Day at City Hall. Scriptless, they were improvising, with mixed results.

# 22

*È un disastro.*

Of a different kind. In the spring, when Willa was six months old, this small family travelled to New York for a dinner in Charles's honour ahead of a new show of his preparatory drawings and maquettes at his Upper East Side gallery. They stayed in a chic hotel in midtown that had nothing to do with children. Charles's choice. Arriving early in the morning after a difficult night flight, during which the pain in Willa's ears caused her five hours of distress, a predicament about which she alerted the entire aeroplane with her piercing cries (though Charles was able to sleep through the racket, as the misleading phrase had it, *like a baby*), Flannery was unable to shake off her intense, nerve-frayed irritation at the throbbing music playing in the hotel lobby and the sinister nightclub red of the front desk lighting. How were these appropriate notes of welcome for her and her infant? She was uncharacteristically short-tempered and fussy about the room not being ready and their lack of a cot for Willa, while the gel-haired hipster at the reception desk fielded her complaints with a restrained voice that had within it, Flannery couldn't help feeling, the chilly implication that such problems were her own fault for getting pregnant in the first place. She stood holding a sleepy, disgruntled Willa against her, and felt awkward and ignorable, like the help that had been brought along to carry the bags and child, while Charles, large and benevolent, stood for ten enthusiastic minutes with some suited professional he'd met leaving the hotel who had to ask if he was *Charles Marshall*, whose pieces at the Whitney a few years earlier he had much admired. 'Oh, you saw those?' Charles boomed to the man warmly. 'Well, thank you. Yeah, I was pleased with how they hung that show. And tell me, what did you think of . . . ?'

So the visit continued. Midtown was a foreign world to Flannery, who knew only the Village, Tribeca, carvings of Brooklyn – certainly not these broad avenues with people who were older, richer and straighter than any Flannery used to brush up against in that city. Flannery was a wife in this Manhattan, and when she met other wives at the gallery she was unpractised in how to talk to them. She was not yet fluent in Wifese. Flannery decided that when she returned to San Francisco, she had better join a moms' group, so she could learn at least one of these new tongues. She knew she could pick it up; she was a quick study.

Certainly up here on Madison or Fifth, near horse-drawn carriages driving tourists around the park and manicured men and women carrying shopping bags, Flannery felt a more than geographic distance away from the streets of Soho, and any ghosts of hers who might still walk there. In her old life and a previous self, Flannery once chance-encountered on Prince Street a charismatic woman with auburn hair and a dry, delicious intelligence whom she had never stopped adoring. Flannery had tried in those few affectionate but awkward minutes to show off that she knew New York now, worked and lived there (while Anne's partner, a silvered professor named Jasper, stood beside her, waiting patiently); but now Flannery saw that the New York she had known then was not the same as the one where she was staying now. Her single effort to meet an old work friend for dinner one evening in Chelsea was thrown off by a last-minute cancellation by the babysitter about whom Flannery had anyway been dubious, seeing as the recommendation came from a hotel which clearly wished children harm. At that point Flannery wrote off this trip as a visit to Charles's New York, not her own, and made peace with how strange it all was to her.

In the end, *non è stato un disastro totale*. With Willa alongside her, Flannery did manage the one crucial dinner with Charles's Manhattan coterie, where he was celebrated and toasted. Charles swelled handsomely in such light. His size suited him then; in fact, it seemed the only appropriate shape for someone of his accomplishments. Even through the miasma of jet-lagged exhaustion, Flannery admired her husband's ease and success in these different arenas – social, artistic, sartorial (Charles wore an elegant Italian charcoal suit, that made you realize that he was a man of Venice, Rome, New York, not only provincial San Francisco). Flannery laughed along with the rest at Charles's jokes, smiled and nodded at Jeffrey's praise of him, then retired early to the minimalist grey hotel room where she and Willa could shelter far from the fame and the fashion.

'It's over. I did it,' Flannery said to Willa as she climbed out of her high heels with a groan of relief. She immediately took off her stockings, too, bunched them up and put them in her suitcase, hoping not to have to wear a pair for another six months. 'God, sweetheart. You have no idea how exhausting these things are.' She lay Willa down on a blue plastic changing mat across the crisp, white-sheeted queen bed, and cleaned her up, before fitting her into a daisy-decorated sleepsuit. Snap, snap, snap. How satisfying it was to dress an infant. She wished, not for the first time, she could wear sleepsuits every day, too.

'You know some people, like your dad, love big fancy dinners. I never have. It's a flaw, maybe, but –' Flannery held her beautiful girl up high overhead; Willa squealed with delight – 'I'd rather just have mashed sweet potatoes with *you*!' She covered her in kisses, drawing delighted gurgles from the child, then placed her gently in the centre of the bed while she got ready, too. Finally, to slow them both down, Flannery started singing a few not entirely appropriate songs – old favourites by Joni Mitchell, and Leonard Cohen – as a kind of mournful lullaby. They were the only tunes Flannery had by heart.

Flannery flew back a few days early with Willa. She and Charles agreed it would be better, so that he could focus on his work connections and she could retreat to their child-friendly hearth on Ashbury Street. That Charles had a two-night stand after Flannery left, with a young nose-pierced video artist, a woman who had the wit (or lack of it) to pick up the hotel room phone and flute into it when Flannery called from San Francisco, was neither here nor there. Flannery was upset with Charles, but not *that* upset, and her internal shrug confirmed something Flannery had begun to suspect, that a drift had started to develop between her and Charles. Frankly, she was still so relieved to be back at home with Willa, away from that awful hotel and the foreign city it was a part of, that she could not bring herself to mind about his infidelity as much as she probably should have.

Flannery had not been back to New York since then.

# 23

Flannery had not completely lost sight of that auburn-haired beauty.

In previous eras a person might lose a love and then not know where she had gone or whether she were alive or dead – until a startling glimpse at a distant market place or town square, or singing hymns in church.

However, in the over-surveilled and close-circuited twenty-first century, former beloveds scarcely had room to vanish. It was easy to find people: their tracks were everywhere. Anne and Flannery, whose bond had been a thickly worded one, their short-lived love nest lined with books and papers, were both in professions that brought them in frequent contact with print.

Flannery knew she was going to be a writer long before Anne expressed scepticism that she could be. ('Ah. You're hoping to write?' Anne had asked seventeen-year-old Flannery, to which Flannery had replied simply, 'Not hoping to. I just do.') As adults Anne and Flannery both were published, hired, connected to institutions. They were, as Californians put it, squarely *on the grid*.

Yet they had corresponded just twice, in twenty years.

When *A Visit to Don Lennart* was published, before the circus of appearances took over, Flannery received a postcard in an envelope. On one side, a Velásquez portrait of a plump, bearded man, *The Buffoon Pablo de Valladolid*; on the other, the familiar slanted hand. The envelope was addressed to Flannery, care of her publisher, and was sent from Anne's university at the time, Emory. Flannery saw the envelope when it arrived in the tarnished brass mailbox in the East Village apartment she shared with Adele, and stood leaning against the scuffed wall on the ground floor, finding it hard, for a moment, to catch her breath.

> *Dear Flannery,*
>
> *Might your Don look something like this absurd but oddly dignified Spanish gentleman? (I like your title's nod to Sybille Bedford.) You always knew your stories would make their way into the world; and I learned early on that you were a person who could make her imaginings real. Congratulations on the publication of your book. I am pleased for the nation's readers that they're being given the chance to relish your voice at last, and have pages of yours to hold for themselves.*
>
> *Anne*

'Pretentious,' Adele judged tartly when Flannery showed the card to her. 'Who does she think she is, God?' (*I might have made her think so*, Flannery thought. *It wasn't her fault.*) Adele had heard enough stories about the wonderful, remarkable Anne to last her a long while. Nonetheless, Adele's judgement did not stop Flannery drafting dozens of replies to the postcard, in her head, on paper, on the computer. She pretzeled herself into knots one day at the Museum of Modern Art with the effort of selecting a postcard whose image would perfectly convey what she hoped to express (Cézanne landscape? Lovely, but bland. Warhol's Marilyn? Trying too hard. Naked Picasso ladies? Suggestive, therefore tacky). The difficulty defeated Flannery, not least because she did not know what expression she was really after. No single image was ideal. No words worked, finally. All remained unsent.

A few years later, when Flannery had moved back to San Francisco, she heard from an old Yale friend that Anne had been hired, in a bit of university poaching, by NYU, and whisked away from Emory in Atlanta (along with, the friend helpfully added, her historian partner, Jasper Elliott). In the teacup of high-end academia, this had created a temporary storm. Still, Flannery knew New York was where Anne had always wanted and intended to be, and that the city deserved her. Taking a leaf from Anne's book – Flannery had always been more likely in this relationship to imitate than initiate – she sent Anne a postcard, addressed from Flannery's art college in San Francisco, to the department at NYU. Agonies again over an appropriate picture, but finally from a trip to LA she found a card of Diego Rivera's *Flower Carrier*. With its dozen lilies and its faceless girl it was, Flannery hoped, not too devotional, but she made herself stop worrying and simply send it. Her words were sparse. It was more a gesture than an actual communication.

*Dear Anne,*

*The city has you back. I'm happy for its university, and for you.*

Unlike Anne, though, Flannery did stick her neck out. In writing – where she had always located her greatest boldness.

She signed the card with –

*Love.*

# 24

Human history could not be written with some different lexicon. You could not search and replace one name for another, once powerful words had been coined. That currency lasted. The verb that described one person's online interest in another person, whether motivated by nostalgia or fascination, lust or regret, sounded like the sound produced by Flannery's own toddler. *Google.* To search on the Internet for information about a person, thing, or place. I google, you google, they google.

Flannery googled.

What had Anne Arden been up to?

Flannery did not use to google. She had, at least, taken a substantial break from it. This was before Willa was in pre-school, during the moms' group era. In early motherhood each phase seems of epoch-defining length: before they hold their head up, when you can still go out to restaurants because they are angelic and sleep all the time; when they start crawling, and you are imprisoned in your home trying desperately to 'proof' the place, as if your child were a criminal or a rodent, requiring lines of defence; and after they start walking and getting into real trouble, a good time to join the moms' group so you have other people who understand the true proportions of these problems, which to the rest of the world seem trivial. Flannery could not understand how any parent had time to watch television, have a coherent thought, or go online. There were simply no available hours in her day. If ever there were, Flannery used them to talk to actual living people – her friends, her mother, Charles.

Now, though, that Willa was at the Blueberry Preschool (that had been Willa at week seven, according to the fruit growth chart), Flannery began to resume relations with her computer. She browsed material she could put together for a part-time job application. And she got back to googling.

Anne had won a teaching prize at Emory. There was a citation on the department website, and trampling through the online jungle further, Flannery came upon a picture of her, small and smiling, with the university's dean. A modest, self-contained expression that compressed a little her musical, lovely mouth. The familiar high-edged cheekbones and Celtic elegance, even in miniature.

Going further back, Anne's book, *The Awakening of Influence*, had been extensively reviewed when it was published in the mid-1990s. 'Brilliant.' 'Challenging, thought-provoking, and meticulously argued.' 'Not only paradigm-shifting but perspective-altering; a crucial step forward in our understanding of modern American literature.' 'To call Professor Arden's profound book a landmark in feminist scholarship is to risk limiting its audience, or overlooking the true achievement of her generous work, which is to expand our humanist understanding of American letters.'

Flannery felt a flush of pride. Her Anne! Though, of course, Anne had not been 'hers' in fifteen years or so, if she had ever been 'hers' at all. (They had laughed about *Flannery* containing *Anne*, but it was a spelling joke – it only worked on the page.)

You did not own people. Marriage was one thing, and might not yet have escaped its association with leashes or shackles, but love was not possession. People were not each other's property. That included children and their parents.

Nonetheless: her Anne! Had shifted paradigms, altered perspectives, expanded humanist understanding. Flannery was not surprised.

Then, deflatingly, a blog post. Flannery might have missed this item, and wished she had. But on looking up at the clock in her improvised office (a narrow room upstairs, formerly used for storage), Flannery calculated that she had ten more minutes before she had to leave to pick up Willa; just enough time to find it. Blogs and posts and tweets, people's endless chatter-blurts about their meals, dogs, travels, interested her not at all. But googling was, as its name also suggested, not entirely unlike ogling; you looked, and then you could not look away. Some purple-haired graduate student in New York wrote an irreverent foodie blog she called *Finger Lickin' Good*.

> Went to dinner at the elegant Bleecker Street apartment of the Kate Hepburn/Spencer Tracy couple of academia, Anne Arden and Jasper Elliott. Or are they more Ullmann/Bergman? Taylor/Burton? No, I think I was right the first time. Arden, star author of *The Awakening of Influence*, is a beauty on the order of Hepburn, while Elliott, a whiz in French history, if not broken-nosed and pugnacious like Tracy, certainly adores Arden the way Spencer did Kate. The intellectual sparks flew between the pair even as they served an outstanding meal of lemon sole and dauphinoise potatoes, to a group that included—

That was enough. Flannery shut the laptop swiftly, before she could read the list of luminaries.

Jasper Elliott, again. Flannery had first met him in New Mexico – an ignominious occasion for Flannery, when Jasper got Anne back. He and Anne had been together for years by now. The golden couple.

The blog put an end to Flannery's googling, at least on that subject. She kept future searches to facts she had forgotten (who starred in that cruise ship movie? What was the name of that Carson McCullers novel?), safety research on plastics or supermarket products, and reviews of schools to which she and Charles might, one liberating day, send Willa.

# 25

Willa grew. She moved more, spoke more, took up more space. It became clearer who she was: a person with a sense of humour, occasionally stubborn, impatient with kids who were fussy, as happy to play with girls as with boys. With each increment Flannery felt the joy of motherhood bite more sharply.

She had been awash with love and astonishment from the beginning, of course, but now, as her head slowly cleared, like the drawn-out morning after a raucous party, Flannery began to see how part of the great plan was the companionship your offspring gave you down the line. Willa's sheer puppyish cuteness transformed into something more satisfying. An acerbic elderly neighbour of theirs, Martha, who had run the pet store on Haight Street for decades and was the kind of deadpan, raspy-voiced dame Flannery might weave into a story one day, visited the house when Willa was a month old, coming in with her fancy, moist-eyed spaniel. She joked, even as she awkwardly held Willa in her arms, that dogs were better value than children, never ungrateful, more easily trained. Charles laughed at this remark – he and Martha often enjoyed a sardonic banter together; she'd known him through a wife or two, sold him chow for an earlier one's Siamese – and Flannery smiled, understanding that offence was Martha's conversational goal. Nonetheless, the comment haunted Flannery in the first months, when her bone-tiredness and the one-sidedness of their arrangement, made more acute by a husband who looked on rather than dove in, sometimes piled high enough to flatten her.

From age three or so, Willa was simply very good company. She listened to her mother and responded to her, and the little girl came to read Flannery's moods more accurately than Charles did. Mother and daughter were able to share jokes over someone they ran into or something they had read or watched together, that did not always need to be explained. They had shorthand, code.

Once, when Charles was on a trip to Frankfurt to tinker with a mobile outdoor sculpture of his that had some technical difficulties, Flannery suddenly decided to take a road trip with Willa. She did not have to sulk indoors like some frustrated housewife. She packed up an overnight bag for them both and drove south an hour to a beach she had loved and played on as a girl. Willa dozed in her car seat on the ride.

As Flannery parked by the rocky wall that bordered the sandy beach and turned off the engine, the scent and sound of surf came in through the open windows of the car, calming Flannery's agitated spirit. She turned around to see her round-faced, sandy-haired girl blinking awake her hazel eyes, still half lost in dream. Flannery smiled, but didn't speak. Willa, taking in the ocean view through the windshield, asked sleepily, 'Are we in Hawaii?'

Flannery laughed. 'No, sweetie, it's still just California. Half Moon Bay,' and it was just like Willa not to be embarrassed, but to join her mom and start laughing, too. 'We would have had to get on a plane, for a kind of a lot of hours, to get to Hawaii,'

Flannery explained, then added, 'You'd know we were in Hawaii if there were palm trees everywhere, and people were doing the hula.' She then did an extremely poor hula dance in the driver's seat of the car, with mimed ukulele music, making her daughter's laugh turn into deeply contagious giggles.

After that, 'Hawaii' became a comic stand-in for any unexpected place they went to, whether it was the Sausalito house of a new preschool friend ('I think this might be Hawaii,' Flannery whispered as they went up the driveway of the luxurious coastal home) or Willa going with her parents to a grown-up event one night at the Palace of the Legion of Honor. ('Mom,' she whispered as they walked past Rodin's *Thinker* on the way into the neoclassical building, 'Is *this* Hawaii?')

They each had ways of dealing with Charles's demonstrative bluster and his excesses, and Flannery sometimes picked up strategies from her daughter. (Don't interrupt him, just let him go on with his rants and they will end sooner.) Willa detailed to Flannery what she was building with her Lego and other plastic pieces, taking imaginative turns Flannery had to be at her sharpest to follow. At such moments Flannery was vulnerable to feeling the parental vanity Charles wasn't too shy to express – 'Chip off the old block!' – but, more than anything, she simply felt light-headed with good fortune that she had been permitted, frankly through carelessness and naivety, to usher this interesting person into their home. For as long as making macaroni and cheese and French toast would keep her, Flannery would enjoy this fascinating, open-faced, funny roommate, and do what she could to make her accommodations comfortable, a place of peace.

# 26

Intelligent though she was, Flannery had never been that good at physics. She liked the *idea* of physics and wished she had been able, like some novelists she admired, to interweave string theory or subatomic particle structure into her stories. She couldn't. Her mind tended to fold, like a poker player with a bad hand, when confronted with infinities, whether cosmic or cellular.

Still, she had questions. For example, was it a basic law that if a person expanded in a new way, another part of her must contract?

Did some equation explain that to the measurable extent a woman grew into being a mother, by that same degree she would diminish as a writer? For every action there is an equal and opposite reaction: was it one of those?

Was there room in one self for author, parent, lesbian, mistress, wife, companion, solitaire? Or was the self finally a fixed size, incapable of containing such multitudes? Didn't Walt Whitman have a comment on the matter?

Was a person expansive, as the universe was said to be, or fixed, like a beaker only fillable to a certain point, before its liquid spilled?

On the ground, at eye level, without the benefit of either

magnification or microscopy, what Flannery saw was this: at Charles's studio or his work events, introduced as his wife, Flannery had little substance for other people. She had visibility – her outfits were important – but no dimension. At the moms' group Flannery was, of course, seen in relation to Willa, admired for the girl's adventurous diet or chided for not fastening in the car seat correctly. As a writer she was as vague and washed out as an old billboard being scrubbed off to make way for a shiny new ad. At best she was 'the one who wrote that Mexico book – right?'

When she had a few exploratory conversations about teaching jobs, it was clear that *Don Lennart* was the only book of Flannery's that was known. It was from a long time ago now (ten years), and the subsequent quiet novel that she was perhaps prouder of was a little-known ghost. Flannery's authorial self had largely drained away.

One day, folding and putting away shirts in her drawer, Flannery had one of her periodic urges to bring order to the jumble. She sorted the garments by colour tone: taupe, white, ash-grey T-shirts of a simple cut by a designer Charles had informed Flannery looked good on her. They were easy to fold, all tailored the same way. Then, at the base of the drawer, an outlier caught her eye. A much-worn, half-faded, turquoise V-neck, made of a cheap cotton, that still faintly said, in orange, *Sarasota*.

Flannery startled, as if she had come upon an old photo or love letter. She held the cloth up to her face but its Floridian scents were long gone, with only the recalled episodes left for her to inhale: the time she bought the shirt, on a beach with Anne, on that blighted spring break journey through Western Florida; and the times she wore it over days of Mexican heat and dust with Adele, across mountains and through beat-up old cities, and even on the occasion she first encountered Lenny. (Flannery was not about to dress up for him. As she wrote in her book, 'Discovering your father is not a black-tie event.') Which meant she was wearing it later that day, when she and Adele rolled around too close to the saguaro cacti.

Same shirt.

Another question for the scientists: where were those selves now, now that she was on the whole a woman who dressed in taupe and ash?

If she put on the washed-out turquoise tee again, would anything come back to her of that more confident, freer, forgotten Flannery?

Or had that person evaporated – turned into air?

# 27

Beaker, or universe? Shrinking, or expanding? Flannery got serious about her job search, to test this physics of the self. It was time to try her hand and mind in the wider world again.

Ostensibly Charles was happy about the prospect. His visible surfaces were shiny with favour – 'Terrific idea, I'm sure it will be good for you' – gleaming with reassurance – 'You realize there's no need to do it for the money, right? So it's OK if it doesn't work out' – and dulled only in occasional patches – 'I hope you won't get too tired. It could be a lot to take on.'

After a round of calls and emails, and the digging up of old colleagues like bulbs in an abandoned garden, Flannery discovered that a woman she had always liked, a Brazilian poet and translator, was going on maternity leave from the Jesuit college, and they needed a replacement to teach introductory composition. This was basic stuff, and only temporary, but the position had the advantage of proximity to Ashbury Street. Still, when Flannery got off the phone with the dean offering her the job, she found herself crying. Charles was not around to see it, fortunately, but Willa was in the kitchen with her. Her puzzled daughter frowned into her mother's streaked face, and Flannery explained how emotions could be *paradoxical*. 'It's a long word, Willerby, but you may as well learn it now.' She sniffled slightly. 'It means something like the opposite of what you would expect. So I'm happy, but I'm crying. See?'

Willa puckered her lips together almost in the shape of a kiss, a characteristic expression when weighing over a line from one of her parents. She was a natural sceptic, and at four she was already well aware that adults lied to you, distorting information to make things simpler or create a prettier picture than the one right in front of you. ('No, I don't know how to put a games app on the iPad. Dad might.' 'I have no idea why your mother is so upset.' 'We weren't arguing, honey, we were just having a discussion.')

'So do people sometimes laugh when they're sad?' Willa asked with the symmetrical logic of a Lego builder.

'They sometimes do.' Flannery reached out for her daughter's hand. Willa's was salty from eating crackers, Flannery's from her brief tears. She had a vivid recollection of herself and Adele in a stuffy hotel room in San Miguel de Allende, in hysterical giggles as they traded impressions of Flannery's father, the preposterous, wizened hippie they had met earlier that day. Flannery was already working up the material about the Malcolm Lowry-spouting antiques dealer, and referring to him as *Don Lennart*, with a faux Mexican accent that mimicked the man's own. Len Jansen had long, thin, mouse-grey hair that fell crookedly, the way hair does on a cheap Halloween costume, and the dome of his head was shiny and bald, though only visible when he removed his dusty Castro hat, as he did when he got hot, or flustered. He spoke in a dated sixties slang and had an inability noticed by both women (though kept out of their comic routines) to look Flannery in the eye. He kept referring to them as 'girls', as if, as Adele said in one sharpish moment, 'he were a hippie Hugh Hefner,' and though Flannery kept laughing at this and at all they were saying to each other, laughing till she could hardly breathe, till tears were streaming down her face, till she was clutching the sore overworked muscles in her stomach, she did begin even then, and certainly later, to consider that the ache might also have as its source something bleaker than amusement.

'It's weird, honey, but yeah. They do.' She gave Willa's hand a salty squeeze.

That paradox had been at the heart of her complicated book.

# 28

Charles was a complex composite, volatile under certain conditions, though even after some years Flannery was still trying to figure out exactly which. In large part, the man was pleased about Flannery's new employment. Yet at points the structure of support broke down unexpectedly, the solid Charles changing form and releasing toxins.

It came out as irritability. As curtness. Most significantly as a failure to appear, when Flannery asked him on days she was teaching to collect Willa from the preschool. Charles, who was punctual when his work required him to be but rarely otherwise, just would not show up on time.

Flannery saw the call come in, silently, in the last ten minutes of her class one Monday when she was trying to explain what a thesis paragraph was. BLUEBERRY lit up the screen on her phone. She breathed in sharply, talked fast, and let her class out five minutes early so she could return the school's call, before listening to their message.

'Oh, hi, Flannery,' said Kim who ran the school. 'Don't worry, it's OK now. Charles just got here.'

'*Just?*' It was a quarter to two. Willa had been due to be collected by one. 'But . . .'

'She was a little sad, but Mercedes stayed with her in the

Apricot classroom and they coloured together. Willa's fine now.'

Flannery found herself caught in a hot/cold, sour/sweet state, wanting to be warmly appreciative of Kim and her staff, while alight with upset at her husband's carelessness. She and Charles had deliberately selected a low-key, homey preschool for Willa – 'Not one of those places that tries to turn out prodigies by dousing the kids in Mozart and teaching them to count to ten in eleven languages,' as Charles put it – and this allowed Charles to believe that, like wives, the teachers at the Blueberry Preschool would be flexible and understanding if he did not arrive at 'the precise minute' he was expected.

'It wasn't a minute, Charles,' Flannery said crisply to him that night, after Willa was asleep. 'It was forty-five minutes.'

'They didn't seem to mind.'

'They were being *nice*. Mercedes had to give up her lunch break.'

Charles shook his head, unperturbed. 'You're letting yourself get way too upset about it. Is there something else that's really bothering you?'

'No! It's this. *This* is what's bothering me. Getting that call.' Flannery steadied her voice, and added calmly, 'I just want to feel I can rely on you.' She touched his arm as she said this, but he pulled away from her.

'I showed up, didn't I?' Charles spread his hands in front of him, a *case closed* gesture. 'You need to work on this, Flannery. Trusting people. Not everyone is going to do things exactly the way you do, but it all works out fine.'

Some recognition of her distress would have gone a long way, but all right – trust. She trusted that he wouldn't be that late again. But he was, a few times, and then a teacher called Flannery one day to ask if it was all right to take Willa with her while she went to get her groceries, as Charles had not yet appeared. Flannery cut her class short again, screeched over to the Blueberry, showing up sweaty and apologetic, and announced, as Willa listened, her eyes wide and probably feeling the tension in her mother's hand, that they would find another arrangement for pickup.

So Flannery did. She was resourceful, like any mother. Elsewhere in the world this might mean making sure enough water had been collected from the well, or bartering services for food; in San Francisco, parental ingenuity was largely spent on transportation. It was all about the car. (In the moms' group Flannery once heard a woman say wryly, 'Why do they call it being a stay-at-home mom? All I ever do is *drive*.') Flannery worked out a midweek plan with one of the other Blueberry families, and also shared childcare with Nick, who had recently adopted an undersized, energetic mixed-race boy named Theo. Flannery enjoyed watching the two kids in her rearview mirror, car seats strapped in on opposite sides of the Subaru back seat.

'They look like an estranged couple at the symphony, sitting as far away from one another as they can,' she observed to Nick once she dropped Theo off.

'"Mozart again! I'm so *bored* by Mozart."' Nick rolled his eyes, channelling his little doughnut-shaped boy as a fussy symphony-goer. 'Seriously, though,' he added, kissing Flannery in thanks. 'These two *are* going to get married one day, right? I'm counting on it.'

Flannery talked about Theo a few weeks later, over a family dinner. Charles had brought home a huge shopping bag of deli treats – Sicilian pizza, chicken wings, green bean salad – for what he called a 'Friday night scavenge'. He laid out the containers on the grey slate counter and let the three of them dive in. It was excessive (there were not one but two fruit tarts for dessert), but Willa loved it, and Flannery was content not to have to cook.

Her story was about the drive with both kids, which took an hour and a half, door to door. Flannery replayed Nick's Mozart joke for Charles's benefit.

'So you see? It all worked out,' Charles said, as he piled a plate high. 'Willa gets to ride with Theo, and you didn't have to hammer me about being late!'

Flannery hadn't thought of herself as *hammering* her spouse. 'Well, kind of . . .' She laughed awkwardly, as if it would be impolite to challenge him. 'Though my head is full now of all the logistics. It blocks out a lot of the rest.'

Charles just nodded. 'Yeah, that was always going to be the tough part about going back to work,' he said. 'If I were you, I might have waited till she had started kindergarten.'

This *If I were you*, spoken casually across their broad, marble table by her daughter's father, clarified the two possibilities before Flannery. She could protest, pointing out Charles's hypocrisy (*Why is this my problem, and not ours?)*, and in the process lessen herself somehow, shrinking as she argued helplessly against assumptions about mothers and fathers, work and responsibility, that were larger than the two of them and their marriage, larger even than Charles Marshall's massive sculptures. A cartoon image came to her mind of a diminutive figure pounding inconsequential fists against a massive, implacable wall.

Or she could swallow her distaste and indignation, in order to keep for Willa something Flannery thought of, with increasing irony, as 'the peace'.

Willa's mother, like countless women before her, swallowed.

# 29

Flannery sought solace in the place she had always found it before.

Not in another person – Flannery knew she must not lean on her beloved Willa that way, the poor kid would topple over – but in stories. Imaginary friends, not unlike those that populated her daughter's world.

But she could not find them. They were flat on her page. The characters did not live or breathe, and they comforted her as much as paper dolls – that is, not at all.

Flannery tried to talk to Charles about her slow, disappointing attempts to write again. He was an artist, she was sure he would understand what she was talking about. Charles worked with passion, diligence, integrity. Flannery loved him for it. However you responded to his pieces (some found them powerful and provocative, others heavy-handed), you knew they were *his*: his spirit, eye, hand, intelligence, ego. Charles Marshall built what he saw, with his idiosyncratic vision, and you felt him in the objects he produced.

'What if it's just . . . gone? The muse, or whatever.' Flannery posed her fear to Charles as she served him a cobbler dessert she had made, on another evening. She sat down and, without realizing it, began wringing her hands. 'What if I've dried up?'

'Give yourself a break,' Charles said, through mouthfuls of hot apple. He exuded comfort. 'Don't beat yourself up about it. Go easy. You're a mother.'

'I'm not beating myself up. It's . . .' Flannery could not work out how to reply. She was not seeking permission to let the work go, as if it were a chore, something to take off her to-do list. 'I just feel . . . you know . . .' She put her hands up over her mouth. 'Muzzled. Like I can't speak. Can't . . . breathe, almost.'

'Oh, Beauty.' Charles gazed at her with his pelt-brown eyes. He moved closer to her.

'Like you would feel if someone, you know, chopped off your hands or something. And you couldn't make pieces. You couldn't work.'

'So violent!' Gently, he pulled Flannery's hands away from her mouth, and kissed them, one after the other. 'Here. Let's take off that muzzle.'

She was bewildered, but she didn't resist. She realized that Charles thought he knew the perfect solution to his wife's difficulty.

*Doesn't he understand?* The question, like a trapped moth, fluttered around Flannery's stifled mind. *I thought he understood.*

She was wrong. They were not reading each other, which made Flannery wonder if they ever had.

# 30

Flannery thought that she had given herself to a man who loved a writer, whom he found attractive. But gradually she realized, in quiet moments – as she drove, chiefly – that Charles Marshall loved an attractive woman who happened to write. After the conversation between them that night, Flannery came to believe that if she did dry up and never wrote another book, Charles would neither mind nor worry. He would do his own work, regardless, and he would feed his many large appetites, regardless, and if Flannery continued to be on hand to help with these nourishments, so much the better.

That such an eventuality, her typing fingers running empty of words, would mean that Flannery herself had disappeared might not present itself as a serious problem for Charles.

Flannery started to sleep less well at nights. The body lying next to her own was causing Flannery's to be tense and agitated, and she found it hard to recapture her sense of warmth toward the man. Her thoughts moved in repetitive insomniac circles.

Then they started taking her to Anne.

Not so much to dwell on the love she and Anne had had, the steep swoop of that passion like a hawk's dive, the hot and lush entanglings. Rather, on something Flannery knew now: that

Anne Arden, twenty years earlier, in the course of a six-month affair, had more truly seen Flannery than Charles Marshall did after these years they had been together.

Flannery moved beyond that melancholy knowledge, however. She drew strange midnight comfort from thinking of the love Anne had with someone else. With Jasper Elliott.

During the wakeful one and two a.m.s Flannery began to perceive what she did not have, and would never have, with Charles – the various ways she had, through her own flaws, gotten her marriage wrong. From there Flannery's itinerant night mind travelled to the ways she imagined that Anne had gotten love right.

The affair between Flannery and Anne ended in New Mexico, over an embarrassing encounter, when with the dumb energy of a clumsy puppy Flannery had flown out to Albuquerque to surprise Anne, who was interviewing for a future job. It was a grand gesture, which failed. The surprise went the other way, when Flannery discovered the company Anne was keeping in the form of the lean, elegant Professor Elliott pouring wine for them both in the hotel restaurant.

A part of Flannery, though stunned to see Jasper, had expected him. Even in the most heated months between her and Anne there had always been a figure in the background – a memory, a history. A future, too, the younger woman now understood. Jasper had been there before Flannery, and he would be after, too; Flannery was a parenthesis, a dependent clause. Anne had not spoken of him directly, though stories from her past often involved an unmentioned, cherished other. Flannery could feel the man at times in the room with them, someone who had already known and treasured Anne. In Albuquerque Jasper became real, with a substance and dimension Flannery wished passionately that he lacked.

A crucial virtue of Anne Arden was that she was not, unlike Flannery, a mumbler or a waverer. Anne enunciated; she was decisive; she did not lie. She excused herself from the table, took Flannery back to her room and, in tactful privacy, delivered her news. Their relationship was over, and she was with Jasper now. Yes, she broke Flannery's heart, but the way she did it was like a merciful monarch: unequivocal and absolute. There was no appeal, and there would be no repeal. Flannery did not cry. She faced the guillotine with a calm strength that surprised even herself.

Flannery had loved Anne truly. And truthfully. She had seen Anne clearly, not covered with the reflective glitter a person acquires if you view them in your smitten, solipsistic state, thinking with excitement, *She is just like me!* Rather, Flannery had that other gift love can give – the capacity to perceive your loved one's curves and chasms, her scars and smoothnesses, an idea of where her secrets are stored and the calm certainty that you should leave them alone. *She has her reasons for keeping them hidden.*

Flannery had had years, since, to think. About Anne and herself; but also about Anne and Jasper. What at first fell on Flannery like a blow, one that left bruising and softness for months after, finally came to seem more like a slap – the restorative, snap-out-of-it slap, to get someone out of a dream state – that allows your head to clear and you to see what is actually what. Anne had wised Flannery up with that sudden break, and forced her to understand. Anne adored Jasper. The fact of their love became an element Flannery could think of with equanimity, and eventually even a peculiar mixture of relief, and awe. They loved each other. They had that!

When Flannery ran into the couple that time in Soho, she saw the ease and grace in the way Anne's neat round shoulder (how Flannery remembered that delicious shoulder – biting it, kissing it) nestled against the tall man's chest. How his arm folded around the petite Anne with a throat-catching *I've got you* gesture. How free they were. Not for him the rigid *She's mine, you can't have her.* Flannery was struck by that vision. Anne was alight and vibrant as she always had been, and animated by the certainty of Jasper's affection, which poured from his face, palpable as light from the sky. Later, when she read *The Awakening of Influence*, Flannery found in the last pages the demure, devoted acknowledgement: 'For Jasper Elliott, without whom there would have been no awakening, and little influence. This book is, like its author, dedicated to him.'

Flannery never forgot this. Anne Arden, a woman who meant more to Flannery than Flannery felt she could ever have meant to Anne, had found the person she was intended for; so Flannery need not be bitter, and never was. Anne loved Jasper, and was loved. What more could you want for someone who mattered to you? Motherhood only confirmed the principle for Flannery. You wanted the people you loved to be happy, whether it had anything to do with you or not.

It was comforting, finally. By the time twenty or so years had passed since the emotional tumult of her passion for Anne, all Flannery ever gained from thinking of Anne and Jasper together was solace. It soothed her on a rough night, when she found the body next to her foreign, and growing unfriendly, to think of that couple. The way mysterious medications can calm your stomach when you are travelling in lurching, abrupt movements over rough and nauseating seas.

# 31

How many loves in a lifetime? One? Three? None? Nine?

Flannery was pretty sure she knew her number.

Had she been writing her own story forward, at eighteen, imaginative Flannery might have told it differently. After her melodramatic heartbreak in New Mexico, the younger woman picked herself up again and grew, wiser, into her adult self. That great first passion for Anne felt at the time exceptional, but perhaps it was just her inexperience which gave that impression. Anne had taught Flannery how to be in love, and Flannery could take this gift, as if it were a gold band around her wrist or ankle, and wear it throughout her romantic future.

It had not gone that way, though. Flannery's love for Anne turned out to be neither a blueprint nor a rough draft; it was not a mould from which she cast other later loves.

What Flannery felt for Anne, and had with Anne, was unique. A one-off, as her old English friend would have said. A private language, a never rediscovered country. All right – a jewelled, irreproducible masterpiece.

So. One. That had been Flannery's allotment of deep, character-altering romantic loves. It was enough, Flannery Jansen felt in her surprising, comfortable house in San Francisco, where a talented man she had married lay largely beside her, breathing heavily as he dreamed. She tended this man, she gave her body to him and her affection, she received his kindnesses and his insults, and together they built something – an installation, a collaborative piece, a bond. That beautiful, beloved child. All in his space, of course. Where Flannery was one of the many assistants, in a sense, working toward Charles's overarching concept. Their love was a project, an endeavour, and it had not seeped down into Flannery's heart to change the nature of who she was. Only one person had ever done that.

It had been enough. One was a perfectly good and fair number.

Yes, hers was far in the past. So long ago you might imagine the memories had become sun-warped, like CD cases used to when you left them out on the hot dashboard of your car. But, no. The elements were still there, pictures, sound, sensations. The unforgotten words that had gone back and forth between the two women during that half year long ago, about novels and olive oil, Paris and palm reading, lipstick and literature. The shape of Anne's lips, and how it felt to kiss them. The hope. The heights. The fall.

One was plenty.

# 32

Charles did not know about Anne.

That is, Flannery had told him about her, a few times in recent years, but it had not stuck. This was not surprising. Charles only had room for so many of Flannery's stories in his mind, after which they spilled and fell out of it, like pieces of Lego from the crate in Willa's room. Much of Charles's squarish head was crowded with his own great stories, thoughts about his work, memories of romantic conquests, and probably furtive desires for more in the future. Apart from a few vivid landmarks, the finer details of Flannery's past were blurry to him, smears out of a train window.

Mainly he knew about Adele. She was the memorable figure – tall, fair, full-lipped, with a sharp humour and double-jointed hands – not least because she was such a colourful, lusty character in Flannery's book. Flannery had described her racily and well.

Also, Charles had met Adele when she passed through San Francisco with her partner and paid the married couple and their little girl a visit. Willa was a year old and unusually ornery on that particular day, wailing and hard to settle, so the stop was brief – though that might have had as much to do with Charles's unnerving demeanour.

'You must be Maddie!' he had brass-laughed to Adele on opening the heavy front door to her. *Maddie* was the name Flannery chose for her girlfriend in the book, to spare some morsel of Addie's privacy, though for the wide circle of people who knew the couple it did no such thing. The memoir was still a delicate subject between the two women, another note Charles had not taken in, apparently. As soon as the child had been displayed and admired, Flannery took Willa aside to calm her, and Charles launched into a few of his favourite scenes from *A Visit to Don Lennart*, as if Adele were a stand-up comedian and he was paying homage by playing her best bits.

'I loved that night when you guys got drunk and started singing Abba songs at the bar,' Charles chuckled. 'And told the Australian tourists you were whatshername's daughters.'

'Agnetha Fältskog,' Adele supplied. 'The blonde one, who was married to Björn.' ('How did you remember her *name*?' Flannery had asked Addie at the time, which she pretended to find offensive. Addie punched Flannery's arm, kind of hard, and whispered, 'She's our mother. How could I forget it?')

'*Dancing Queen . . .*' Charles crooned, doing a brief, lamentable shimmy. 'I bet everyone at the bar loved you.' Flannery could see that Charles's trying too hard, uncharacteristically, was related to his desire, touching in its way, to prove his affability to his wife's former girlfriend. 'Also, the time you dressed like a man so you two would look more like a straight couple.' If Flannery had not been holding Willa, she would have made that cut-off gesture to stop him talking, though it might not have worked. 'So you'd be safer. I'd love to have seen that. Flannery calling you *Albert* for the whole long bus ride.'

'Good times,' Adele deadpanned, shooting a look at Flannery, and then both women contrived to bring Willa back to centre stage, to change the subject, and her partner helped shift the focus from Adele.

*A Visit to Don Lennart* had broken Flannery open as a writer, lifted her career up to improbable elevations, forcing a fundamentally shy person into an uncomfortably exposed position. The book's success also meant that many of Flannery's recollections ceased to be her own, transformed both by being shared with a large public and by the very process of her writing – the slight altering of timings or details to make them work better in print. The narrative was tight, funny, and coherent, and the colourings Flannery gave her experiences overlaid the originals, the way a restorer makes a Renaissance masterpiece brighter with modern colours. Addie became Maddie, and Flannery, playing an exaggerated version of herself, was alternately brave and cautious, sophisticated and naive, playful and withdrawn. She did not make herself a hero, which was central to the book's charm.

Nowhere in those pages was Anne. Flannery's telling Charles about her first lover from her Yale days had been off the record, and Anne had therefore faded from his mind. No wonder Charles did not remember her. Unlike Adele, or *Maddie*, Anne had never been a bestseller.

# 33

She sent him the link.

There were always ways of half telling important facts to the person you lived with. Classic strategies would never go out of style: mumbling, imparting information when the other was clearly distracted, mentioning a controversial plan while out with other people in order to quell your partner's initial hostile reaction. Mobile phones multiplied the opportunities for miscommunication, running as they did on the fractional attention their owners tended to pay to them. The effect could be achieved through simple lies – *Damnit! I'm going into a dead zone*; *That email must have gone into my spam filter* – or diversionary tactics like the one Flannery used, in this case. She sent Charles a link at the end of an email, suspecting he would not find the time to click on it.

> So, I want to try to go to this conference in October. I think it would be a great place for me to 'network' and connect again with other writers. As you can see from the link they've got some great people coming . . .

Flannery's experience of Charles was that at unpredictable points he would recall, as a person might a pleasant vacation taken some years earlier, his enjoyment of Flannery's status as a well-regarded, if minor, author. If the job of Charles's wife primarily involved sexual availability, attentive audience, childcare and logistical support, nonetheless Flannery's writing, when recalled, could be a kind of reputation-burnishing extra (his reputation, that was), like having a nanny who spoke Mandarin, or a personal chef who made documentaries.

Flannery tried him one night, when they went out to a new restaurant on the fringes of Hayes Valley. It was one of the new rustically designed joints with paint-peeling walls and tables made from wood reclaimed from some Midwestern barn, and a name that meant 'cupboard' or 'pantry' in Italian (Flannery didn't catch which). The menu featured hemp powder and garbanzo dust, squid ink reduction and loquat foam. Flannery always endeavoured to keep her palate up to date, but that night she prepared to eat a lot of bread. She dipped a wedge of pain de campagne into a saucer of olive oil whose deep green made her think of the swoon-inducing colour of Anne's eyes.

Charles, in his element, launched into one of his lengthy chats with their server, a honey-skinned beauty named Paola who had plenty to say about ingredients and provenance, and with whom, Flannery guessed, Charles might happily have lapped up some loquat foam, if given the opportunity. When he finally ran out of questions Paola retreated, with a fake chuckle (or, who knew? Perhaps it was sincere) at Charles's parting joke.

'Did you see that link I sent you to the writers' conference?' Charles was smiling, but tablewards, savouring the aftertaste of his own wit. 'They've got some good people coming.'

Her husband's face, flushed slightly from a cocktail that had citrus muddled with an aperitif Flannery had never heard of, remained benevolent.

'Definitely,' he answered. Ambiguously. He popped an *amuse bouche* into his mouth. 'Wow! That's fantastic.'

'My old TA is going to be there,' Flannery made herself add. 'I think I've told you about her. Anne Arden? She wrote this important book called *The Awakening of Influence*. Anyway, she teaches at NYU now.'

'Huh!' Charles said, looking around the restaurant to see if he recognized any of the other diners. One of Charles's many arts was appearing to absorb what a person was telling him, while also evidently distracted. Though you could never tell how deep the distraction: Charles might accurately quote back a fact or line you thought he had not taken in; or deny having been told a key detail you were sure you had given him. It was perhaps his way of playing the miscommunication game, too.

They were brought small pewter plates, each with a sculptured pile of microgreens scattered with flavour nuggets of a fried unknown crustacean.

'I swear,' Charles said, examining the tiny pan-fried being between his curious fingers, 'these restaurants must have in-house naturalists, whose job is to scour the ocean for new creatures we can eat.'

'And botanists,' Flannery agreed, 'digging up heritage wheats and ancient grains.' She pressed on: 'So, I'd only have to be gone five or six days. Alicia Delgado is happy to teach the one class I'd miss. I did her a favour last semester.'

'Right.' Charles grimaced in response to the strange food's flavour. That, or this subject, did not entirely please him. 'And what are you going to do about Willa?'

Flannery looked levelly at her husband. A few tart remarks came to mind, something like *It is more a question of what I'm going to do about you*, but she smothered them.

'I thought,' she said slowly, grinding a sea creature between her molars, 'that you might be able to handle Willa. It will be less than a week. You could have some father–daughter time together.'

'Listen, I'd love to.' The man was nothing but amiable, as everyone around them would hear, especially as he spoke at volume. 'But I've got to be in the studio dawn to dusk, like I told you. For Detroit.'

Flannery took a deep breath, but before she could exhale, he continued.

'Here's an idea,' he said, after sampling and then assenting to the sommelier's proffered bottle of pinot bianco. 'Why not take Willa with you? She could have a little adventure. See her mother's alma mater. The maternal alma mater.'

The pun pleased him.

'I don't think I'd be able to participate in a conference with Willa there. The sessions go on for half the day.' Though there was a passing sweetness in the idea of showing her daughter those streets, that place, one day. 'It's a six-hour flight. She'd miss school. It would be expensive, then when I got there I'd have to find a babysitter.'

Charles shrug-nodded, then sipped his drink with one hand while, with his other, he took out his phone and started flicking his thumb over its surface. 'Women Write the World, eh?' he said sceptically. 'It looks more like New York, to me. New Yorkers always think they're the world.'

'I think that's why they want me. In this context I'm diversity. I'm the West.'

'I don't know – *Times* columnists, a poet,' Charles continued to read, as their plates were cleared. 'It sounds kind of academic. Andi Chatterjee is funny, she'd be great, but I don't see who else is *that* big a name on this list.' He grinned at her, in a way meant to be winning. 'Present company excluded, of course.'

'Ellen Kessler's work is very important,' asserted Flannery, who had been intending for years to read it. 'And Lisa Sahel Jefferson is the Poet Laureate.'

'OK.'

'I just think it's important, you know, for me to stay connected. The way it is for you.' She allowed a beat. 'I'd like to go.'

Her mother, of course. That would be the answer. Flannery would ask her mother to help. That is what it came down to in the end. Mothers and daughters.

'Sure, sure. Andi Chatterjee. Who knows? Maybe you'll get your big break in TV, if you talk to her. The small screen, at last!'

'Maybe so,' Flannery said, weighing whether Charles was mocking her. 'Though my heart, you know, is always going to be with the printed page.'

A platter of roasted waterfowl descended to the centre of their table. It nestled on a bed of root vegetables and something that looked a lot like seaweed.

'Leg or breast?' Charles offered Flannery chivalrously, holding a fork and spoon above the meat. 'Because you know me.' He winked at her. 'I like both.'

# 34

Flannery's mother agreed to step in to make the trip work.

'Though – will Charles mind my being here?' Laura asked.

They sat together over cups of tea at the broad marble table, while Willa played in her room. Flannery could never get past the sensation that her mother, who appeared ordinary-sized in her single-storey ranch home on the Peninsula, always seemed diminished in this house of Charles's, on which Flannery herself had made only a faint impression. Charles filled the space with his material and immaterial presence: his art on the walls, his expensive modernist furniture, the industrial bookshelves, the complexly mastered lighting; and his music, keyed into the house system, his sensibility in the air. When Flannery and her mother were alone at this vast, dramatic table she felt as though they were two dolls placed in an outsized dwelling, meant for different toys.

'I'm guessing you'll hardly see Charles,' Flannery said. 'He has a lot of work to do, a big piece for the Detroit Institute of Arts.' Passing this along, Flannery heard the pride in her own voice. So there was that – the ego burnishing could go the other way, Flannery admitted to herself.

'Gosh! That will keep him busy.'

Laura Jansen's bearing toward Charles veered between the

deferential (as if he were an eminent CEO, and she a demure, obedient secretary) and mildly condescending (as if he were a precocious student who conceived of grandiose projects for himself, and she was too kind to point out his delusions). Flannery sympathized with this duality; the glare from Charles's reputation sometimes made it hard to see the actual shape of the work he was doing, and you could not tell whether you were shielding your eyes from the brightness or the bluster. 'He's constructing a giant head made of molten old kerosene lamps, car headlights, torches . . . It's called *Enlightenment*.'

She and her mother exchanged ambiguous expressions.

'It sounds important,' Laura said faintly.

Flannery tried on occasion to enlist her mother in sharing her frustration at the ways Charles was so erratic in his attentions as a father and a husband; but as Laura had never had a man for any length of time in either capacity, she generally retreated into a mute uncertainty about what was to be expected. She adored her daughter, while not fully understanding her, and carried that same slightly baffled doting on to her granddaughter. Those were the constants.

'Grandma, can we play Candyland?' Willa asked, coming into the kitchen with a game box slathered in pictures of candy canes and gumdrops. Flannery's teeth hurt just to look at it.

'Of course, honey.' Laura brightened. She was great at playing board games with the little girl. Flannery had a terrible habit, tsked over disapprovingly by her daughter, of reading a magazine, or checking her phone, between turns. 'Let's set it up.'

Flannery's mom gestured to the table, though the notion of the garish, psychedelic board being spread out on its suave, grey-on-grey surface was a jarring one.

'Can we play on the floor?' Willa said, collapsing onto the nearby Gabbeh rug. 'It's softer.'

'Sure. Flan? You joining us?'

'Why not?'

So, in varying degrees of comfort, the three generations sat cross-legged together on Charles's elegant, cinnamon-coloured carpet, guiding their plastic pieces through the Lollipop Woods and Peppermint Forest, as they tried to reach the Candy Castle and victory.

# 35

The ways kids nose things on the air, like dogs sensing plates shifting before a quake, or catching the scent of explosives in luggage. Children's senses are sharper, attuned to frequencies adults have elected to forget. Willa felt a gust blowing between her father and her mother. There was a new gap there; she sought to close it.

'Can we go to Dad's studio?' Willa asked one warm October afternoon as Flannery was strapping her into the car seat after school. Soon, with a couple more inches on Willa, there would be no need for such equipment. Flannery could hardly wait. She had jettisoned the gear of each stage of Willa's childhood (bottles, cribs, strollers) with a bolt of joy, as Willa got closer and closer to being a regular person, whose constraints in the world would be only virtual, rather than plastic fiddly things you had to fasten.

'Today?' Flannery was caught off balance.

'Yeah. It would be fun.'

Would it?

'OK!' Flannery chirped, that false cheerfulness parents put on to hide discomfort. Willa probably heard that, too. 'Sure we can.'

For Willa, her father's studio was an emporium of wonder.

For her mother, it was impressive, alarming, and fascinating in equal measures. Its dangers were everywhere – blades, nails, poisons, and machines that could pierce, melt, sever, flatten – yet from its noisy stench and brain-wrecking cacophony great entities were born. Though as both child and adult, Flannery herself leaned toward quiet, it pleased her that her daughter was learning not to be afraid of noise; or at least that interesting things could come out of it.

The immensely spacious aluminum-roofed warehouse was in a flat, southern part of the city known as Dogpatch. When Flannery first told Willa this strange name, her daughter said, 'Oh, like pirates!', an association strengthened by the studio's proximity to the city's shipyards. But Dogpatch was one of the many parts of San Francisco getting altered now by tech money, which nurtured new kinds of businesses – laptop case makers or recycled rubber goods boutiques. Willa's clear favourite was the bespoke chocolatier who had moved in to a small storefront around the corner from Charles's studio, suffusing the neighbourhood with a divine cocoa aroma.

'Sarah said at her sister's birthday party they had a chocolate fountain,' Willa said conversationally, as she climbed out of the back seat. Once on the sidewalk the kid inhaled dramatically. Flannery sensed that a cookie stop had been part of her daughter's master plan all along. 'But I don't believe her.'

'Well . . .' Flannery considered Sarah's parents, who had organized pony rides to celebrate Sarah's birthday the month before. 'It's possible.'

'Really? That's something you can have, a chocolate *fountain*?'

They were inside the store by then, standing in front of a glass cabinet filled with cookies and brownies as well as more grown-up concoctions (chocolate truffles with chilli pepper, or alcohol). 'I've never seen one,' Flannery admitted. 'But I've heard of them. Like a unicorn, I guess.'

'Yeah, but unicorns aren't real.'

'So you say. Do we know for sure?'

The woman behind the counter smiled patiently at this exchange then helped mother and daughter to two warm cookies, each in a tidy paper bag, and Flannery thanked her. Flannery considered her conversational Jekyll and Hyde as a mother – her wish to establish, when she was with Willa, *I don't only talk about unicorns, you know*; paired with her equally strong urge, when she was in some shop or bakery without her daughter, to smile with extra indulgence on other people's children, to show that she was on the side of people with kids.

'Mmm. Warm chocolate. Is there anything better?' Flannery said to her daughter as they ambled up the street together. Flannery was content. She gave Willa a sideways hug. She was travelling east in less than a fortnight, and was just beginning to feel the pull of a near-forgotten freedom.

# 36

Flannery opened the heavy metal door and stepped inside with Willa. They were not, for the first instant, seen by the men at work. Flannery always wondered at the collaborative nature of Charles's creations, which made them seem almost more like pieces of theatre or film. Her own prose sculpting was so solitary: just her chipping away at the hard, rough rock of language. She often felt, when she and Willa came to the studio, that it clarified the ways her daughter's and her husband's inventive leanings were related: their interest in substance and implements, matter and how to shape it. They shared a wish to explore balance and space, a passion for the third dimension. Flannery's safe, deskbound work was a long, silent, effortful endeavour to build a world in two.

Within the wide, high-ceilinged room there were materials (stacks of wood; bins of reclaimed metal; long steel rods and columns; a 'fabric hamper' Willa loved to play with, that contained rags and samples; a treasury of adhesives; toxic paints and fixatives of all sorts); hand tools (a fantastic gallery of hammers, pliers, wrenches, drivers, that seemed almost like living creatures, with faces); two workstations of enduring industrial steel, with beat-up clamps attached at points; and the power instruments (drills, blowtorches, soldering devices). Willa's father's studio was a serious, less primary-coloured version of the worlds created by Richard Scarry in his brilliant depictions of work and construction, picture books that Willa loved to pore over, still. For Flannery, who had known Seuss's wide-eyed rhyming creatures and Sendak's mad underworld dreams, Richard Scarry had new information. How to build a road! The way you wire a house, and plumb it! This was, of course, the tenth or hundredth beauty of loving someone new: you were introduced to books you had not read before.

The high-pitched whine of a saw over a base layer of radio, atop a track of give-and-take insults: this was the soundscape of the team assembling and affixing the pieces of Charles Marshall's *Enlightenment*. In a cluttered corner, sandy-ponytailed, laid-back Baer was skilfully eviscerating what looked like a hurricane lamp, as a transplant surgeon might save what he could from a cooling corpse. Baer was a twenty-seven-year-old with the flexibility and muscle to assist Charles without buckling, as previous assistants had.

Standing more uncertainly, at a nervous disadvantage, was an etiolated boy named Lowell, the seventeen-year-old son of one of Charles's friends, who had the idea that assisting in an artist's studio would be cool, and incidentally look good on his college applications. At seventeen, as Flannery well recalled, you did not always get into situations with your eyes open; you dove down, eyes closed, nose blocked, into the cold and wet, then waited to find out when and where you'd surface afterwards. Lowell looked convincing enough, in an ironic T-shirt advertising a fifties cleaning product over skinny jeans with ragged knees. However, the task he had been set – sorting scrap from several outsized bins – seemed to bore him. Distracted, surreptitiously checking his phone, he looked up and was the first to spot Willa and Flannery. His eyes widened and he moved to get the attention of his boss, who was using a powerful table saw to do something shrill and violent to a sheet of metal. Charles looked up in sharp irritation at Lowell for bothering him, a fraction before he saw the reason why.

The aproned artist powered down the saw, which brought instant aural relief, then flipped up his safety visor. 'My *girls*!' He came over to envelop Willa in a thick embrace of sweat and affection, before doing the same, only slightly less effusively, to his wife. Whatever else went on, when the tap was open, the flow of the man's warmth was a good thing. 'What brings you out here to the Patch of the Dog?'

'Someone wanted to see their dad,' Flannery said, 'and possibly also score some chocolate. Hi, Baer. Hey, Lowell.'

Baer nodded at them, his hands full, and Lowell gave a shy half-wave before turning to wander over to where Charles had been working.

'Art and chocolate,' Charles said, wiping sweat away from his nose. 'Two of life's essentials.'

'Have you ever heard of a chocolate *fountain*, Daddy?' Willa stood looking up at her father, her arms crossed, an endearing smear of the stuff at the corner of her curious mouth. 'Like a fountain, that's made of chocolate?'

'I told her it was in the same category as a unicorn,' Flannery said. 'Maybe fantasy, maybe real.'

'Oh, they're real,' Charles stated. 'They're just overrated. But look at this, Willamuffin!' He gestured proudly to the evolving creation that took up the centre of the studio. The assembled jumble already stood taller than Willa.

'See what I'm making?' The use of the singular pronoun to describe his work came naturally, as if Baer and Lowell were mere ghostwriters. 'Pretty cool, right?'

Willa could only agree, as she stared at the form taking shape from other forms. She touched it, tentatively. 'Is it . . . a head?'

'You got it!' Charles laughed and then ruffled the top of hers with his oily hand, a gesture his daughter had told him repeatedly she did not like.

In his corner, Baer was intently focused on his dissected lamp, getting ready to solder a reclaimed piece of metal onto a long, powerful ledge of what was probably this metal giant's jaw. He was putting a pair of goggles on as he sang along, loud and tuneless, to the rock song blaring from the old transistor radio that stood on a low, wide sill.

The sun shone for a full minute. Then there was a brief sudden whirr of a motor from the opposite end of the room, and Charles turned his ferocious attention to the high school kid, in shadow.

'*Lowell!*' he bellowed, rending the air. 'What the FUCK are you doing?'

# 37

Lowell leapt back, as if from a live wire. He was over near the table saw.

'Sorry . . . I just . . .'

'Get *out* of there! You fuckwit.'

Baer, across the wide warehouse expanse, flipped up his goggles to see better, and stopped singing. He had been around his boss long enough to know when a dressing-down was on its way, and he did not intend to miss it. Everyone with any connection to Charles had been through this. There could be a sinister gratification watching it happen to someone else.

Flannery, however, felt differently. This explosion was the opposite of therapeutic for her, vibrating with memories of all the times she was the one receiving his nasty slapdown. The occasions had been both large and small, at home, or on the road: when Charles felt Flannery had poorly handled a press call for him ('It was just incompetent, that's all. You need to stay away from my professional dealings'), or lost it one evening about a dinner of chicken tenders Flannery had cooked ('Jesus! I don't want to eat this crap. What am I, *four*?). Here they came, in sequence: Charles's spit of contempt, the percussive slapping of hand against table, like a butcher's cleaver, and Flannery had no schadenfreude at all. She just felt sorry for the kid, in his torn jeans and Brillo tee, standing with his arms folded, head down, his pale face peachening with embarrassment. 'Sorry,' he mumbled.

'Were you listening to me *at all* when I explained to you how to be safe around these machines? Are you in grade school? Do you even *understand* circuitry?'

Not only that, there was Willa.

The little girl took the dancing dog she had brought in with her – a soft, cross-eyed toy whose tinny music, prompted by pushing a button on its fluffy leg, simultaneously delighted children and enervated adults – and folded herself into her mother's arms for ballast. She was familiar with these storms too, of course. She petted the brown and white dog to reassure him, though she did not press the button. If she had, a decelerating voice – the batteries were wearing out – would have started singing, *Dream dream dream dream dre-e-e-eam*, and Willa had the good sense to know that might push her father over the edge.

'Charles.' Flannery approached him, hand outstretched. Willa slid away from her arms and retreated to an aluminum stool near the door. 'Look, Lowell didn't get hurt. It's OK. He's not—'

'He wouldn't have gotten "hurt",' Charles barked. 'He would have lost a couple of his fucking fingers. You have any idea how bloody that is? No? Well, guess what? I do. I've seen it. It happens in *two seconds* when morons ignore basic safety principles and get their clumsy hands on serious equipment.' Charles's face was livid, the colour of a beating heart. 'This isn't nursery school here, Lowell. The blades are sharp, the poisons are toxic, and these tools aren't pretend. They're the *real fucking thing*.'

'OK, OK.' Flannery's own face was becoming red now. She

knew she had to get Willa out of here, but she wanted to try to calm Charles. She put a hand on his arm. 'Don't you think—'

He whipped his arm away from her angrily. 'Stay *out* of this, Flannery.' Charles's face was transformed: curled lip, narrowed eyes, high choleric cheeks. In this state, Flannery had had the thought before, he looked like a drunk. 'This is my studio and I know how to run it. For Christ's sake. You think this is a *playground*, a place for chocolate and chit-chat and stuffed animals. You don't have the faintest fucking idea of what's going on around here. You never have.'

Flannery turned her back on Charles, and his crew. 'Come on, Willa honey.' Her voice wanted to waver, but she would not let it. 'Let's go home.'

Charles was not about to dissuade her. He returned to the matter at hand, hollering and humiliating. Flannery couldn't save the young man. It was women and children first: she had to get herself and her daughter out.

# 38

'Are you crying?'

They were back in the car, Willa strapped in to her seat, the automotive throne of childhood.

Flannery was indeed crying.

'Not really.' She wiped her face clean. She attempted a watery smile, but could see in the rearview mirror her daughter's flatly sceptical face. It was wrong to lie into it. 'I mean, maybe a little,' Flannery admitted. 'I just . . . I don't like it when your dad talks to me like that.'

Willa nodded.

'And I don't think it's that great for the people who work with him, either.' Though, thin ice: don't disparage the other parent to your kid. Everyone knew that, no matter their background. Even if their own dad had been a spacey hippie living down in San Miguel de Allende. 'We just –' Flannery tried to fix this – 'have different ways of doing things, Dad and I, and so sometimes . . . we . . . disagree.'

Willa was silent.

'And . . . it's upsetting. At times.'

Silent a bit longer. Then:

'Why did you marry him?'

Flannery nearly swerved into a turquoise *taquería* at the

question. Her daughter was known to be direct, but this was exceptional. To stall for time, Flannery laughed, as if it were a joke. '*Why?*'

'Yeah. Why.' Willa, a patient judge, remained serious.

They drove up and over Potrero Hill, an elevated area of nifty restaurants and sloping stores. Flannery was considering her answer. The only way to frame it honestly was in terms of her daughter.

The origin story. You should be able to tell it to your child – whether you were married or not, in a couple or not – shouldn't you? Every kid wanted to have one. Your father was presented as a boy from a good background, with decent prospects, and I was supposed to produce for him an heir. Or: your mom and I went down to the fertility clinic and selected a donor together. Or: we were so in love with each other that we whispered in the dark, on the beach, *I want to make a child with you*, and that is what happened. Or: we had intense and accidentally unprotected sex, and I found out I was pregnant.

'We wanted you, sweetheart.' Flannery spoke this limited, careful truth into the mirror, and the earnest acorn-shaped face reflected in it. She was slightly obscuring the timeline, but it was the best she could do. 'Dad and I were eager to meet a person named Willa – and so we got married, in City Hall, under that big gold dome. And, you see, that led to us meeting *you*.'

The response pleased Willa, appealing to her child's innate solipsism as it did. She was central to the story, then. 'How did you know I'd be called Willa?' she asked, but a smile played about her face now, as she tapped into a telling she had heard often, comforting as a piece of toast with melted butter.

For Flannery, too. 'Because I had known for a very long time,' she said, as one recites a fairy tale, or the lead in to a song, 'ever since a friend introduced me to a beautiful story called *The*

*Song of the Lark* by someone named Willa Cather, that one day I wanted to have a daughter.' Flannery thought of the red-haired friend who had given her the novel. An unexpected emotion rose in her throat, and she gulped it down. 'And when I did, I would name her Willa. And that daughter –' she looked in the mirror again – 'that was you.'

# 39

There was one last person who Flannery needed to inform about her journey.

Flannery and Willa returned to their neighbourhood for dinner at their favourite Build Your Own Pizza place on Haight Street. The first time Flannery took Willa there her daughter had been disappointed that the restaurant did not live up to its name. The restaurant had, she thought, promised exciting culinary construction projects. 'You mean, it's just like choosing toppings? That's all it is?' However, the six-year-old had reconciled herself to the place's limited offerings, and settled in simply to enjoy the pizza.

'So, sweetie, I'm going to go on a trip, in a little over a week,' Flannery told her as they sipped from giant plastic cafeteria-style cups of water, sitting at a broad formica table, speckled like a hen. 'For about five days. To the East Coast.'

Willa stared at her. 'Why?'

'For a writers' conference,' Flannery answered. 'A bunch of writers get together to talk, you know, to students. Compare notes.'

Willa frowned. 'Why couldn't you do that here?'

'Well . . .' Flannery cleared her throat. 'I do, actually. At the college.' Again, looking at her daughter's face, Flannery felt the importance of not being evasive. 'There are some interesting people going. And some people I haven't seen in a long time. Old . . . friends. A woman I once knew, named Anne. The one who gave me *The Song of the Lark*.'

Willa sipped her water indifferently. Old friends of parents were of little import, unless they were right in front of you, offering presents or outings.

'It was nice to be invited,' Flannery added.

'And will it just be me and Dad here?'

'And Grandma. She's going to stay at the house too in case Dad, you know . . .' *Flakes out*. 'Has to work a lot.'

Willa sighed, just audibly, and Flannery, to silence the unspoken accusation of her maternal neglect, said defensively, 'Honey, it's not just Dad who has to travel for work. I have to go places for my writing, to promote my books.'

'Why?'

'Why? So people know about them.' Flannery realized that since the passing, glamorous period of her writing life well predated Willa's existence, this claim might sound fraudulent. 'I used to have to do more of it, right after my books first came out.' She tried not to think about how long it had been, and to distract them both, played her career ace. 'I was on TV once, to talk about one of my books.'

'*You* were? On TV?'

Willa's open-mouthed shock made her mother laugh. 'Yeah, me! For my first book, *A Visit to Don Lennart*. A long time ago.' So long. A different self.

A new respect came into her daughter's hazel eyes. Without question a television link was more enticing than anything printed between two hard covers.

'What was it like?' Willa asked. 'Being on TV?'

'You know, I was so nervous, the whole thing was kind of a

blur. Everything went super-fast, everyone was pretty and shiny, there were a lot of lights – then it was over. And we were done.'

'It sounds like the Giant Dipper.' Willa named a rollercoaster at the beachside amusement park Flannery had taken her to the previous summer. Willa, just equal to the height requirement for the ride, emerged from the two-minute vertiginous experience pale and nauseated, saying clearly, *I'm not doing that again till I turn ten.*

'It was very like the Giant Dipper,' her mom agreed. 'Almost exactly like that.'

Willa's pizza came then, descending like a cheesy UFO onto their table, and the child got to work dismantling what she had built and eating it, as they sat in a companionable silence for the rest of the meal. One of a thousand things Flannery loved about her daughter was that she knew how simply to be; she did not always have to talk.

# 40

Willa fell asleep early, out of tact or tiredness, and after she was safely under, Flannery called Adele. Occasionally, when she felt aswim, she had to hear her ex-girlfriend's voice. That Adele had met Charles and Willa, even briefly, meant that she was somehow a bridge for Flannery, linking the person she had been in her twenties to . . . this person. Whoever Flannery was now.

Within a year or two of their split, any hard feelings had washed away between the two women. Jealousy, betrayals, anguish, rage – it was all drawn back like a tide into the wider forgiving ocean, and only affection and familiarity remained. Charles and his ex-wives fell out of touch with apparent relief after their divorces, like actors turning their backs on a panned production, but for Flannery her ex was like a cousin, extended family.

'So,' Addie said, hearing the quaver in Flannery's voice. 'How's life on the Prairie?'

Delivered in Adele's native Minnesotan accent, the reference made Flannery laugh. 'I don't know,' she replied in a drawl. 'It was kind of a tough summer.'

'Drought? Fires? Pesky government ministers driving you from your land?'

'Something like that.'

'Just don't let that adorable kid of yours fall down an abandoned mineshaft. That episode nearly killed me.'

Flannery missed Adele. Her humour, especially. She knew they could never have stayed together, and not only for the obvious reason that both women eventually started sleeping with other people, in their flailing attempts to find an exit strategy after the book broke big and the balance that privacy ensures had permanently shifted. Flannery and Adele's compatibilities were related to the period of their lives they shared – the adventurous but haphazard mid-twenties – and at heart they both knew that when they properly grew up, it would be into different kinds of adults. Adele was a lawyer, the practical, Superbowl-watching type, who would play in a Sunday Ultimate Frisbee league and take biking vacations with her girlfriend; while Flannery, writer and ponderer, would have her head in an imagined cloudscape, while she hiked in the hills or wandered around an art museum, with . . . well, whoever she shacked up with, in the end.

Once, during a long bus journey on the Mexico trip, the two women got into a lengthy faux-argument about kids versus dogs, and which were more essential for a happy life. Adele claimed that dogs were more loyal than children, who were 'hardwired to turn thirteen and then hate and betray everything about you'. Flannery had riposted: 'True, but dogs are not going to look after you in your old age, or make you cute cards on your birthday and Mother's Day.' They declared the debate a tie, then Flannery took some time to look out the window at the dry scrubby landscape and take a short nap. She could still remember Addie half whispering, an hour later, when she thought Flannery was asleep, 'Ah, you'll be a great mom one day, Flannery. I know it.'

It took some imagination to see a maternal quality within

Flannery in those dusty Mexican days, and Flannery would always be grateful to Adele for her confidence. Certainly Flannery lacked that clarity herself. It wasn't till the shock of the double pink lines in Charles's black bathroom that Flannery understood that the stirrings within her were maternal (and came to recognize, like picking out a dimly lit face in a cave, that her shadow self had participated in the couple's birth control error); and it was only when Willa the peppercorn started growing toward blueberry and then kumquat that Flannery began to read her own narrative differently. Perhaps the restlessness of her twenties had been less a deep search for her father, her younger self's truth, than it was the force that propelled her, circuitously, toward becoming a mother. On the baby's light-drenched arrival Flannery finally saw the mother within her, seated on the bench right next to the writer. She had been there all along.

'Seriously. How's that cute kid of yours?' Adele asked, into a silence that had begun to yawn.

'She's great.' If Flannery kept her sentences short, she would manage.

'And Charles?'

'Well. He's . . .' But it was too complicated to put into a late-night telephone call. 'How about Jamie?' Flannery's voice was muffled. Addie's partner was an airline pilot, which Flannery found impressive. Another person, like Charles, who commanded large machines. They had joked about that.

'Flying high, expanding her carbon footprint.' There was a pause. 'So, Flan, what's up? Why the call? Not that I don't love to hear from you, but . . . you sound a little . . . stressed.'

Flannery wanted to speak. She fully intended to. She had the phone pressed close to her ear. She had inhaled, prepared an opening sentence and everything.

It was just that the moment she opened her mouth, her breath caught, and she knew that if anything came out, it might be frogs, or sobs, or something else inappropriate and embarrassing, and of no use to either one of them.

'Flannery, sweetie?' Adele said gently, dropping the irony. There was concern in her voice, which made it all the harder. 'Are you still there?'

It was a question without a straightforward answer.

# 41

Charles came home late and beery, but no longer angry. Beery she could manage. In fact, before she called Adele, Flannery had poured herself a fairly tall glass of wine. Like any couple, Charles and Flannery used alcohol as an irritation suppressant and a douser of bad memories, while knowing that the effects sometimes went the other way.

How was it with Anne and Jasper? Flannery wondered. She stretched out on the electric-blue couch, pretending to watch an episode on her laptop of a new show everyone was talking about, but as the people on the small screen glared and argued and kissed and made up, thoughts of Flannery's past rose to the roiled surface, stirred up in part by talking with Adele. The television characters did not have the power to speak more loudly than the dialogue in Flannery's own mind.

She remembered how Jasper had looked, pouring wine for Anne that night in the hotel restaurant, in Albuquerque. Flannery's young yearning eyes might have been on Anne, at first, but when she saw the expression on her beloved's face – such warm, humorous intimacy in her eyes – Flannery had to turn and take in the object of Anne's affection, too.

You can tell so much from so little. Even when you are eighteen and unschooled, you can. The man with the strong jaw and sly smile was not trying to impress Anne; he was simply happy, deeply happy, to be with her again. The 'again' was clear from their bodies, which did not carry the wariness of strangers, but rather the vibration of recognition – loose limbs, a known affinity. Anne's small, manicured hand rested on the table, and Jasper's rested loosely over it. The hands said everything.

The front door opened, and allowed Charles back into his house.

'Hey.'

'Hey.'

The simplest post-argument encounters were usually those that ignored what had happened. Certainly now, so soon before her East Coast escape, Flannery felt she could hold the day's events in a small carry-on in her mind, and need not unpack it here, late, at night – with him. The artist, father, boss, shouter. Husband. Charles would not, Flannery knew from experience, apologize for how he had spoken to her, or for what he had said, and if she mentioned the episode, it would only make Charles angrier again. Apologies, even half insincere ones, require an awareness of the effect you have on another person, and Charles, though full of a sense of self, spared himself that awareness. Flannery's outrage about this pattern was old and dried, a hard crusted layer over which regular life carried on. She poured her husband a small glass of scotch, brought it to him, and let him unspool. Charles would tell Flannery some complex, diverting story as a means of establishing quieter waters between them, evidently believing that was the way to make up for his earlier aggression. Flannery hardly had to respond, he simply needed her to sit and listen in a posture of sympathy. Her mind was free to wander its halls, listen to silent music.

'It was like an epidemic of incompetence today. Baer totally fucked up the soldering he was supposed to do. I had to take it apart and redo the entire thing. In Detroit they're pissing around with the transport of the piece, which is seriously threatening the timeline they're harassing me about. Then little Joey thinks it would be awesome to play with the cutters and hack off a few fingers.'

Charles sat in the vast leather armchair that was, by daylight, Willa's life raft or hibernation den, depending on the game. He sipped his scotch.

'It always happens: you try to do a friend of yours a favour. Sure, bring your son into the studio, he's a smart kid, right? Not an idiot? No, no, he's very responsible, he'll be fine. He just wants to help if he can, he's really grateful for the opportunity.' Charles shook his head. 'That'll teach me to be a nice guy.' He looked up and semi-focused on Flannery, his eyes somewhat malted over from the beer. 'I *did* see someone lose two fingers once in a table saw, at a fabricator's in New York. Well, I didn't see it happen, but I saw the guy afterwards. Fucking gruesome. I had to make that kid understand.' Charles carried on, convincing himself that he had saved Lowell from serious injury. 'He thinks he's hot shit because he used a lathe in shop class once.'

Charles wiped his mouth. 'And so after this bullshit day' – Flannery guessed there had been another explosion or two – 'I just threw in the towel, and took the two fuckwits out for Mission Chinese. They'd never been there, and the kung pao burrito blew their minds.'

'Cool.' In her imagination, Flannery walked by Anne and Jasper's home – on Bleecker Street, hadn't that blog said? So maybe a lovely old brownstone in the Village? Where the couple were seated quietly together, reading. Perhaps Jasper was massaging Anne's feet absentmindedly, letting go only to turn the pages. Jasper asked Anne if she'd let him read aloud a sentence from his book, and she raised an eyebrow and nodded. He read the line, she smiled, then returned to her pages. They breathed in a syncopated rhythm. The room was hushed. Or was there music? Anne loved Monk and Coltrane, and Jasper had been, Flannery was fairly sure, the reason why. They both had on their palates the aftertaste of the meal they had made together, a Moroccan dish, preserved lemon and cardamom, spiced harissa.

'So it's going to be up to *me* to negotiate with the trucking company, because the people in Detroit can't figure it out. It's only their job, that *is* their job, but . . . whatever. I can't trust Baer with it, Christ knows, because he's got his head up his ass . . .'

It was an idle gear turning over in Flannery's literary imagination, the creation of the brownstone haven. Her own private version of a romance novel, and as soft-focused and indulgent. Some people escaped their lives by tracking Hollywood couples through their marriages, infidelities, divorces. Flannery had her fantasy of Jasper and Anne.

'Let's go to bed,' she invited her husband, the best and quickest way to stop the flow of his complaints. She had heard enough, and knew the offer would get him to shake off these irritations about assistants and incompetents. It might return him to a better, more cheerful self.

In her romance novel, the other couple made love on the couch. The two books fell gently to the floor as they reached for one another with hungry, knowing hands, while notes of jazz dreamily suffused the air, like the lingering aroma of cardamom.

They could resume their reading in the morning. Now they had better things to do.

# 42

How many places can you be while having sex? The possibilities are as infinite as a distracted mind. You can be making childcare arrangements. Or mentally rescreening scenes from a film you watched a few nights before. You might be planning how to get from that hectic unpleasant airport in New York to the university, for the conference. Wondering whether you could leave luggage at the hotel before the room was ready. And. *And*. When might you see her? When?

Charles moved on top of Flannery, thrusting himself into and out of her, and though he was single-minded, with a clearly formed goal, he was neither inconsiderate nor clumsy. He paid her the attentions that were due, out of courtesy, and a wish that she would have pleasure, but he was soon on his own trajectory. Flannery considered it her – what, job? Responsibility? – to help her husband get there. She had lost interest, for herself, in making the same journey. She remembered the waypoints, but did not miss them much. At thirty-eight, Flannery's own sexual satisfaction was far down on the list of items she wanted or felt capable of getting. Willa's well-being and happiness; space, if she could ever find it again, to tell her stories; good days' teaching; companionship and conversation with friends. These might be attainable. Sex did not feature in her plans. Flannery thought of the first hothouse months with Charles and their frenetic couplings, or of that majestic, desolate stretch of the Mexican desert where she and Adele had enjoyed their legendarily erotic scene. Both seemed equally fantastic and unlikely to her now. Had Flannery ever actually been that bold? That wet?

Charles murmured a few endearments afterwards, told her she was beautiful, exhaled scotch and satisfaction into Flannery's ear, then fell into a heavy sleep.

Flannery breathed.

Not in tandem with Charles, or with anyone. She lay awake for a while, jumpy. Sex with Charles tended now to leave her this way: restless, seeking some other form of fulfilment. That picture she had of Anne and Jasper's languorous lovemaking on the couch still warmed her imagination, and Flannery found herself with the dangerous, prurient urge to browse.

She reached for her phone. Why not? Where was the harm? She googled Jasper Elliott, to see if his image, even if older, matched the one she had still in her mind. Perhaps she would find him, as if by telepathic magic, dozing away on a comfortable sofa, curled up fondly in the arms of his Anne. A cosy photoshoot for the *New York Times*.

Flannery already knew some recent items about Anne: she had published another book; authored introductions to a set of reprinted Cather novels; was listed as faculty on one of those alumni cruises around scenic European waterways (Italy and Croatia). But what about Jasper Elliott? How had he aged?

Flannery's pale face was illuminated by the cell phone's silvery green, as if by an underwater light. She sat up in bed next to the snoring bulk of Charles, and she tapped and scrolled. Ghost-hued, she furrowed her brow, as she read the fine print more closely.

Teaches at the École Normale, Paris.

Paris, that must be a commute for them – New York to Paris. Well, Flannery could imagine that, too, one great city twinned with another, each academic the master or mistress of the realm. *Shall we meet in New York in October? Actually, love, it would be better if you came to Paris, this time. We can walk along the Seine together . . .*

Lives with his wife and two sons.

The light flickered, or perhaps Flannery's vision did. That could not be right. Wife and sons. How could that be? Wife and sons – in Paris?

No, not sons. There were never going to be children. Not for Anne. That had been a certainty pure, hard and clear as a diamond, right at the heart of her.

If there were sons, Flannery knew, then Jasper Elliott's wife could not be Anne.

# PART TWO

## August

# 1

*Americans Abroad.*

They were too innocent, or not innocent enough. Falling in love, or recovering from heartbreak. They sought a cultured break from the moneyed jumble they had come from in New York or Boston, hoping to trade that in for the suaver soothe of European history and art. Television programmes were made of such stories now – rich American Cora bailing out hapless Lord Grantham, while their mostly well-meaning servants served, and strove – but in a previous era these encounters and exchanges had been the stuff of novels.

And novels were the stuff of Anne Arden's work.

Anne's fingers paused on the laptop keys, touching them lightly. Ready to tap out the words of her next thought.

She sipped her coffee, and licked its bitter taste off her lips.

Anne was preparing a talk, but not for her usual New York University undergrads. This, the *Stella Maris*, was a floating classroom for an older set. When she looked out the window here, instead of the silvered icons of Wall Street or the squirrel colours, browns and greys, of Greenwich Village, which was the view from her desk at home on the twenty-seventh floor, Anne saw the shifting labradorite surface of the Adriatic.

The ship, an elegant vessel, sailed with stately grace toward

Dubrovnik, its next port of call. By now, over halfway through the six-day voyage, Anne could anticipate its rhythms and noises the way she might a lover's – the way of turning from side to side, the feel of a body subsiding into sleep. Though she hid her roots well and had erased any trace of the original Michigan in her accent, Anne had retained the Midwesterner's wariness about the ocean and had not expected to enjoy this journey. Yet she was developing a fondness for the *Stella Maris*, and had almost gotten over her frank shock at the physical pleasure of being on board. It was as though at forty-eight Anne had been given chocolate to taste for the first time, or introduced to a new sensual experience. *Now I understand what people have been talking about.*

The phrase 'super yacht' might invoke images of playboy politicians or Russian oligarchs, but travelling with Anne on the *Stella Maris* was a more prosaic mix of faculty, crew and alumni passengers, primarily Americans. It was for the latter that Anne was shaping the talk she was to deliver the next day. She intended to share a scattering of European light from fictions of Edith Wharton and Henry James: American Italophiles who in life as well as art knew their way around the churches and gardens, the beckoning decadence and old-world charms of Rome and Florence – and Venice, the ultimate destination of the *Stella Maris.* Anne planned to draw on a lesser-known Wharton novel that included a cruise ship meeting and scenes on the Venice Lido, and James's *The Aspern Papers*, with its avid scholar pursuing an old woman and her cache of invaluable letters from her long-ago lover. Romantic missives of younger selves from an early, life-shaping passion: it was good material.

Anne's hands hovered over the keys as her memory briefly hovered, too, over her own earlier loves. *Laptop dancing*, Jasper had once called it as a joke, the tapping out of sentences by

Anne's lithe fingers. She was fast and dexterous, translating her thoughts onto the screen.

*Americans Abroad*. They had revelations while away from home. They found themselves, or lost themselves. Whichever was to be preferred.

Whichever made for the better story.

# 2

'I've never cruised,' Anne demurred during the previous December, when her friend Margaret Carter first suggested it. Margaret was calling Anne from Yale, where she taught and where Anne had received her doctorate, twenty years before. It was a place Anne nicknamed the *Lock*, out of an innate reluctance to show off its old New Haven name, one that brought Bushes to mind, and Clintons.

'I wouldn't know how,' Anne added. 'I don't have the outfits – or the attitude.'

'I thought that before I did it, too. You'll adapt.' Margaret, herself long married, was one of those friends who had been lately urging Anne to *get out more*. 'Though I was on the North Sea when I cruised – hardly "sun-kissed", as this one will be. It says so in the description.'

'Hmm.'

'Anyway, you can acquire both,' Margaret encouraged her. 'Attitude and outfits.'

'Pale linen jackets? Chanel scarves?'

'Exactly. You'll look fabulous.'

Anne considered. She knew what Margaret was doing; Anne's friends at NYU were attempting the same. Anne's partner of a couple of decades, Jasper Elliott – *Jazz*, as he was to her – had left her the year before, and the hopeful helpers were lining up to try to fill the Jazz-shaped hole in Anne's life with travel, activities, outings. Men.

Anne found that she did not necessarily want the time or space filled, however. The benevolent friends had it a bit wrong. Sometimes – not all the time, granted, but a good deal of the time – she was enjoying the newfound silence in her Bleecker Street apartment, and the hours alone led to new ideas. Solitude consoled. In its way.

'Don't you have to talk to people non-stop on these things? I'm not at my most sociable these days.'

'You'll have a nice cabin to retreat to.'

'I don't know. It all sounds a little . . .' Anne sought the right word. '*Nautical*.'

Margaret laughed. '"A Voyage Around the Adriatic"? I'm not going to lie to you, Professor Arden. You'll be on a ship.'

'That's my point.'

'But ships are relaxing! Why do you think all the old folk do it?'

'Perfect: A Voyage Around the Geriatric.'

'Now, now, missy. We're all getting there.' Margaret was in her early fifties, and sometimes liked to play the head girl. Not many people attempted that with Anne, and she loved Margaret for it. 'They won't all be geriatric on this one. It's rated as "moderately active" – there are walks around Byzantine churches, and old walled cities. Besides, you end in Venice. Or, as they call it, *Serenissima*.'

Anne snorted. Her laptop was open while she spoke on the phone, so she did a nanosecond of research. 'Hmm. 2013 will be a year for the Biennale. Perhaps my sister could join me in Venice – she'll need a vacation by then. She's been looking after our unbeloved mother.'

Anne's sister Patricia, who still lived near Detroit, had the stationary sibling's task of tending the ageing parents, though now only their mother was left. Mild Frank Arden had died, bitten round the edges by Alzheimer's, a few years earlier, of a massive stroke, leaving bad-tempered, dependent Irène, whose heart was failing too. They had been an unmonied pair, not people who took educational cruises around Europe.

'Good idea.' Margaret sounded satisfied. 'Shall I tell Steven Marovic you'll do it? He's an interesting man, by the way. Was a politician in Croatia in his early life, before he became a historian. He's probably buried a body or two.'

Anne was not fully listening; she was in a dark winter apartment in New York, imagining a hot, crowded August in Venice. By then, Jasper's new twins would be a year old. (Not that Anne was tracking such things.) In their years together, he had been the couple's assigned map-reader and logistics sorter. Where to stay, how to get there. Across the blank new sheets of Anne's summers and breaks, Anne was learning to author her own holidays.

'Thanks, Margaret. For thinking of me.' People were trying to fix this for Anne. It was good of them. Even if it was unfixable. 'Yes. Tell Steven I'll do it.'

# 3

How had he loved Anne? He used to count the ways. For her to do it would have been vanity, and Anne loathed vanity – in part because she knew she had it, like a mercury trace, within her.

He loved her appearance. He called her exquisite, stunning, ravishing – Jasper was old school, in his chivalry and his vocabulary. He loved her body, showering it with praises and caresses. He invented nonsense names in French for his favourite parts of her, and tended them devotedly. When they were separated, he said, he felt the emptiness next to him as a concavity, and a moral hollow.

A cinephile, Jasper reached for leading lady comparisons. The names changed with the slant of Anne's haircut, which film they had recently watched. Though he favoured redheads like her. 'What are you up to, Huppert?' Coming up behind Anne as she worked at her desk, and planting a kiss on her inviting neck. Or: 'You were doing your Sarandon, and he couldn't resist you,' humorously, after they went out for sushi with another couple and he saw Anne flirting, meaning no harm. In a sombre period – Anne was susceptible to lightless stretches, a thick curtain falling across her mood – Jasper once compared her to Piaf.

He loved Anne's capacity for truth. Not just the intellectual truth in her work, but emotional truth, without which the other would have been empty anyway.

'Don't lie to me,' Jasper said very early on, in the first months they were together, when Anne was still a graduate student, he a new professor. 'Lying erases the other, diminishes him. You don't need to do it.' His voice was gentle, not chiding, though pitched as instruction rather than request. 'I can take the truth from you. It's what I want.'

Anne came from a home where secrecy and evasion had worked better than openness, so it took her some time to understand something different. It was a geological act, to realign habits and self-protections she had learned from fraught years in her family. 'Lying,' she told Jasper, 'was the best revenge, with my mother.' But gradually, like a child learning to play an instrument, Anne found she could present Jasper with truths, even those she had expected would alarm him. Hidden pettinesses she felt were unworthy. ('I'm afraid I often do judge people by their shoes.') The times in her life she had injured others. ('When I broke my mother's beautiful china vase, not only did I deny doing it, but I allowed her to punish both of us, though Patricia had nothing to do with it. Of course, only I got the beating.') Her ambition, a difficult admission. Yes, she was gratified when people knew her name and her work.

Jasper loved her anyway, he assured her, all the more for Anne's honest accounts, even of what was not beautiful within her. He absorbed her stories, whether they took her to pain or pleasure. 'It is all part of our knowing each other. I'm not frightened of who you were before we met, or who you might become. I hope you feel the same about me.'

A few years passed before Anne could receive this grace from Jasper, and return it. But she did, slowly, come to feel known, forgiven, and granted emotional shelter; and to feel the same way about Jasper. Anne respected the boy he had been, from a prominent Amherst family; admired the college student who studied for a year in Aix-en-Provence, which ignited his passion for France and the French; and had no reason to fear the man he would become, as he grew into his academic life with her.

Though that last, finally, proved a confidence misplaced.

# 4

Required.

Unrequited.

'Define your terms,' Jasper said.

They were driving from Albuquerque toward Taos the first time they had this conversation, and they revisited the question across the years and geographies – in Atlanta, Paris, New York – unhappily. That first time, Jasper wore mirrored sunglasses as he drove the sports car he had rented for their trip, and though Anne was unsure whether or not this showing off was ironic, she was falling in love with him again, in any case.

'Define them? You know what they mean.' She had to speak loudly over the road noise. Anne loved arguing with Jasper, who was never offended or put off by her challenges. They could talk about anything. It was like exercise: essential. 'Requited love is mutual. Unrequited isn't. Heartbreak occurs when love is unrequited. These are in Love 101, these terms. You'll find them on the handout.'

'No. It's a flawed glossary.' Light poured over Jasper, over them both, the alabaster southwestern light that meant a sudden storm was an hour off, or less. 'There is no such thing as unrequited love. It's a logical impossibility.'

Anne lifted her own shades a moment to fix her eyes on him sceptically. 'Explain.'

'Certainly.' He was enjoying himself. To be in love, he declared, was to create a beautiful system, a call and response, a treasuring and a being treasured. Mutuality was at the heart of it. The system did not work unless both people were in it: the gears otherwise did not move, the belt did not turn. 'You can't have a tennis match with just one person,' was his concluding analogy. (Jasper watched hours of the sport, was an avid Agassi fan in that era.) 'It's not tennis. It's just a person standing alone on a court, holding a racquet.'

'So how do you explain heartbreak?' she asked. 'Lovesickness? Poetry? Decades of sad country songs? The blues?'

'Ah,' he had said with relish, and the private smile he showed when Anne offered him a question he had hoped she would.

He had thought about this, of course. As a French historian, he had to know his way around the subject of love. The figures in his narratives struggled and succumbed, just as literary characters did. Napoleon and Josephine. Louis and Marie-Antoinette.

'Because that sensation – that pain – does not come from love,' Jazz said. Jasper's hair, longish then, was blowing across his forehead from a partially opened window, giving him a wild look. 'It's wounded pride. Pride is a very sensitive organ, and it hurts like hell when it has taken a hit. The bruises last, and from them people write sad songs. And poems. The wailing of a battered ego.'

Anne considered this. 'All right.' There was a difficult issue between them to discuss, and they were heading right at it. Recalling his exhortations to seek the truth, she held course. 'So for these past months, when we were not together, there was no moment of unrequited . . . yearning?'

'No. There couldn't have been.' Jasper spoke calmly, as if

their having spent a year apart did not worry him. They had recently reunited, and Jasper exuded confidence. 'Besides, the decision to split was mutual.'

'True.' Anne looked out at the scrub-scattered mesa for a few moments of recollection. Yes, it had been mutual. The two of them had hit edges and coldnesses in each other that could not, it seemed, be softened or warmed, and decided to uncouple. In that time they had each found romance elsewhere: Jasper had a fling with a voluptuous Italian chef ('I don't need the details,' Anne had told him, firmly), while Anne, in the late stages of dissertation writing, fell into a hothouse swoon with a smart and pretty undergraduate.

They approached an exit for the sanctuary in Chimayo, a place famous for its solace. 'I'm not saying we didn't ache.' As the car slowed, Jasper spoke in a quieter voice. He raised his mirrored shades to wipe away a grain of sand or salt, and for a moment Anne saw his azure, expressive eyes and knew that he could still feel that ache, however cavalier he appeared to be. 'Though each of us did find another woman to comfort us.' He gave a wry smile. Anne believed it was her Sapphic excursion that had stirred the embers of Jasper's jealousy. As if he heard her thought, he added, 'Then I decided it was time to try to set our beautiful system in motion, again.' Jasper had worked, artfully and successfully, to draw Anne back to him. And here they were.

That pretty undergraduate. Anne sighed, with a sadness she chose not to translate. Flannery had come all the way to Albuquerque from New Haven, poor reckless thing, hoping to surprise Anne back into her arms. The thought of their painful encounter made Anne wince. Anne knew that Jasper would never concern himself with what that lovely young woman was like; how bright she was, how surprisingly fierce the spark within her; how passionate she had been.

'I'm not sure my young friend would agree with your theory.'

'Perhaps she wouldn't. But when she's older' – Jasper had the victor's magnanimity – 'I expect she'll come to see it.'

Jasper did not waver from this conception about the non-existence of unrequited love; while Anne was never sure he had convinced her, over their itinerant years, through the move to Atlanta together and later to New York, when NYU hired them both and the couple enjoyed a decade of delicious, conversational life on Bleecker Street, on the twenty-seventh floor. They swore no vows, but they kept their promises, and Jasper was right, it was a flowing, rhythmic system the two of them shared, a relationship others tended to idealize and envy.

Until it stopped.

Jasper sought something different, met someone else, moved somewhere new.

Anne had doubted Jasper's picture from the safely distant belief that she would never have to explore the question from her own experience; she doubted it from excruciating proximity when he left her. By his definition, the man she had loved for a pair of decades, Anne could not call what she felt for him after that *unrequited love*. If it hurt to lose him (and yes, it shredded her, hurt like hell as he had said, it was agonizing), that was just the nerve endings of Anne's pride made raw. Their system had simply ceased. The gears stuck. Jazz discovered in his fifties that he wanted a child, and Anne never did, nor would. Young, French Sophie would have to oblige him.

Yet Anne could not stand alone on the court.

Without Jasper, there was no game.

# 5

Anne sat with Steven Marovic at a sidewalk cafe on a stony, uneven avenue in Dubrovnik, a wave-inflected light scattered across their faces. Marovic, a bald, bespectacled man with the ambiguous, unscarred face of an operative and an accent inflected by tragedy, had just given a good talk about the famous forts of the beleaguered coastal city, its geologic layers of defence against a shifting set of enemies. It was a matted internecine history, and he was witty and incisive as he threaded through his lecture a few personal stories (his brief encounter, as a young man, with Tito; his uncle's torture by the fascist Ustaše during the Second World War). Marovic held the alumni rapt. Anne's subject apparently interested them less, at least the men. Literature was all very well – with its houses and marriages, affairs and inheritances – but history was real. Assassinations, wars, religious persecution. Walls, graves, ruins. What could be realer? Pages in a book?

The two of them sat companionably, sipping espressos, enjoying for a moment a break from their professional duties. A violin and cello duo began playing at a cleared area near their table, and Marovic's face brightened.

'Bach,' he noted, then looked embarrassed, as if perhaps this were too obvious. He suddenly seized up with a shy silence. Anne could have that effect on people.

When someone made the flutter of their ruffling evident to Anne, her core tended to harden, and the scrim came down. It was like an involuntary climate change within her. She became still, cat-like, and her wide eyes gazed at the other as though at a different sort of creature, something small and furred that knew it was prey. She could not, quite, help it. Now that she was single, she should try to change this internal mechanism, but did not know how to.

Jasper had not quailed at this power of Anne's, and for that she had adored him. He was the same size as Anne, as she saw from their first encounter. Not physically, of course; he was birch-tall and sturdy to Anne's curved and petite, so she could lean against him in the moments she felt frail. Species-wise, though, she and Jasper were the same. Each knew the role of the mesmerizer. It was not a gimmick exactly, as it required the willed submission of the other, student or acolyte, colleague or lover, who gave themselves over by choice. Jasper and Anne's particular alchemy came from the fact that when they met neither one lost their sense of self, or dissolved. There was no submission.

Anne remembered this as she watched Marovic, ostensibly gazing out at the musicians, absorbing Bach's intricate tonal patterns. His strong head looked sculpted, with a few surprising juttings and indentations, as if made by an artist with an impressionist flair, and Anne saw how someone would find him attractive. (What had Margaret hinted at? Marital trouble, Anne recalled. It was why Steven was travelling wifeless.) She felt the confused heat from the man now and noted the sweat darkening under his arms. He would not hold Anne's gaze, though she had seen his eyes darting to her shirt's low opening.

Anne folded her arms across her chest and closed her eyes for a moment. She was not yet ready for that kind of attention. Not from him.

'I was thinking of West's line about Dubrovnik,' she offered. 'Calling it "a city on a coin".'

'West!' Marovic appreciated the diversion. Perhaps he was self-conscious about the sweat, the suggestive heat, and sought escape from it. 'She is essential, of course, though an apologist for the Serbs. I referred to her briefly.'

'Yes – it was a good talk. I like the inscription on the fortress . . .'

'"*Non bene pro toto libertas venditur auro.*"' He patted the back of his neck with a wrinkled handkerchief. '"Freedom is not sold for all the gold in the world."' The *r* in 'world' rolled in his throat, a hinted thunder.

'That's it.' Anne smiled in acknowledgement. She kept herself still, uninviting, while wondering if Jasper mesmerized his new wife, or if they were equals as he and Anne had been.

'Tell me more –' Anne improvised, to draw her mind elsewhere, and Marovic's too. She shivered slightly, in the Dalmatian sun – 'about your heroic uncle.'

# 6

It was the last full day on board, and they were headed toward Ravenna. For her closing performance Anne had chosen a heather-grey tailored shirt that cast a cool light on her auburn hair, and a steel-blue pencil skirt: she wanted to look smart, in all senses.

Anne had never understood the stereotype about frumpy academics, men in leather-elbowed corduroy jackets or women in shapeless skirts and baggy sweaters. Jasper would not have let a corduroy jacket across the threshold of their apartment, and disdained in equal measure tennis shoes and the clunky brown boots favoured by some of his colleagues. 'Ron Edwards wears those,' he said to Anne once, gesturing to a pair, when they were shopping in Soho. (Jasper had liked to shop for clothes with Anne, a fact that caused Margaret to protest, when Anne mentioned it, 'Are we *sure* he's a man?')

'It makes him look like some bleak character out of Beckett,' Jasper continued. 'Perhaps that is how he feels,' Anne suggested mildly, and Jasper had had to agree that after Ron's interminable tenure review, this was possible.

Anne had to stop thinking about Jasper. The sting might have dulled somewhat since he left two years before, yet the image of Jazz's angled smile of greeting, wearing one of his striped shirts – magenta aligned with turquoise, or mauve with ochre – gave Anne a sudden grief-seizure, that phantom limb pain. *Americans Abroad*: just don't mention the ones living in France with their new wives.

She stepped closer to the mirror above the walnut dresser and applied slate liner and smoky shadow around her gold-green eyes, a plum shaping on her lips.

The knock on the door came as Anne smoothed a last concealing fingertip over the grooves in her skin, where anger or laughter preferred to dwell. That her years showed had begun to bother Anne, but not as much as the fact that her face reminded her more and more of her mother's. Irène Arden had died in June at the hospice, angry and unaccepting, attended by Catholic nurses, and though Anne remained certain she did not mourn her, embittered as their relationship had been, still she found her expressions now taking on the slant and accent of Irène's. It made her feel haunted.

'Yes.' She pulled herself away from the mirror to break the spell. 'Come in.'

At the door stood the pert German purser Charlotte. Trim and tidy in her dark uniform, she wore her hair boyishly short, and a slight smirk that Anne read alternately as playful or impertinent. Charlotte had been flirting with Anne over these several days, in the galley outside the dining room or in a chat on one of the dapple-lit decks, and Anne, entertained, had flirted right back.

'Good morning, professor.' Even the salutation had a suggestive edge, though that might simply have been the slant of her Teutonic accent.

'Good morning, Charlotte.' A slight raise of her eyebrow. 'Can I help you?'

Charlotte looked down.

'Ah, no. I'm to help *you.*' Her Bavarian cheeks had cherried a deeper red, bright against her black hair. 'We're to confirm where you'd like your luggage sent when we dock in Venice. You're not staying on with the group . . . ?'

'For the Venetian Postlude?' Anne and Margaret had joked about the suggestive phrase, but she thought better of trying to translate that for Charlotte. 'No. I'm going to stay for a few days at a flat in Cannaregio.' There was a beat, to allow an instant of fantasy. 'With my sister, who's coming to join me.'

'All right.' Charlotte nodded properly. 'If you give us the address, we can have a taxi waiting at the dock to help you there with your luggage.'

'I'll find it. It's in my email.' Anne collected her books and papers and placed them in a leather satchel, though she had only to travel half a ship length to deliver her talk. Still, the gathering was part of how she prepared. Anne felt calmer when organized. 'And you?' she asked. 'Do you have any time off to enjoy Venice?'

'Two nights. Then back to the *Stella Maris*, and we'll retrace the journey in the other direction. With an English group – we'll have to make sure we have enough beer on board.'

'Our replacements.' Anne empathized. 'Like classes of students at the end of a semester: all those names and faces you've learned and then have to forget, to clear space for the next lot.'

'Yes. Some quite happily forgotten.' Charlotte allowed a subtle eye roll, and Anne laughed. There had been passengers who were demanding, or complaining, or both. There always were. Students, too. 'But then there are some –' the dashing German very nearly clicked her heels, as she took her leave of Anne, though her voice dropped suddenly, for emphasis – 'we will remember.'

# 7

Anne stopped in to the ship's 'library', an elegant, contained space where in spite of its name books were less in evidence than electronic devices, as passengers unfolded their laptops or unsleeved their tablets and reconnected with the worlds they pretended to have left behind. *Escape the flurry of everyday life as you travel in luxurious comfort aboard our star of the sea*, the brochure had encouraged, yet people did not really want to escape that flurry, in Anne's experience. Wi-fi anxiety was cross-generational, and the people around Anne were nearly as wired as the twenty-year-olds at NYU. Few on the ship were taking time out on the canvas deckchairs to pen postcards, Anne noticed, though most did come to the library to check their email. The world of *The Aspern Papers* was more imaginable to these alumni, who must have distinct memories, at least, of correspondences that required ink and paper, and left behind tangible objects, cards and letters, in boxes stored in dusty attics.

Anne's simple task was to find the address of the apartment she had rented for Tricia and herself; however, having opened her email, it was impossible for Anne not to notice a subject head on a note from Margaret. It wouldn't hurt (Anne glanced at the laptop's clock; she still had time) to read it.

From: Margaret Carter
Subject: Women Write The World

Hi there, dear A. Hope the sea breezes are relaxing you and you have discovered your inner sailor.

So that's a good title, isn't it? Women Write the World? But is the line descriptive or prescriptive? Perhaps you can help us decide! I'm sorry to interrupt your idyll, and I am eager to know whether Prof. Marovic has helped you find your sea legs, ahem. But more than that I'm trying to finalize the list of names for the conference we're organizing in October. Could I possibly persuade you to moderate a panel, lending your elegant celebrity to the event? (Flattery will get you everywhere . . .)

So far we have some good people. Melissa Green of *The Times* and the Poet Laureate, our very own Lisa Sahel Jefferson. We need a few younger names on the roster, though, so this too doesn't turn into a Journey Around the Geriatric. (Sorry, but hey, you started it.) Can you let me know a) if you're in, as moderator, and b) if you can think of anyone under forty (no offence to all of us who are pushing fifty or in my case have ACTUALLY PASSED it) who would be good to invite? Thank you. Yours faithfully, forever in your debt, hoping you'll have a limoncello for me, etc. . . .

M xox

Anne stared at the letter for a long moment, while her thoughts wandered over old territory. *Flattery will get you everywhere*. Writers under forty. Graduates of that university. Women.

She could think of one, yes. Possibly a flicker of the energy Charlotte had carried into Anne's cabin brought this person to mind. Possibly the thought of her, recently, was less far away. A woman Anne once knew. Like a piece of polished sea glass, the name was there, surfacing above all the other students, the numberless undergraduates she had known. That memorable colour catching her eye amidst the many bland grains of sand in her mind.

Flannery Jansen.

Surely it wouldn't hurt to suggest her?

# 8

She was a fetching girl, and she had touched Anne in a place Anne had not been touched. Even by Jasper.

A bonnie lass. Anne liked 'bonnie' because it sounded sunny and golden as Flannery Jansen was, on the surface, and the word had a fairy tale, yesteryear resonance which matched the girl's otherworldly quality.

Girl! She was not out of her teens, for God's sake. *Look at you, babe!* Anne sometimes wanted to say when Flannery had been clever, but she came to see that that head-patting impulse had to be resisted. Because Flannery was smart, too; very smart. You did not want to underestimate her intelligence or her resilience. Both were deeper than they seemed on first appearance.

First appearance. Anne and Flannery met at a diner, a tiny, no-frills joint near the campus, since transformed into a print shop, though its perky name, The Yankee Doodle, lived on in T-shirts sold at the college bookstore. Strictly speaking, the two women saw each other there but did not meet. Anne had been reading, over a cup of coffee, a book required for the comp lit class for which she would be assistant teaching. Into the diner came a tall, fair student, half ducking as if to apologize for her height, a general air about her of having run away from home and being down to the last few dollars in her wallet. But beautiful. She looked around, bewildered – no make-up or adornment on, which made it easier to appreciate her smooth skin, the curved fall of her buttery hair, and the darting, unmistakable look of hunger she threw Anne's way after she sat down. It was a diverting paradox: she was checking Anne out without realizing she was doing it. Staring at Anne, then turning away, blushing, unable to finish her breakfast. Anne had tossed a teasing joke her way, and the stranger had fled, like a frightened deer.

Anne had returned to her reading, her concentration altered.

She saw the stuttery, pretty girl a few days later in one of the sections she was teaching for the comp lit class. There she learned her improbable name: *Flannery*. That this apparently self-effacing person should be saddled with a name so ostentatious was amusing enough, but when it turned out that the young Flannery wanted to write, too, it was hard not to smile. Might this flaxen-haired Californian not have opted for something less loaded, career-wise, further from her nominal home – animal husbandry, say? Civil engineering? To their mutual relief, Flannery transferred out of Anne's section, without which move none of the rest might have followed. Anne probably teased her about that move, too.

Anne had not been at her best at that time. She was trying to claw her way out of graduate school, completing a doctoral thesis which she had been told was 'potentially' brilliant but required an undivided attention she did not have to give it. The split from Jasper had given relief and grief in equal measure: Anne had been finding Jasper overbearing, somehow too much to manage, but their separation nonetheless had left her brittle and unbending, like some soft confection that hardened in the air as it cooled. Anne had to hand only a small amount of patience and a vast sum of sarcasm.

But Flannery Jansen, that cute crushed-out freshman, developed an infatuation for Anne and was too inexperienced to hide it. Teacher-love, if not the oldest story in the book, was certainly one from a tattered, dog-eared edition, and Anne was familiar with its generic conventions. These crushes generally faded, if you left them alone, like an untended fruit that ripens then dies on the vine. Yet watching this young woman go through the motions – trying to hide, yet somehow often being in the same places Anne was, the all-night convenience store, the campus book shop, the library, of course, making a flicker of eye contact then looking, pinkened, away – stirred something in Anne, awakened a tenderness in her. As she finally prepared to leave Yale, she was moved by a naive and lovely newcomer who scarcely seemed to understand where she had landed. Both were outsiders to the place, though Anne had gone deep in the hiding of her roots. The two women were ships passing in the New Haven night. Anne Arden was almost gone, heading west to teach, and here was this eager young thing trying to blend in, not yet with success, to the bristling East Coast.

For a while, Anne's feeling seemed big sisterish – *Look at that poor kid! Someone needs to talk to her* – but there came an evening, that fall, when Anne recognized that Flannery was an adult, not a child. At a raucous off-campus party, a mixture of grads and undergrads, Anne saw a lithe, tank-topped Flannery dancing, and the rhythms of Flannery's hips and her long limbs entranced Anne, and opened her to a risky possibility.

The two women traded verse and wordplay, drinks and banter. Anne loaned her young friend a book of poetry. She was flirting, and did not pretend to herself she wasn't, but neither did she expect it to lead anywhere other than perhaps to a brief, sweet fling.

Flannery kept deepening, though. She continued to get

older, and bolder. She had the courage to bare herself to the core, make the ultimate offering. She wrote a poem for Anne, then waited in a dawn train station to give it to the object of her devotion, before Anne headed to New York City for Thanksgiving break. 'Pages for You'. Remember?

When Anne read the poem, alone in a Metro-North carriage, she felt that steel clench of significance. *Someone is giving you something, here. Pay attention.* This young woman whom Anne hardly knew was willing to *risk* – embarrassment, revelation, mistake – in order to communicate to Anne that she loved her. And wanted her. There was no way to look at this offering and mock. Or turn away, even. By the time the train reached New York, Anne had determined to call Flannery (there were no cell phones; the world did not yet email) to invite the young woman to come to the city so they could meet.

Anne realized that 'Pages for You' could be thought of as an innocent's error too, an adolescent overstepping. She wrote you a *poem*? Come on! But it wasn't a mistake. This wise and sometimes still foolish young woman had done the right thing. Flannery's intricate words were her own; and then Anne's; and then theirs.

Anne told Jasper about Flannery, later. The women's hot winter passion, their spring cooling, a March vacation to Florida that went pretty badly wrong, with storms and sunburn and blistered tempers. But Anne never mentioned the poem Flannery had written. She did not want to have to show it to Jasper. Not out of shame, or for that matter pride, but simply from a sense that the heart of what happened between the lovers was private, entirely, and should not be shared.

It was a gift, those months she had had with Flannery.

And they belonged just to the two of them.

# 9

*'When Americans went abroad in 1820 there was something romantic, almost heroic in it, as compared with the perpetual ferryings of the present hour, the hour at which photography and other conveniences have annihilated surprise.'*

Anne wrote this sentence in her neat sloped hand across a whiteboard on which lingered the ghosts of consonant-thick Slavic names from Marovic's lecture the day before. Now, as the *Stella Maris* crossed the Adriatic back to Italy, it was time for Anne and her Europhile Americans.

She stood, exercising her gift of stillness, while they gathered. There was an art to this too: to waiting. In order not to have to engage in chatter as they entered, Anne regarded the faux-yellowed maps that hung on the lounge's tasteful ochre walls. The Mediterranean, the Baltic, the Adriatic. So many seas!

The passengers fluttered in and settled like birds – a parliament of owls, a scold of jays. There were some of each. Among the owls, a famous diminutive psychoanalyst and her besotted second husband, a pepper-bearded man who bore a more than passing resemblance to Sigmund Freud. (It was impossible not to notice.) They were a cultured pair and engaged readers, and Anne had written a portion of her lecture with them, particularly Barbara, in mind. Then there were the two women companions from Maine, one pulling a draped rose cardigan closer over her shoulders, the other holding underarm a half-written-over legal pad, as if on her way into a city council meeting. Settling in to two of the yellow leather chairs were the good-humoured Knudsens (timber money; Anne recognized the name), a couple modest about their wealth and their learning, from whom Anne hoped still to keep the fact that she, too, was from Michigan.

Then, the jays. Entering theatrically with his cane, more prop than necessity, was a Tennesseean named Winter, a retired tobacco lawyer, whose egg-white hair was combed in even strips across his florid forehead and whose knowledge of antiquity came largely from the novels of Gore Vidal, to whom he was distantly related. Anne could have done without Winter's joking interjections and wandering hand, which had a way of finding one's forearm (and once, at a lunch table, her thigh) but preferred them to the abrasive voice of the implausibly dark-haired film executive from Los Angeles, whose wife had the distracted eye of an alcoholic, watching the clock for the next drinks hour as if waiting for a train. Last to arrive, walking slowly and with a slight limp to a chair near Anne, was an imposing Austrian woman in a previous century's floral dress, her expression ever a mixture of haughty scepticism and intellectual curiosity.

It was a mostly energetic, outward-looking group, whose years of experience gave them peculiar advantages in a discussion of, say, the nature of envy, or regret. In classrooms at home, Anne was used to her students representing a *place she had once been* (young, striving, proving; confronting urgent dilemmas of the self), rather than a *place she might be going* (older, having striven, having proved; confronting the prospect of death). Orphaned, Anne had no one standing between her and the grave now. She was turning fifty in a couple of years, a waypoint she dreaded – she had not needed Margaret's joking reminder. An English colleague of Anne's, an older man, once warned her, 'Watch out for fifty. It does your head in.' She could not shake that line from her mind.

It was time to start talking.

'More than a hundred years before Facebook, or Instagram, or Twitter, people were already beginning to feel that the adventure of travel was over,' Anne began, wondering who in the room might know what Instagram was. She turned back to the quotation on the board.

*Henry James, The Aspern Papers.* She paused, then added: *1887.*

Chuckles bubbled up from Winter and the analysts. The Austrian looked grave. One of the Maine women jotted down the quotation and the date.

'It wasn't, of course, over,' Anne said. Her lucid emerald gaze met that of her listeners. 'The adventure of Venice – of discovery – was not over then, and it's not over now.'

Professor Arden had their attention, and they were ready to believe her.

# 10

It was the farewell dinner aboard the *Stella Maris.* Laughter, conversation, and alcohol overflowed, a rivulet of flirtations and indiscretions. From shore, onlookers might watch the vessel alight, alive, and speculate about those who animated her. Anne was seated at the captain's table, a phrase that brought to mind images of Bette Davis in *Now, Voyager* or some other forties film in black and white, though the captain himself, a chiselled Swede named Sven Magnusson, was nicely in colour and right beside her. Marovic was on Anne's other side, flushed and lively after a couple of potent cocktails, and patrician Winter a safe distance across, where his heavy paw had most likelihood of landing on Austrian Greta, who, now brightened with blue eyeshadow and some form of schnapps, looked like she might not mind.

Marovic had found a Californian lawyer and his wife, also of Croatian ancestry, with whom he was trading stories about foods and family members, striking the occasional tart note about his soon-to-be ex-wife. Over the earlier cocktails, Anne had heard more about the historian's unfortunate, drawn-out divorce, details she did not feel obliged to track, though she felt empathy for Marovic on his effortful path toward liberation.

Magnusson was, by contrast, chivalrous on the subject of his wife in Gothenburg. A broad-faced, weather-tanned man with a kind mouth edged by a short silvered beard, the captain attracted Anne, his understated Scandinavian humour appealed to her, and though she believed the aquavit tint in his eyes had no real intent, she leaned in as he spoke to her of his many travels. He was telling her a well-practised tale about a trip to Patagonia with a batch of American adventurers ('So sure they knew everything – and that they were immortal!'), and she allowed herself a vivid moment to imagine his wide hands holding her in that mobile rhythm of the ship he knew and guided. *A Voyage Around the Adriatic.* Well, you had to be allowed such fantasies; wasn't that what these journeys were for? The aquavit had loosened Anne, too.

All over the ship the married passengers did carry on as flirtatious as, if not more so than, those who were single. There was something about marriage that pushed its inhabitants into a state of tense, never to be satisfied anticipation – a dog straining on the leash, the dish just out of reach.

Had Anne resisted marriage because her mother's and father's was so miserable, or was it her sister Patricia's wedding when she was much too young that had put Anne off? Anne had been too embarrassed to bring Jasper to Detroit for the occasion, and was relieved that he had missed the flowers and dress-up and ornate rites of the Catholic mass, performed over a union it seemed likely would end in alcoholic divorce – as it did, a decade later. Perhaps, Anne considered recently, as she tried to reshape her understanding of her own decisions, it had been magical thinking on her part – her irrational hope of inoculating herself against heartbreak – but seeing these 'train wrecks of marriages' in her family made Anne determined not to have one herself. For his part, though in their first several years Jasper raised the question with Anne, he seemed to settle happily on this rebellion against his class and background, in the form of their undocumented partnership. 'No papers,' Jasper and Anne told each other solemnly. They were not hippies or free spirits, but felt they were acting with integrity. 'No legalities. Just trust, and honesty – and love.'

So Anne and Jazz had not married, and Anne had not regretted it. They shared companionship, domesticity, sex, loyalty, encouragement, affection, forgiveness; but never marriage.

Nothing inoculated you, though. Nothing kept you safe from heartbreak. Anne looked around at the energetic exchanges on the *Stella Maris* and knew that some flirtations that night would damage marriages, and others would not. She smiled deafly at a joke delivered with great hilarity at the captain's table. Anne had missed it.

Nothing, she now knew, made you immune.

# 11

*Serenissima.*

They sailed toward Venice. It was the sixth and ultimate day, and Anne was, the daily printed schedule informed her, *at sea*. 'Yes, yes, I know,' she muttered to the sheet, alone in her cabin. 'No need to remind me.' How pervasive nautical metaphors were in the language of adventure and return, security and its opposite: adrift, at sea, tossed on the waves; or anchored, ashore, safe harbour. Run aground. Sunk. *Iceberg dead ahead.*

Which was she, now? Forty-eight and parentless, mateless. Was Anne free, or unmoored?

She could not decide. It depended on the day. Anne could feel either.

She had been told – by the captain the night before, in a voice that might have been poetic or simply practical, Anne could not tell – that it was difficult at first to feel your legs firm on land again, even if you had been disembarking and going ashore during the journey. That, of course, was another part of the lure of the cruise: the lyrical, floating suspension away from reality, the wilful turning away from the earth of every day. Anne was looking forward to having solid ground underfoot again; though rejoining the real world, somewhat less.

Which made Venice the right place to conclude her voyage,

a city that was anyway half water, and half magic. In Venice, with her sister, Anne would reacquaint herself with the rhythms of regular life, though still in the heightened, near imaginary environment of that city.

Having time to herself would be a relief. By now Anne had become wearied by shipboard existence, especially its social demands. She had predicted correctly that she would have little appetite for the *Stella Maris*'s many small talk exchanges, which moved inexorably toward questions about her romantic and family life. Having, and even avoiding, such conversations brought with it a particular emotional lag in Anne; and conferences produced this same sensation. She enjoyed dialogue on the page more than poorly scripted snippets traded in the bar areas of hotels – or ships. Margaret's October gathering would require more of all that. It was the main reason Anne had not yet committed.

Venice, though. *Serenissima.* What ghost stories might it raise?

Anne and Jasper had travelled to Venice together. Of course – they had travelled widely. Some couples had children, or dogs; Anne and Jasper had geography. One sabbatical year they lived outside Nice while Jasper was finishing a book, and Anne too, months spent working and walking and cooking, the kind of life about which people wrote bestselling memoirs that became lush, touristic movies. From there the couple had taken a trip to Venice. They stayed in a charismatic, dilapidated hotel, looked at art, ate well, and gondolaed, even.

But a shadow travelled with them. A month earlier, in Nice, Anne had had an early, hygienic abortion, and Jasper planned the Venice trip as a healing distraction. In a shop that sold fashionable leather bags and belts Jasper found Anne a purse, but in discussing the purchase in Italian he misspoke so badly that all three of them – Anne, Jasper, and the angelic young man helping them – collapsed in bilingual laughter. Later, when a sudden *acqua alta* made San Marco an impassable lake, they had walked like circus performers along the rickety wooden platforms that appeared as if out of hidden cupboards, to ensure a dry crossing, but then Anne stepped deeply into the water anyway in order to help up a distressed child who had fallen. Anne's chic shoes were ruined in the rescue, but the child was restored to her parents, who were a minute behind, and very appreciative of Anne's assistance. Back at the hotel, Jasper had dried and warmed Anne's feet and said she deserved a medal of valour for her effort.

Venice was just ground, Anne reminded herself. Nothing hallowed about it. You must simply go over it all again – the crooked pavements, the arched bridges, the flooding piazzas – and tread firmly over memories. If Anne only ever went places she had not once been to with Jazz, how narrow the brilliantly wide world would become.

In the future Anne might set foot in places she had never been to with him – Jaipur, or Melbourne. Johannesburg, where a friend of hers was working on a film project. First, though, the recanvasing of a place she had known. Tricia would be good and bracing company, as long as they were able to avoid argument, and could negotiate any posthumous parental matters that required sorting. From the outside, the holiday seemed a chance for the sisters to come together to lament their lost mother. Given their complicated feelings about Irène, however, it might turn into something else – for Tricia, Anne supposed, a chance to recuperate from the task of managing Irène's final decline (and mention her irritation that Anne had not helped out more). On Anne's part, the grief she had still to shed was for someone else.

*Serenissima*? Not yet. Anne lay down in her cabin at sea, wondering when she would get there.

# 12

The *Stella Maris* moved into the harbour, the famous cityscape gradually sketching itself in the passengers' sightlines. The silver domes of the Salute, the ochre and terracotta and taupe of canalside *palazzi*, and the puddle colours of the canals themselves, navigated by striped and photo-ready gondoliers. The *vaporetti*, Venice's water buses, lumbered from one stop to another like heavy carthorses, while darting speedboats, sleek thoroughbreds, overtook them easily. *The perpetual ferryings of the present hour.*

Most were out on deck with their cameras and their phones, ready to chronicle their arrival, though Anne held back. Her itch to be alone was by now unignorable, so, explaining to Marovic that she was not going on to the last, grand lunch, she went through several goodbyes, simultaneously sincere and superficial. 'Please do email me your article on Wharton, I'd love to read it' (Barbara, the analyst); 'I'll send you pictures from Lecce' (the Knudsen husband, who had a surprising eye in his photographs); 'Now I'm determined to go home and read Mary McCarthy. I'd always avoided her before' (a spry ninety-year-old whose eyes were a blue that rivalled that of the Murano glass the group had seen being blown in the famous factory). As for Marovic: he had given Anne a formal embrace, hangover-chastened, with kisses back and forth three times on her cheeks. He had heard from Professor Carter that she might be at Yale in October for a gathering, and perhaps he would see her then? Anne smiled noncommittally.

As Anne watched the city draw nearer to them, she felt an eagerness to move through its streets for herself, having read and taught the city and handed out famous quotations about it. Venice, and clichés about Venice: could the two ever be disentangled?

It was the same with love, probably, Anne thought. Jasper might have said as much to her. Or grief. *No point in trying to be original.* She had read that somewhere; a line from an English book floated through her mind, Barnes quoting a friend of his who had said, about leaving his wife for a younger woman: 'People tell me it's a cliché. But it doesn't feel like a cliché to *me*.'

That was the trick, perhaps, Anne thought as the ship slowed, close to the dock: to walk through these alleys and clichés with your head held high, as though no one had ever been there before you.

# 13

The apartment suited. It was modest, discreet, quiet. Not far from the madding crowds, since in August Venice was mad and crowded every inch of it, but, Anne judged, a good place for a private coffee in the morning and a respite from art and commerce in the later humid afternoons.

It was midday when Anne arrived, her gait still slightly uneven from her sandalled encounter with the odd solidity of land. She spoke her adequate Italian to the weather-beaten landlady, who avoided looking Anne in the eye, as if it were too much effort to read even one more tourist's face. Anne heard how to use the windows and shutters, the broken tap and erratic plumbing. She accepted the keys – a heavy, dungeon-like set with the enchanted quality of so much in Venice – thanked the signora, and then the thick oak door closed with a portentous click.

Anne moved into a high-ceilinged living room that seemed to list slightly. She recognized the simple furnishings from the stamp-sized photograph she had seen online. It was the same as Internet dating, Anne guessed: you imagined yourself in the photograph on your screen, then met the actual place, or person, and judged for yourself how much truth the photographs had spoken, or how deceptively flattering the angles had been.

This one did not disappoint. A camel-coloured sofa with a few textured orange pillows, a rectangular glass coffee table scattered with magazines, and simple prints on the wall – the dome of Santa Maria della Salute, a bowl of apples, a low boat in a timeless mist. On the warped wooden floors a pleated cotton rug, also orange. Anne recalled Jasper telling her about the palette Turner had created for his Venetian paintings: swatches of salmon, terracotta, clementine, as well as shades of the city's many watery blues.

Anne breathed in sharply, a lungful of the city's distinctive scent of salt and sewage. It permeated the apartment in spite of the eighteenth-century building's effort to shield its inhabitants from the atmosphere. She made herself a cup of fragrant chamomile tea.

What you lose with all the rest is the person who knew the cast of your personal drama. *The death of the evil queen.* If Anne were in contact with Jasper now, she would have told him, of course, about her mother. How would he have reacted? He had known Irène Arden less as a person than as an imprint on Anne – or perhaps more of a negative space around her. A negative space, now absent. Would Jasper have called that paradox a positive? Even if Anne believed she was not mourning, she felt that Jasper would have helped her understand, and not just logically, the shape of her loss.

*Be patient with your sister*, Anne could imagine him saying. *She may be grieving more than you are. Don't presume to know.*

Anne reached for her book. She had a sudden, keen appetite – not for food or rest, but for reading. Sometimes, if it had been too long since she had settled into a book, she started to feel faint and hollow. Stretched out on the camel sofa with her book and a cup of tea, her mind and body finally relaxed. It was Wharton's *The Children*, the novel she had mentioned in her talk. She came across a good line – 'He loved Palace Hotels; but he loathed the mere thought of the people who frequented them.' It made her think of her friend Cynthia, who taught a class called 'Money Can't Buy You Love: The Wretched Rich in American Fiction'.

One symptom of Anne's current nameless condition was how much more distractible she was than usual. The Internet invaded. It was relentless as a sea, breaking wave after wave on the shores of her vulnerable mind. A solid shoal of concentration was broken over months and days into something granular, endless tiny pieces of attention, as the mind's solidity slowly dissolved. Anne was, it seemed, helpless against it.

She put down her book across one of the orange cushions, and reached for her laptop. She wrote a quick note to Cynthia with the line from Wharton, then saw another new note in from Margaret.

> Bellissima! Brief one here – to say thanks for the suggestion, we've a note out to Flannery Jansen. But in yours you artfully dodged the central problematic: will Prof Arden herself preside? Sorry to bug you . . .
> Can you let me know? M xo

Anne closed her eyes. It would be better to resolve this now.

> Ciao Margaret,

They had a note out to Flannery. That did not mean she would be there, though, and Anne's participation could not depend on it. Still, she owed Margaret thanks for getting her on that Voyage Around the Adriatic. She would not have been in Venice, now, without her.

> *Si, certo!* I'll do it.
>
> Sorry I didn't make that clear before. Let's chat details when I'm back . . .
>
> Axx
>
> PS Sorry to be brief – my sister's arriving shortly, and I'm still getting used to solid ground. And as you know, Venice is anyway none too stable . . .

Anne folded shut her laptop. She picked up her book again, but found that her mind now seemed to be travelling elsewhere.

# 14

'I can't believe they call themselves an airline.'

Such was the exasperated greeting that met Anne on her opening the outer door of the apartment building. There stood her sister: eyes slightly bloodshot, her hair damp from sweat and heat and the stale exhalations of other passengers on the overnight flight. 'Delays, incompetence, rudeness – I should have just come by cruise ship, like you did.'

Had Tricia rehearsed that opening, knowing the reference to Anne's more pampered existence would immediately wrongfoot her? The younger sister stooped slightly to allow Anne's embrace, a moment of touch that returned them both to that fundamental animal closeness of family.

Tricia's familiar features had not quite fallen into focus, as if they had not caught up with a body that had travelled too far, too fast. 'They lost my luggage,' she said, though her intonation was defensive, as if someone were about to suggest this was her fault. Tricia often spoke this way, fending off imagined criticism. A different aspect of the Irène legacy. 'They're delivering it here this afternoon. *Supposedly*.'

'How annoying. Well, come in. Shake the plane off.' At work Anne was known as fair, though given to a cool impatience when others made mistakes, but with her irascible younger sister she took the role of the calmer-downer, the soother. 'It's a nice apartment,' she said as she walked up the broad marble steps that were bevelled in the centre by a couple of centuries of climbing boots. 'If a bit overly orange. There's a nice little balcony. I let you have the larger room.'

'Hunh,' came from Tricia as she climbed, a sound pitched between a grunt of exertion and a note of thanks. 'But I'll have to stay in these gross sweaty clothes until the suitcase gets here. Nothing of yours would fit me.'

'You can cool down, anyway. I'll get you some sparkling water, and lemon.'

Siblings, unless they are graced with that rare gift, an even-handed upbringing, always end up owing each other something. There are lacks that must be made up for; unfairnesses that cannot be erased or forgotten. If Irène had managed a brusque, condescending affection with Patricia, she had forever withheld from Anne her maternal love, or even liking. Then again, from early years their mother made it clear she considered her younger daughter homely, and not thin. The French–Polish cocktail of Irène and Frank Arden had not blended as successfully in the second child, so though Patricia's face was broad too, she did not have the high cheekbones that defined it; Tricia's eyes were a flat shade of grey, not green, and tilted at a slight angle. Her chin had an elfin point, like a character in a children's story.

Anne, for her startling beauty, had been punished, at times viciously, by their mother, for whom Anne's appearance was a deliberate act of defiance. She behaved as though her daughter was threatening and disloyal – which, of course, allowed the bright and feisty girl to become both. Their fights were fierce sparrings that sometimes ended in a sour slap on those broad, pale cheeks. In this later era, Anne had reflected, her mother would be considered abusive; in the time and place where Anne grew up it was just called being mean.

Their mother's favouring of Tricia, and her resentment of Anne, were naked and unignorable. Their father Frank, a quiet, industrious engineer and a subdued member of a mother-dominated household, gave his sympathy in silence, and by showing a fairer hand with his affections. Anne was rewarded in the wider world, as her mother was furiously sure she would be, with the love and attention of men, and propelled by that favour and Irène's disdain, Anne left as soon as she could for the far East Coast – for university, adventure, and an exile that felt more like the discovery of a world in which she properly belonged.

Tricia stayed in Michigan. She was educated and employed, married and divorced, all within a hundred miles of where the girls grew up. Their parents supported her, in the mildest sense, witnessing Tricia's marriage and its unpleasant dissolution, accepting visits from her with their grandson Mitchell, faintly congratulatory when she started work at the Detroit Institute of Arts. They also relied on Tricia increasingly for assistance advice, and as the person to whom they could complain about her older sister, who hardly ever returned. It was Patricia who helped make the two mismatched Ardens as comfortable as possible in their fading years – as decent, stay-behind daughters do. She visited their father regularly at the assisted living facility, until the stroke that kindly took him some years before, and she nursed Irène during her last illness, and navigated the move to hospice.

Anne had sympathy and appreciation for her sister's dedication. But she stayed resistant to guilt; raised as she had been, the guilt could have flattened her, if she let it. That, of course, was the other major debt that Anne owed her sister: emotional reimbursement for her own success at escape, and Tricia's decision to stay in Detroit with Frank and Irène. Though – did either have a choice, really?

They had last seen each other at their mother's funeral in May, a poorly attended occasion at a church associated with the hospice centre rather than the one familiar from their childhood. This was a relief to Anne, to travel to a suburban church outside of Detroit that had no family association, though it was unnerving to listen to a priest speak rote redemptive words about a woman he had never known. Still, she shed no tears for Irène Arden. That day, or since.

# 15

'Oh, Pellegrino. Perfect.'

Tricia had been sober for several years now, having by her own account turned into one of those 'weepy winos' during her first post-divorce stretch of single motherhood and precarious finances. Her work and home life had settled since, and if Tricia was too proselytizing about AA for Anne's taste, clearly it had helped stabilize her, and would prevent the alcoholic viciousness that had sometimes soured the sisters' time together in the past. It also meant Anne would be drinking alone, a melancholy prospect.

'At least I had a clean T-shirt in my carry-on, so I feel like a human being,' Tricia said, and, showered and refreshed, she did look more herself. 'Honestly, I haven't travelled in a while, I'm out of practice.'

They settled on two cast-iron chairs that occupied nearly the entirety of the bathmat-sized balcony, from which they had their view of Venice: a murky green lapping diagonal of their nearest canal, below a collage of taupe and terracotta rooftops and variously sized sky-shaded domes.

'I've counted eleven different churches here named for Santa Maria.' Anne sipped an Aperol, her free hand resting on the guidebook she had been reading. 'Her mercy, her rosary, her visitation. Her health.'

'Dad's favourite lady.' Tricia sighed. 'She was his great comfort.'

'More than our mother was.'

'That's for sure.'

Santa Maria had without doubt helped Frank Arden to tolerate, or at least endure, over five decades of marriage to a bitterly dutiful wife who yearned to return to France, and possibly someone she had known there.

'That wooden Virgin he kept in his room . . .' The couple had not shared a bed for as long as either sister could remember, though for years Frank continued to refer to where he slept as 'the spare room'. 'He prayed to her daily.'

'I remember her,' Anne said. The Madonna had been modelled after the figure in Lourdes, a subdued saint, her head down and her hands pressed together in symmetry. 'I helped drive her over when we moved him to the facility.'

'Yeah,' Tricia confirmed. 'Mary, clothes, a few books – that was pretty much it.'

'And the Chopin sheet music. Though I doubt he played.'

It was one of the coinages of families, economical means of summarizing previous arguments. *I tried to be there for our father. It was only our mother's care that I left up to you. I couldn't be part of that.* 'He travelled light, when he left their house.'

'Can't blame him. He left Chère Irène to deal with all the boxes of photographs and letters. Not that she ever did. We'll have to sort through them.'

'Chère Irène! God. I'd almost forgotten about that.' Anne shook her head.

'Really?' Tricia's grey eyes had a cool scepticism much like Anne's own. 'Come on.'

'Well,' Anne said, truthfully, 'I have tried to bury most of those occasions when –' she searched for the right euphemism – 'our mother had a heavy hand.'

They were children at the time – Tricia was eight and Anne twelve – and up in the cluttered attic they rummaged like squirrels, making a nest amongst the boxes. Tricia was busy physically building the nest from musty old coats and blankets, while Anne started looking through letters. For what, she was never afterwards sure, though she knew it when she found it. In one old shoebox, a set of old blue air letters, in French, addressed to *Chère Irène*. 'Come on,' Tricia said to her, bored. 'Let's play.' But Anne could not stop herself reading, as well as she could, a foreign hand and a language she was more proficient in to speak than read – but words that she knew, with shame and growing excitement, were speaking of love. They were not from Frank. The letters were signed *ton amour dévoté, Edouard* and Anne was too fascinated by the import of what she had found to register the danger in the discovery, or the sound of her mother's steps up the attic stairs. '*Démon!*' was all she hissed at her daughter before pulling her by the wrist down the attic stairs to issue a beating to her, out of little Tricia's sight though not her hearing.

'That was one of the worst times.' It had been her face, a hard slap, followed by a twisting of Anne's ear. She would not cry, but it stung for days.

'Yeah.' They both allowed the silent equation to move through their minds: *I was the one she slapped. All right, well I'm the one who changed her bedpan.*

The Venetian air hung between them for a moment.

'I'm going to one of these churches this afternoon.' Anne gestured at her guidebook. 'The Santa Maria dei Miracoli. It's near here. "A gem." Do you want to come?'

'You go,' Tricia said. 'I'm not really in shape for the Virgin today. I'm going to call Mitchell to let him know I got here. Maybe take a nap. Hope the airline shows up with my bag.'

'I'll send Santa Maria your regards.'

'Yeah. Do that.' Tricia drained her glass. 'Tell her to keep going with the miracles. God knows, the world needs them.'

# 16

You did not have to be religious to find solace in churches. Whether God lived in them – or only human dreams about God – along with errant sparrows, patterned windows, and cold, stone saints, the lofty heights of those consecrated spaces gave room for the spirit to breathe. Anne would not have said any of this to her no-nonsense sister. But it was why she had come.

Anne approached the five-hundred-year-old building in an ochre afternoon light, and inhaled like a child at the sight of it. No density of tourists outside clicking their phones or cameras could lessen Anne's sensuous pleasure at the facade's inlaid grey-veined gold marble, its intricate slate and yellow roses, the burgundy cross above the Virgin and her infant. Anne entered a *chiesa* built to celebrate Mary's miracles, with its own stone-wrought miracles that were purely human. Lombardo had carved beauty from stone – Francis and Clare, the angel Gabriel and the Virgin – and it must make a man feel something like a god, to be able to do that. Anne sat down on a pew and dipped her head, a few rows behind two women, one older than her and one younger, who sat together, praying.

It was just as well, probably, that Tricia had not joined her. Anne would have felt more constrained. The last time the sisters had sat in a church together, at their mother's funeral, Tricia had allowed herself a brief whispered sarcasm about the bishop's hypocrisy (though that didn't stop them both from taking communion, out of respect for Irène). Their long-ago hours spent at Detroit's Saint Aloysius, being instructed in all the ways people could stain themselves with sin, gave Tricia the native's right to chafe at Vatican pronouncements; though for Anne those Sunday hours had at least provided respite from the caustic unhappiness at home. Mass had still been in Latin then, and the language stirred Anne; it fed, like a distant, concealed spring, her present-day Italian, and French. She did not have faith, almost definitely. Yet her lips moved along with some words in her mind, possibly something resembling prayer.

Behind her, a dozen Germans started singing softly, a Teutonic hymn. A nougat-shaded light suffused the air about Anne and she tilted her head back to catch the consoling sound of human voices in harmony.

Were they singing, in particular, to the Virgin? Expressing gratitude, or requesting mercy? Did their verse run anywhere near the thoughts moving through Anne's own mind? *Please, allow me to find peace. Allow me to accept.*

On the last, painful occasion of a conversation between Anne and Jasper about unrequited love, Jasper came at it from a desperate new angle. The desperation, Anne knew, came from not being able to tolerate hurting her.

'There is always love,' he insisted, though his characteristic confidence was undermined slightly by the rasp in his voice, 'the other, deep, groundwater kind – whether you feel it in every instant or not.' It seemed that this was the facing side of his earlier conviction. If passionate love could only exist as a two-person system, then this other essential love could keep two people bonded always, whether they saw each other or not, whether one of them died or not. Jazz had sketched this idea for Anne one night in their apartment, after he had delivered the darker, awful part of the picture, that he had fallen in love with someone else. Jazz's mind had always been of endless interest to Anne, its intellectual and especially its moral capaciousness, but this contradictory cosmology struck her as weak, born, of course, out of apology. 'You know I'll always love you . . .' Even as he left her? How did his words have any coherence?

On the Germans sang, though not comprehensibly to Anne. She had only a nodding acquaintance with German, whose order she admired, along with its mechanical approach to word construction, as she understood it. The voices carried up to the prophets and saints painted neatly on the vaulted ceiling, and Anne assumed that holy collective could translate the choral message, whatever it was.

Forget the strictures of the Church, and its dogma. All you needed was right here in the room. Anne allowed the reverent sung offerings of others to give her, as the wooden Mary had her father, a precious, immaterial comfort – the sensation that somewhere in this hallowed space, within these high stone walls, there was understanding and grace. Even for one's self-imposed losses. Especially for those.

# 17

It was not a question of betrayal and forgiveness but rather of change and acceptance. Acceptance required discipline, and that was one of Anne's tasks. She did not care for Tricia's curt summary – 'It's a story of men chasing tail, as men have done for millennia.' Anne saw the situation differently. A desire shared by two people breaks into two different desires, and the couple breaks with it.

Anne had never wanted to have children.

She knew this about herself as soon as she knew anything. It was an obligation of life, not just of love: *know who you are*. Anne's certainty that she would never be a mother came at the same time she absorbed the possibility of an expanse of opportunity far from her parents' unhappy home, where intelligence could be rewarded not suspected, and her pretty mouth and the sharp sayings that came from it would be appreciated rather than slapped shut. The piano, an instrument Anne was benched in front of aged three and forced to practise for hours a week long into her teens, need not be played obsessively. She could quit. And she could leave. Anne applied to colleges several states away from Michigan, and as a young woman fulfilled the fantasy she had had since she was small, of placing all her possessions in a spotted handkerchief at the end of a stick balanced on her shoulder, and walking away.

Anne told Jasper her feelings about children from the beginning. It was an essential Anne never covered over, a central vein at the core of her, something no one with integrity could hide. Do you want to be a parent or not? Speak now. Or forever hold your peace.

Anne spoke. When they first met; when she was twenty-eight and they reunited; and again over the years. This truth remained constant, and Jasper listened and agreed. Work was more important. Neither could abide the idea of the leaking out of self, time, energy and imagination that parenthood required, and they were comfortably united in their views. Child-free, they travelled together, read, made love, worked. They slept late, or they woke early. When colleagues with young children made envious jokes, Anne always thought: *Well, you could have chosen this, too.*

The only wavering came when Anne once got pregnant in her early thirties. The couple was living in Nice. For Anne, the decision to terminate was so clear she hardly felt the need to discuss it, and the only issues were practical: where to find the best care and treatment. She trusted Jasper to locate that for her – for them.

He did not hesitate. Speaking the better French, Jasper explained the situation, booked the appointment, arranged the soonest possible date. But the morning they were to go to the clinic, he asked her to walk with him around their local streets for a few minutes before they left.

'I have to ask you this, love.' His voice had a slight rasp, as though it had been worn down. He looked underslept. 'You don't want to . . . leave it behind, do you? Teaching, the university . . . ? Just run away from everything and, I don't know, tend grapes, have little . . . Pierre –' he laughed, as if at his own whimsy – 'help out in the vineyards? Live together a stone's throw from the Mediterranean?'

She smiled indulgently, as if at an imaginative joke. 'I know so little about viniculture,' she said. 'But I'll come visit you at harvest time, and trample a few grapes.'

'So,' he continued, and suddenly Anne saw that this was Jasper's main point, and he was serious. 'No Pierre then? No new life?'

'Why are you asking this, Jazz? Is that what you want?' Her voice had a sharpness that came, she felt it, from panic. Fear did that sometimes: transform, in the speaking, into anger. 'A baby?' Her voice sounded accusatory; she could not help it.

He heard her edge, and stopped and turned around, abruptly, to walk back toward the car. He tried to relocate the notion that it had been a passing fanciful idea. 'No, of course not. I want you, darling.' He wasn't looking at her, though, and he sounded subdued. 'Above all. I want you. Let's go. *Allons-y.*'

Part of Anne knew they should talk more, right then. Exactly then. But she was too angry, and did not trust herself.

When they travelled to Venice after, there was no noticeable trace of regret in Jasper. Certainly not in Anne. It was a wonderful, romantic few days there, of art and food and churches – at Jazz's urging they went to Santa Maria dei Miracoli, among others – and Anne had put the preceding episode behind her.

It was years later, during a fraught dinner conversation, when Anne thought of that moment in Nice again. By then the couple had been settled for a decade in New York. The reward for their professional singlemindedness came when NYU offered posts to them both, along with an ample apartment in a high-rise on Bleecker Street. They had a living room that looked toward the giant edifices of the financial district, and a generous study each. Anne had published two books and, especially with her first, *The Awakening of Influence*, had built a room of her own within the broader cultural argument about literature. In their books, both Jasper and Anne had shifted paradigms. As they were meant to.

When their conversation began, Anne had a dizzying sensation of the slippage of time – how the past bleeds right into the present, and events that had seemed separated safely by many years can really be, somehow, simultaneous.

# 18

A wine-lit night, a candle-warmed meal, on a restorative stay-in Saturday after a week filled with students, lectures, bureaucracy. For her married-with-children friends, Anne knew, evenings at home could seem like a continuation of work and noise, the tasks of a different, familial kind that also involved organization, rules, instruction. Anne and Jasper's night was a luxury: two people simply agreeing to cook and delight one another at home. Talking, and then what followed talking.

Jasper roasted a whole seabass encrusted in salt. 'Poor creature,' he said as he slid the fish into the oven, 'you can dream that you are still in the ocean.' Anne worked alongside Jazz in the narrow apartment kitchen. It required a good deal of elbow jostling and culinary dancing, but they managed good-naturedly, with passing jokes and the occasional neck-kiss. Anne tossed an endive salad with lemon juice, avocado, and toasted hazelnuts. Jasper opened a bottle of wine and they sat together in the living room, Wall Street glittering through the darkness while the scent of the cooking fish gradually filled the air.

'Ron Edwards' daughter came by today. While touring the campus. A nice girl, very clever,' Jasper said. 'Wants to be a doctor.'

'I'd have thought she would find it constraining to go to the university where her father teaches.'

'I know.'

'Or even the same city, frankly. Don't children usually want to get as far away as they can from their parents?'

'Well, they have a nice relationship. It seemed very easy. Though she's looking at other campuses too, of course.' Jasper paused. He held his glass in his right hand, and studied its white-gold contents. 'Seeing them together made me think again, though,' he began slowly. Jasper was not one to hesitate when he spoke, and that he did now caught Anne's attention. 'About having a child.'

Anne swallowed with difficulty. Her appetite disappeared. She placed her glass very carefully down on the table, as if it might otherwise shatter in her hands.

'What?' she said, unnecessarily. She felt the sudden racing adrenalined need to slow everything right down. Hold on, hold on. Wait. *Arrête!*

There was Jasper's face beside her, so known, every curve and angle. The handsome, truth-speaking mouth; the long nose; the sandy, silvering hair falling across the broad forehead she loved to soothe. His eyes, cobalt blue in this light, were liquid with an emotion Anne had not seen in him before. *Doubt.* Jasper had not doubted himself around Anne before, not even when they discussed, as they occasionally had to over the years, infidelities or strayings. Jazz knew Anne, and he knew himself around her. That knowledge had been the unbreakable strength of their bond.

'Do you think about it, love? A child?'

Suddenly, it seemed breakable.

'Jazz,' Anne said in a low voice. She had found that nickname for him near the very beginning. Jazz was their shared music, and the way she came back to the piano, gradually, after all those childhood years playing Chopin and Mozart. Jasper had encouraged her. 'I've told you. You've known from the start. I will never be a mother.'

Jasper slid his eyes away from her, and drank.

'Of course, you've said that.' He waved a long, supple hand at the ghost child they were – *he* was – conjuring. Anne felt that the gesture suggested that her earlier words had been not much more than an opinion, one she might have expressed about a film or play they saw together. 'But at the risk of sounding clichéd . . .' He smiled sorrowfully, fetchingly; or so he must have imagined, for Anne could see with a cold dismay that he was acting for her now. She felt herself to be sitting a great distance from Jasper on this familiar sofa – perhaps she was out there on Wall Street, where the lights endlessly shone, or beyond Wall Street even, splashing in the gentle waves of the blackened river. 'I thought you might change your mind.'

'Why? Why would I do that – at forty-one?' And now there were other vibrations in Anne's tone, not just, *How can you pretend not to know this?* But also, *Why would you raise such a question again, now, when I'm this age?*

Jasper drained his glass, folded his arms, sat sideways, angled, on his chair. He too looked out at the postcard view through their plate-glass windows.

'People do,' he said simply. 'People change.' A chill came into his voice and for the first time she heard a novel note – of condescension. She would hear more of it in the painful time ahead. 'Though you seem very clear. Very sure of yourself.'

'I am.' Yet in uttering those two words, Anne could hear that what had seemed a strength in her before, admirable, lovable to Jasper – Anne's clarity, her decisiveness – was being cast in a souring new light. Suddenly she was stubborn, or trapped, or unbending. How swiftly your image in the other's eye could alter, if the other was himself altering.

Anne could hardly eat the dinner they had made together, that Jazz served silently at the round table over which would ordinarily have travelled talk, ideas, in-jokes. Untold that evening. The fish turned to ash in their mouths, the salad had wilted and browned. Their bed was quiet that night, two bodies touching only by accident.

The specific question was folded up and vaulted, but gradually, over the months that followed, Anne heard creeping into Jasper's voice a new wistfulness. A softening toward his younger self, a revisiting of his childhood town and family members he had not seen in a long while. A revived interest in his sister in Los Angeles and his niece and nephew there, whom he sought to visit and befriend. A seed grew within Jasper, and Anne knew this man well enough to sense it growing. His wish to be a father. More than that: his determination to be one.

It was his condescension toward Anne which enabled Jazz, she realized, to edge away from her. She came to believe, when he finally left two years later, that Jasper's departure had begun that night, in their apartment. The actual details – the chef Sophie, where they met, how their affair began – hardly seemed important. It was not a new passion that Jasper sought, exactly; it was parenthood. By definition, that was an adventure Jasper had to have without Anne.

# 19

By early evening, Tricia was rested and ready to wander. And Anne, having been to church, was eager for secular pleasures.

'They came with my bags. Some grouchy, swarthy guy out of the *Godfather* movies. Al Pacino's brother. We couldn't understand each other.'

'That doesn't sound so bad,' Anne said. 'Sometimes a language barrier is a fine thing. Isn't that what they call a meet-cute?'

'It could have been.' Tricia slung a yellow leather purse over her shoulder, which Anne touched, admiringly, and as they headed down the stairs and into Venice Anne noticed something: her sister was walking straighter. Looking lighter. The travel weariness had been just that. 'But actually,' Tricia continued, 'I'm spoken for.' Her voice sounded almost girlish.

'What? *Who?* Who speaks for you?'

'I'll get to that,' Trish said coyly. 'Over dinner. First, what about you? Are you seeing anyone?'

They wove in and out of shops and tourists as they spoke, falling into a sisterly rhythm they hadn't enjoyed for too long.

'I've always found that such an odd verb. *Seeing.*'

'Oh, for God's sake. Don't be such a professor. *Are* you?'

'Well. I saw a nice enough man getting out of my bed a few

times last spring, if that's what you mean.' Another sororal eye roll.

'So? Who was he?'

Anne shook her head. 'It doesn't matter, honestly. Tim. He was a consultant. But it was fairly mercenary on both our parts, that's all.'

'Mercenary?'

'I just mean we were both in it for the sex. Which was fine. There wasn't much more to it than that.' Anne had embarked on this brief affair chiefly so she could tell concerned friends that she had. To put some distance, or at least a body, between herself and memories of Jazz. It had not been especially effective.

'You're a cold fish, sister.' Tricia peered in the window of one of countless glass-offering stores: little glass elephants, swans, giraffes.

'I am, at times. I looked up restaurants, there's one nearby that sounded good, and not a tourist trap. Are you hungry?'

'Starving. So what about your cruise? Any romance there?'

Thoughts of the Swedish captain and the German purser drifted across Anne's mind. 'Sadly, not.'

'No millionaire widowers you could hook up with?'

'Well, there were a few of those.' Anne laughed. 'But they tended to have overgrown ears, and wandering hands. And hold forth at length about Julius Caesar.' She gave a brief comical sketch of Winter. 'Maybe Greta got lucky. But no, I resisted the millionaires' advances.'

'Huh. And you're supposed to be so smart!'

'*Book* smart.' Anne corrected her. 'Not the other kind, that matters more.'

It was an old quotation from their mother. When it became clear that Anne's intelligence would be her means of escaping from home – then, as with her beauty, her mother had to consider it a major character flaw. Chère Irène tolerated her older daughter's academic success – a PhD from one of the nation's most famous universities, teaching positions, the publications of her books – only by insisting it came at the expense of the life achievements that were, for a woman, more important: marriage and family. That this view was held by a woman who herself had little warmth for her husband and no obvious sense of fulfilment from motherhood was beside the point. Irène had been consistently dismissive about Anne's long unmarried partnership with Jasper – whom she met just twice, on strained occasions – and it was a source of acute distress to Anne that her mother lived long enough to know that Jasper and she split up. At the family's last Thanksgiving all together, a grim meal at their father's assisted living facility served in the shadow of Irène's diseased wheezing and Frank's agitated, circular confusions, Irène said succinctly to her daughter, 'I never understood why you didn't marry. It said something, I think. About his intentions.'

This was delivered with a smugness she did not bother to paper over with pretended kindness. It was as though, in Jasper's leaving of Anne, Irène's suspicion of him had, like a long-term bond, finally and with great profit, cashed out.

Anne returned to New York on the first flight out the next morning. Tricia drove her to the airport before anyone was awake, when the Detroit air around them was still icy and dark. 'Well, now she can die happy,' was Anne's sole tart comment to her sister on what had happened, and though Tricia sometimes tried to excuse away their mother's cruelty to Anne, in this instance she could not say a word.

# 20

Anne and Tricia sat together at a lively canalside restaurant, elbows brushing their neighbours', a mixture of languages peppered over plates of silver-bright anchovy and lightly fried coils of calamari. Tricia thought fussiness over food was pretentious, preferring not to stop to notice the flavours and textures they were presented, and rolling her eyes if Anne did. So Anne savoured silently, then said, after a salty mouthful:

'All right. Your turn.'

'Well!' Tricia brightened. 'I've met someone.'

'Mmm. That's very good . . . news.'

'Yes. It is.' Again, Tricia sounded defensive, as if Anne had suggested the opposite. 'He's a nice guy. Salt of the earth. For once in my life, I'm not dating an asshole.'

It wouldn't be polite to agree, but in the ten years since Tricia's divorce from a smart engineer with a serious drinking problem, as she largely single-handedly raised their son Mitchell, Tricia had shown a consistent knack for locating men whose interest in her was cursory. At best, they offered company for baseball games with Mitchell, and presumably sexual companionship for Tricia, but they had never been men you hoped would stick around.

'Even better,' Anne said. She tasted rosemary; the sweetness of slow-roasted tomatoes; and olive oil of a pungency that made the ordinary stuff seem like dishwashing liquid. Half a lifetime ago, Anne recalled, in her New Haven kitchen, she had given Flannery a bossy lesson in the importance of olive oil. 'What's his name?'

'Paul.' Tricia's cheeks turned pink with pride, an emotion Anne had scarcely seen on her sister's face, except when talking about her son. 'Castellanos. He works at the Institute too. So, you know, it's an office romance, you could say.'

'Tsk, tsk.' Anne feigned disapproval. 'And? What else? Tell me about him.'

Paul Castellanos worked closely on the museum's Diego Rivera pieces, tending the Detroit Industry frescoes that made up the core of its modern collection. He was overweight, Tricia admitted, but she didn't mind; this was offset by the fact that he had thick dark hair, and, 'Attraction-wise, having a head of hair makes up for a lot in a man.' Anne, considering Marovic, agreed.

'We met at the Spring Gala. I hate those things, having to get all dolled up and talk to donors and all that crap, but you feel like they're going to fire you if you don't go. You were supposed to dress up as either Diego or Frieda Kahlo.' Her sister had a gallery of eye rolls, one for every occasion. 'I didn't bother with the costume, and neither did Paul. You can imagine, for a large Mexican American man to dress up as Diego Rivera seemed kind of redundant. Or offensive. Or both. Anyway, that's how we got to talking.'

'Sounds like fate.' Anne tipped her wine glass toward her sister, a gesture of cheers.

Tricia tried to see whether she was being mocked. She took a gulp of water and for a moment, Anne suspected, wished she could lean over and sample Anne's wine. 'It was luck. That's for sure. He and Mitchell really get along too. If he's as good a guy as he seems, it will be more like a miracle.'

'A miracle,' Anne repeated softly. She was happy for Tricia; and did not intend the note of melancholy in her voice. 'So Santa Maria has been at work, after all.'

Tricia smiled. All the cynicism had fallen from her face. She looked like the girl Anne remembered, who used to braid Anne's hair for her. Then Anne would braid hers; they took turns.

'Bless that lady,' Tricia said. 'She has.'

# 21

'Are you in touch with Jazz at all?' Tricia asked.

Her tone was uncertain, and Anne was uncertain how to hear it. From her sister's roundly inquisitive face Anne perceived that Tricia's sympathy, ampler now from her own nascent contentment, was competing with a primitive satisfaction that for once the younger sibling was somehow ahead. It was hard for anyone from a conflictual family to be purely sorry for one member's sadness. And it was anyway maybe a zero sum game. One can only be as happy as the other is less so. Was that right? Or was it Anne's second glass of wine that suggested this cynicism? On the one hand, when younger, Tricia had clearly wanted her glittering big sister to achieve, to be a worthy object of her adoration; when Anne was valedictorian at their girls' school fourteen-year-old Tricia radiated nothing but pride. On the other hand, if Anne fell, she guessed that the pressure on Tricia lessened greatly, and Tricia's divorce shrank in importance. At Irène's funeral, Tricia confessed to Anne that their mother had never been kinder to her than in the last months of her life.

'No,' Anne answered, about Jazz. 'I'm not. What would be the point?'

Tricia looked away. She had always had a slight crush on Jasper, it seemed to Anne, which didn't bother her (though her appropriation of Anne's nickname for him did). Jasper was interested in Tricia's work and friendly to her, and to her son Mitchell, when they came to visit. The three of them used to play poker together, a game Anne appreciated but did not join.

'I still have a hard time seeing him as a dad. How old are the twins now?'

'One.'

'He never seemed to want that before. I mean . . .'

'People change.'

'Sure, of course. But after twenty *years*—'

'Twenty-one.'

'I don't know,' Tricia began. 'I still think that if you'd—'

'*Don't.*'

Anne's voice was low and sharp, a knife-thrust.

When they were children, Anne learned early that her voice could pin Tricia down more effectively than any wrestle hold. She was physically strong when she needed to be, and Tricia was timid around her for that reason, but it was the voice that scared her little sister most. Throughout Anne's life, at work and in love, she commanded with her voice. It was a weapon, as well as a charm. It could utter endearments at a warm, stirring vibration only audible to her lover; or it could deliver a slap as cold as that of Irène's own hand.

Tricia looked away, her eyes dipped like a scolded dog's.

'Just . . . don't,' Anne said again.

The repetition was unnecessary.

# 22

After a silence, Tricia pulled out her cell phone and examined it. While she tapped out messages, Anne asked for the bill. They settled it and left.

They ambled without talking along a sidewalked canal lined with buildings of autumnal colours, then across the pretty Ponte dei Pugni – the word meant *fists*, though this didn't seem a good time for Anne to mention it – and on through a populated *campo*. Anne was poised between aggravation at Tricia's intrusion and regret at her own loss of temper; Tricia, by the look of her, between apology and defiance. That stalemate could have continued, but finally, the third time Tricia stopped in front of an elegant *palazzo*, smiling into her held-up phone to take a selfie, Anne issued a peace offering:

'Here, let me take it. They come out better.'

'OK. Thanks.'

Tricia posed, Anne obliged and handed the phone back. 'For Paul?' she asked, and Tricia, checking the image, nodded. 'He told me if we couldn't do this trip together, the next best thing was me sending him pictures.' She seemed to sense the imbalance in the moment and said, 'Look, I didn't mean—'

'Forget it. Let's move on.'

They continued walking.

'The curator's notes, for the Biennale –' Anne tried to bring them back to neutral – 'had a nice line about the worlds we carry in our cell phones. The way an image of a loved one becomes a kind of talisman.'

'This is the guy who pulled together *The Encyclopedic Palace*?'

'Yes. Though it sounds better in Italian. *Il Palazzo Enciclopedico*.'

'Everything's better in Italian.'

'True.'

'Like *gelato*,' Tricia said, as they approached a tiny vibrant shop selling some. 'I mean, how much classier than ice cream? You know it can't have as many calories, with a name like that.'

'Shall we?'

'Absolutely.'

They chose *gelati* the colours of flags of nations – Brazilian green, Spanish gold – and a brilliant cherry-streaked *stracciatella*.

'Heaven,' Anne announced.

'It really is.' Tricia hummed with satisfaction. 'My boss at the DIA, Beal, told me that the show is about trying to contain all the knowledge of the world in one place. Just that, you know. No big deal. Just everything.'

'Right. Like Wikipedia, in a way. Gioni calls it "delusions of omniscience".'

Tricia looked sideways. 'You suffer that occasionally, don't you, sis?'

'More than occasionally, even.' It was Anne's way of apologizing for snapping earlier. 'A hazard of my profession.'

They crossed back over the Grand Canal on one of the spare undecorated gondolas known as *traghetti*. It was a simple, inexpensive ride, no singing, no accented lectures about the city's architecture, just a stand-up crossing to the other bank. Anne considered making a joke about Charon crossing the river Styx; but knew that would only have proved her sister's point.

'So,' Tricia said, as they moved through the teeming evening alleys. 'The word from Beal: Israel is fascinating, South Africa inspiring, France is lame.' She sounded like a god, looking down on his world. 'China's total crap. America's genius.'

'I've heard that.' Then, so that her sister should not think Anne was unable to revisit her own history, she said, 'The year Jasper and I came, in the nineties, the American Pavilion had a bombastic piece with lots of weaponry – a Kalashnikov rifle, landmine, grenades – and then scattered bloody dove feathers, plastic hearts. *War and Peace.*' She rolled her eyes. 'Get it?'

'That was Charles Marshall.'

'Right.' The name lit a synapse in Anne's brain. 'Jasper had some time for it, but to me it seemed like a one-note idea.'

'Well, that's Marshall. If he finds a note he likes, he'll keep playing it. He's doing a piece for us, did I tell you? It's way overdue, and he's a nightmare to deal with, but it's a coup for us to have gotten him.'

'Congratulations.' Anne was slightly distracted, though, recalling a gossip item that had startled her some years earlier. 'I think he's married to someone I used to know.'

'Still?' Tricia barked a short laugh. 'He changes wives pretty often. Wives and dealers.'

'I read this a while ago.'

'Well, he used to be married to that movie star, what's her name? The one in all the sci-fi blockbusters. Hell, what is her name? My god, my memory. Middle age is eating it alive.'

'No, this woman is a writer. Flannery Jansen.'

'I don't know.' Tricia shrugged. 'All I can tell you is, he's an asshole. Charming, but an asshole. Always blaming everyone else for what goes wrong. His assistants, us, some metal supplier – whoever.'

*I might be seeing her in October*, Anne thought of mentioning, a prospect which suddenly brought a honey flavour to her tongue that blended with the icy vividness of the gelato. But as they picked their way through the hot crowds, her sister had carried on to a story about Charles Marshall. Something about enlightenment.

# 23

Was it any more pleasant to stand jostling next to sweaty, noisome people on a boat hopscotching over low, wake-made waves across a broad canal than to do the same on a bone-rattling train a hundred feet underground?

It was, Anne decided the following morning, but only marginally and because you were nearer to fresh air, even if 'fresh' did not seem the right word precisely to describe the sultry Venetian atmosphere in August. Anne and Tricia stood on a busy waterbus making its slow way up toward the gardens of the exhibition. Tricia kept nearly stumbling at the boat's jerky movements, reaching for Anne to steady her. The gesture's metaphor disturbed them both – the younger sister leaning on her older one for stability – but it was preferable to leaning into a rank bearded man on her other side.

'Well, it's not the *Stella Maris*,' Anne muttered, briefly missing that ship's dignified rhythms, its engine's leonine purr.

'Or even the Beaver Island ferry,' Tricia concurred, referring to a crossing they made a couple of times as children across Lake Michigan.

'*Giardini!*' called a harassed black-haired woman with a pink forelock as the boat pulled up, swaying like a drunkard, to a basic dock. The conductor, if that was the word for her, made a cursory effort to secure the vessel to its mooring. A heave of tourists vomited themselves out of the *vaporetto*, leaving behind a scum of chocolate wrappers, used tickets, and the occasional abandoned pair of sunglasses, or stray hat.

'The Italians are so inefficient,' Tricia announced when they were on solid sandy ground again. 'They never even check that you've paid. People must rip off the system all the time. No wonder the country's bankrupt.'

'People in glass houses . . .' Anne said. 'For someone who comes from Detroit, which is thinking about selling off van Goghs to pay off its debts, I'm not sure that scolding the Italians—'

'*Don't*,' Tricia said, in an exaggerated but plausible rendition of her sister's voice. 'Just . . . don't.'

It was a risk, as a joke; with sisters, teasing could always go either way. It could start a fire, or create a new thread of comedy.

Anne laughed. They both did, then made their way companionably through the Biennale's stone entryway to a landscaped maze, where thirty countries had separate pavilions devoted to their art.

# 24

In Russia, umbrellas were handed out at the entrance to fend off coins falling from the ceiling; the piece had to do with lust, and capitalist greed, and somehow gender. (Only women were allowed into the room that rained coins.) In the Netherlands, imaginary newspapers decorated the space, Japan had a ball thrower and sums on the wall, while the United States housed rooms with ornate and delicate assemblings that spoke of issues of work and time, precision and entropy. So the sisters decided, anyway. They marvelled at Sarah Sze's whittled table legs, egg-like deposits of stones and boulders, and otherworldly contraptions that looked like machines you might design in your sleep, to complete jobs that had not yet been conceived. Tricia was a sharp guide, drawing on more awareness of material and technical challenges than Anne was used to from Jasper's cerebral excursions.

Outside each nation's building, whether configured as crypt or town hall, igloo or banqueting house, crowds milled cheerfully. Children ran about unmonitored in the close heat, and pairs strolled arm in arm under the high plane trees. More than Anne remembered, it was like being at a fair. She half expected strong men or painted ladies, stands selling snow cones or cotton candy.

So many couples. This was something you did with your mate: travel. Like the *Stella Maris*'s amiable Knudsens or the cardiganed ladies from Maine, the affectionate analysts, a third entity was created when two people came together. In that configuration they could go further, see and hear more, touch and know better. It was all part of the system she and Jasper used to talk about, the call and response, the gears moving, as new geographies led to traded perceptions that were part of layered conversations, which in turn became memories on which you continued building, brick by brick, your adult self.

Still. The self was still there, after. Even without the other. It did not crumble. Sometimes Anne required her own professorial sternness to remind herself of this. *Yes, you can bunk alone in your cabin and sleep perfectly well, the ship's rhythms will soothe you. You can let your younger sister take you through an international art exhibition and tell you what she knows. It is good for her to be the one in charge for a change.*

This was not an original revelation, Anne realized, but for the bereaved, and the adjusting, it bore repeating: the world need not be less colourful, just because you were moving through it now uncoupled.

The women paused between Hungary and Finland to get their bearings, when the sound of a thin, chirping alarm came from Tricia's purse, like a little electronic chick. From a chaos of tissues, euros, pens, coins, receipts, lipsticks – Anne shuddered to see the cluttered guts of her sister's clutch – Tricia extracted her telephone, and on seeing its playing-card-sized surface, her cheeks bloomed with maternal pleasure: the flattered face of a parent receiving the attention of an adolescent son.

'It's Mitchell! He's FaceTiming me.'

There was no chance Tricia would not have answered the

call. If the Internet invaded, the phone positively trampled over whatever conversation it happened to find in the field, and your only choice, as the other person, was not to mind. Tricia pressed a button and Mitchell's face and voice were suddenly with them on the gravel path in Venice, under the shade of the high green trees.

'Hi, honey!' Tricia's voice grew louder and warmer as she smiled at the device in her hand. 'It's early there! Is something wrong?'

'No. I'm just getting ready for work.' The miniature Mitchell yawned. 'But I have a question about the car.'

'What is it? Say hi to your Aunt Anne first.'

'It's OK.' Anne held up a fending-off hand, but the phone was flipped around before she could move, and captured her face like a spy's swift recorder. 'Hi, Mitchell,' Anne conceded, as her image was beamed into a bedroom thousands of miles away, where her nephew waved to her, then cutely brushed a mop of sleep-mussed hair off his forehead.

'Hi, Aunt Anne. How's it going?'

'All right, thanks. How are you?' Anne tried to ease the strain out of her voice, and make her smile relaxed rather than taut. It wasn't Mitchell's fault that she had not felt ready for her close-up. Tricia, satisfied, took the phone back from Anne, then held it above her head and waved her arm in a wide, slow circle through the air, as if she were the pope bestowing some kind of magical benediction on the crowds.

'Look! We're here at the Biennale!'

'Cool,' Mitchell obliged.

Anne moved away from her sister and the son-containing cell phone as they began talking. What did the Check Engine light mean in the car? Did Mitchell have to, actually, check the engine, meaning take it to the mechanic? Should he ask his dad for help with it, and if so . . .

'You can catch up with me,' Anne called, unconsciously issuing the classic older sister taunt, but Tricia just gave her a silent salute, like a busy executive dismissing an associate. Anne ambled over toward Australia, which neighboured Germany, while a memory came to her of her nephew when he had been a young, rambunctious boy visiting New York, and her fear for him had nearly slayed her.

# 25

Mitchell was seven at the time. Tricia had secured permission from her ex-husband, as if the boy were a valuable artwork that required travel insurance and special packaging, to take him to New York for a few days to visit his aunt and uncle.

From the start, Anne and Jasper's apartment had found it hard to contain the child. It was like trying to keep a dolphin in a bathtub. That Anne's study was transformed into a room whose unfolded sofa bed was littered with T-shirts and toys, shoes and underwear and odd snack bags of foreign foods already required an adjustment. But that the boy himself – large, energetic, loud, somewhat clumsy – moved at speed near the large plate-glass windows caused her hourly anxiety, and meant that Anne was hardly once, in the time they visited, truly relaxed. A slab of deathly cement awaited Mitchell when he might finally break through the postcard view and, lacking superpowers, plummet the twenty-seven floors down. Anne could not get that image out of her mind.

Her nephew was lovable, though, and Anne adored him. Kinship was not an issue. Plump and fond as a puppy, a natural flatterer (the habit apparently enhanced by his parents' divorce, and his role as morale booster to both), Mitchell mopped up attention like an eager sponge. Of the two of them, Jasper might seem the more forbidding to a young person: restrained, ironic, speaking in a register children recognized as not quite straight. Jasper did not fawn or talk down, but if you met him where his humour was, you did well, and Mitchell swiftly figured that out. The boy was smart and amusing, and early on established a few running jokes with Jasper, the first of which had something to do with burned toast. This led to an impromptu lecture about M. F. K. Fisher, whom Jazz revered, and his plucking one of her books from their shelves.

He showed it wordlessly to sandy-haired Mitchell, who read the title, then looked quizzically at Jasper. He wasn't alarmed, but he was curious.

'And does it really tell you that? How to cook a wolf?'

'I think it might. Shall we find out?' Jazz asked, then sat with the boy on the couch and started reading. Jazz loved to read aloud and was good at it, with a resonant voice and an ability to captivate. Mitchell was entranced. When the phone rang for Jasper, Anne came over and took up the reins. She found a favourite cookbook as well, butter-smeared from frequent use, whose pen and ink drawings could serve as illustrations for Fisher's culinary musings. There was an unparalleled pleasure in sitting beside her nephew and reading, then showing him the pictures, his head tilted comfortably against her shoulder. She loved him, simply. When Tricia said later she was amazed they had gotten Mitchell to enjoy a book, he never wanted to read with her – 'What did you do? Hypnotize him?' – Anne felt a thrill of auntly pride. The visit had, up to that point, gone so well.

But something happened on the last day of their trip to New York.

Jasper had gone off to teach, and Tricia was at a work meeting at MOMA. Anne planned to take Mitchell into Soho, where a filmmaker friend of hers lived in a marvellous, enchanted loft with a toy-like dachshund. Anne had little liking for dogs, large ones with intrusive noses and small ones with a tendency to yap, but she thought Mitchell and Minnie might move at the same speed, and appreciate each other's noisy enthusiasms. It would be fun for the boy, she hoped.

There had already been a problem, so Anne's nerves were frayed. While she was getting her bag Mitchell had left the apartment without telling her and gone down in the elevator alone. Anne spent several anxious minutes assuring herself that he was not hiding in the apartment before calling the lift, her heart pounding as she stood outside it, while she considered the possibility that he had left the building and ventured onto Bleecker Street by himself. When she got to the lobby, she found Mitchell chatting in a friendly way to the security man, Ronald, who gave Anne his customary smiled greeting and made good-natured jibes about Mitchell being a Detroit Tigers fan. Anne quelled her temper in front of Ronald, but in a low voice as they left the building she made it clear to Mitchell how displeased she was that he had gone out without letting her know. 'That is *not* acceptable,' she heard herself repeating in a tone of deep disapproval, as though the boy were a college student who had produced a shabby piece of plagiarism for his final paper. She shuddered with Irène recognition, which only rendered her tenser.

The incident followed just after. It took an instant, as attitude-altering events often do. The two were waiting at the edge of Houston Avenue, that vast four-lane car-river of a thoroughfare that marked the southern edge of Greenwich Village. Anne was trying to hold Mitchell's hand but he squirmed away from her. Then he skipped for a mischievous second out into the road.

*Killed.*

He was going to be killed.

Her heart somersaulted up her throat and Anne grabbed the boy by the arm, shouted '*Mitchell!*' with guttural ferocity, and yanked him onto the sidewalk.

'Don't you *ever* do that again,' she whisper-spat.

Then she slapped him.

Mitchell was too stunned to cry. They both stood for an instant in shock. It took Anne a beat to understand what she had done.

'I'm sorry, Mitchell. I shouldn't have . . .' Her left hand wrapped her slapping right one, as if to conceal the evidence of what had happened. 'I'm sorry. You frightened me.' Her voice was shaking; hands, too. She tried to still them by touching his shoulder in reconciliation, but he pulled away. 'I should not have . . . That was wrong. But –' she was not talking just to the boy, but also to a galley of imagined jurors – 'you just can't jump out into the street like that. Do you understand? You could have been *killed*. People do get killed on city streets, every *day*. It isn't funny.'

He wasn't laughing. Nobody was.

Anne alternated between contrition and condemnation while the child remained silent, lapsing into a long-lasting, mute resentment. He told Jasper later (he wouldn't speak to Anne again that evening, just squeezing out a 'goodnight' on his mother's insistence) that it was a joke, he was going to jump right back, there was a space in the traffic, he hadn't been in any danger. The bus coming at them was, the boy was sure, 'a mile' away.

Anne tried to recover, and finally decided to take him to her friend's place anyway, as she didn't have a better plan. Mitchell was sulky, uninterested in Rachel or her loft or the dog, asking in a monotone if he could watch television, which Rachel, sensing the discomfort, let him do. While cartoons animated the boy back to ordinariness in the other room, the adults sat on stools in the minimalist kitchen murmuring over coffee, and Anne tried to calm herself, though she was still trembling, then and for a long while after.

# 26

For the rest of that day Anne had a sense memory of how sharp her grip had been on Mitchell's young arm, and could feel in her palm how hard had been her slap. His cheek stayed pink for half an hour; his arm was not visibly bruised, but Anne knew she had left a mark, whether or not it showed. Of course she would have to tell her sister about it, humiliatingly. Jasper had proved adept at re-establishing normalcy with Mitchell, playing a game of chess and collaborating with him on their evening meal. 'Shall we cook a wolf tonight?' he asked him. 'What do you think?'

'You mustn't make too much of this, love,' he comforted Anne that night in bed. 'He was naughty, you were provoked, these things happen. He's OK.'

'I suppose so.' Her frown lines were deep. 'Is he, though?'

'He really is. You didn't kneecap the boy.'

She agreed, to placate him. What Jasper did not realize was that Anne was horrified not only by how she could so easily and without thinking slap her nephew's sweet round face, feeling her own mother's harsh voice and violence surging through her; but by the moment just before, when she saw this beloved kid step out into the lethal road. Anne's heart poured out of her mouth with the certainty of what was about to happen to him: the animal terror that she was going to watch Mitchell get fatally hurt.

'I could never be a mother,' she told Jasper in a ferocious, terrified whisper that night, tears pooling in her eyes.

Jasper had shushed and consoled her. But years later, when he prepared the case for his departure from their home and their life together, he allowed himself to invoke this incident, to use it against Anne.

The once love-laden living room had become a site of more and more wrenching conversations, including the one in which Jasper finally made irrevocably clear to Anne that he was choosing a different life. With Sophie. That they wanted to have children together.

Anne had closed down, most of her internal mechanisms had gone cold and still. She was in a kind of hibernating, or power-saving, mode, where the only part of her alive were her fiery green eyes. And a boiled pain on her lips, that she was trying not to speak.

'Of course, motherhood is not something you wanted, or ever felt able to do.' To sell his decision to himself, Anne saw, Jasper had had to recast Anne, the woman he had so adored. 'Which was clear from the beginning, of course – in fact, we agreed for a long time on that preference – but I didn't realize till that day with Mitchell that it was really an impossibility for you. You remember that day.' And now Jasper's face was twisted, slightly, with the effort of distorting the truth. 'You were clear – you said as much to me – that you could not care for a child.'

How Anne had loved that strong and intelligent face. She had counted on it for truth and for understanding. He had taught her to. Yet Jazz had allowed himself to take away the wrong conclusion from Anne's arm-grab of Mitchell, the standing on the edge of the abyss, the slap that followed it. Or he pretended to have, which was just as bad. He had filed the episode in the place a person keeps in his mind, even if he is deeply in love, in case the couple one day breaks apart, and evidence is required for the one who leaves. Jasper was not, perhaps, in every fibre the romantic he had always promised himself, and her, that he was.

*I could never be a mother*, she had told him.

Anne had thought the second silent clause of her remark to Jazz that evening on Bleecker Street was clear. Only years later, as Jasper prepared his exit, did she realize that perhaps it hadn't been.

*Because I would care too much.*

# 27

There was only so much art Anne could look at before starting to feel faint, and she needed some solid reality. Like a sandwich. Their last stop was the bright installation of Great Britain, called *English Magic*. One room had a painted kestrel flying with a diminutive Aston Mini in its talons; another was screening a video, which drew a younger crowd. Anne sat down on a broad bench next to an alert little boy. She could never tell children's ages; perhaps he was eight or ten. Together they watched, mesmerized, as kids and adults bounced cheerfully up and down on what Anne saw was a rubbery joke – an inflated model Stonehenge. Tricia came in and found Anne, sat down on the other side of the boy. The piece was called *Sacrilege*.

'We should take a break,' Tricia said, and Anne agreed.

They found a cafeteria, then sat at a round aluminum table in a crowded yard, eating panini of tomato and mozzarella, the perfect food. They were surrounded by students and families and voracious pigeons.

A group of English women nearby erupted into laughter. The spirit of this exhibition seemed to lean that way – into hilarity, or at least good humour. Then a tidy, grey-haired man approached their table and asked politely, in what might have been a Dutch accent, if he could take their third chair. The sisters assented, then watched him carrying it back like a slain beast to the table around which sat a fair-haired younger woman and two toddlers, a plum-cheeked girl and a check-shirted boy. Anne knew that she and Tricia were making the same silent assessment: was the man the children's grandfather? Or father? Parental ages were not what they had been. The man and woman interacted pleasantly, helping the children with their pizzas; then the children fought over something, a glass was knocked over, and the girl started wailing. The woman leaned in to scold the boy, help the girl, mend the problem; the grey-haired man sat back, as though the situation no longer interested him. He caught Anne's gaze. She looked away.

'He's the father,' Anne declared softly.

'Who?' Tricia feigned surprise. 'Oh, that guy?'

'Yes.' Anne put her sunglasses back on, embarrassed to have been caught staring. 'He acts grandfatherly, but is actually the children's father.'

'Could be.'

'He did not quite know what he was getting into – fatherhood, at this stage. He hadn't realized how much pizza would be involved.'

Tricia laughed. 'Chicken tenders. Burgers and fries.' She got into the spirit of it. 'Anything at all, as long as it's fried or you can put ketchup on it.'

'He's disappointed,' continued Anne, with an edgy glint of humour, 'that he hasn't yet found the children receptive to his lamb tagine.'

Tricia snorted. 'No. They wouldn't be.'

'To his dismay, he finds that there seem to be a lot of messes to clean up.'

'Oh, sure,' Tricia agreed. 'Runny noses. Vomit. Trips to the bathroom.'

'Though he lets his wife do most of the work.' With her glasses on, Anne glanced back at the now calm table. 'It's part of the deal they made at the start.'

'And are we still talking about that man over there?' Tricia asked her. 'Or are we talking about someone else?'

# 28

'I'll tell you what happened,' Anne began, and even before saying more she felt relieved. At last she could tell this story. 'Jasper became very fearful about death. He saw sixty coming, and it flicked some kind of alarm switch in him.'

She was hesitant, uncharacteristically. It would take only the slightest misstep – if Tricia smirked, or made a joke – to seal the story back up within Anne. But Tricia simply waited. Anne's own trick: staying quiet.

'Obsessive, almost.' Anne had not spoken of this to anyone. 'He could not sleep at night, which hadn't happened before. Jazz was always a sound sleeper; I was the one who had insomnia for years. I could even put a light on, it didn't bother him.'

Her sister listened.

'Then . . . he started waking up too. He was restless, agitated. He spiralled down into very dark moods. Really, an existential despair. That's the only way to describe it.' Anne remembered the ashen quality of Jasper's sleepless face. How hollow his eyes looked. This man she loved was, in those bottomless nights, terrified. 'He once told me that all he could see was blackness, and . . . the end.'

Tricia took in this picture. 'Was there anything you could do, or say? To help?'

'Nothing.'

Anne had herself known depressions, she was the one of the pair who occasionally succumbed, and Jazz had been the rallier, the rock, the soother. She wanted to be able to do the same for him. It was his turn. 'I couldn't seem to help him at all.' Anne's voice was reedy and thin. She sounded like a child, admitting defeat. *I didn't finish the race. I got too nervous to play at the recital.* In a tiny sigh, nearly a whisper: 'I tried.'

Anne felt a hand on hers, which startled her. She almost pulled away, instinctively, but made herself leave it on the metal table, allowing Tricia's to anchor hers there.

'I suggested the obvious things. Anti-depressants. Sleeping pills. Jazz wouldn't do any of that.'

'Therapy?' Tricia asked tentatively. Anne was glad of the question as it made her laugh, abruptly, a laugh with a sharp note of grief in it.

'Can you imagine?' she said to Tricia. 'Jasper Elliott on the couch?'

Tricia laughed a little too. 'I can't,' she admitted. 'Honestly. No.'

'Well.' Anne pulled off her sunglasses, rubbed her salt-tinged eyes. Let them, unprotected, look at the crowd around them. This part of the narrative became easier, and Tricia knew pieces of it anyway. 'It was in that state that I sent him off to visit his sister in LA. He had started talking about children. His niece and nephew. And also, the way children give you a link to the future. They made – he actually said this – *the grave less dark.* Or maybe it was *less stark.* I was never sure which.'

Her sister raised her eyebrows in something fairly similar to an eye roll, but that was all right with Anne now.

'Yeah, I know. Anyway. Whether his sister Harriet knew any of this is unclear to me, but certainly she was the one who introduced him to adorable Sophie.' Anne's voice was steady now. 'Pretty, young French Sophie, recently divorced, and eager to start a family.'

Tricia didn't speak, so Anne said her line for her. 'The story of men chasing tail, as they have for millennia.'

'And women wanting children,' Tricia added, 'as they always do.'

Anne removed her hand from the table but leaned in for a moment first.

'Well, Trish.' She smiled, though tautly. 'Not always.'

# 29

'Let's stay in and have an orange evening, at the apartment,' Anne suggested, after they had finished their art marathon. 'I've had about as much omniscience as I can take, for one day. I'll cook us something simple.'

'Thanks. Nice idea. But nothing too carby. I don't want to have put on five pounds by the time I see Paul again.'

So Anne found a few fillets of fresh fish and a couple of leeks, two small comical purplish artichokes, and, with a minimum of fuss, created an easy meal for them both to enjoy out on the mini balcony.

'OK,' she said, serving them. 'You have a story too, I know. Tell me.'

It had been too soon, at the memorial, for Anne to have asked in detail about Chère Irène's last weeks. But now, after a few months, Anne felt that the only way she could begin to balance the ledger – though the debt was fundamentally unpayable; nothing equals aiding one's parent through her dying – was to give her sister a stage and a setting. How the story ended: as Anne knew from her work, everyone always wanted to know that.

So Anne heard of the spring crisis in the hospital, where their mother nearly died of pancreatic failure, and a long list of organs and scans and specialists and treatment, how when Irène woke after hours of intensive medical interventions to a Kuwaiti nurse in a hijab taking her blood pressure, she nearly spat with horror, even in her weakened state. How adamant she was that she be moved to the Catholic hospice, which took some effort on Tricia's part but where, Irène told Tricia gratefully, it was an enormous relief to be tended to by Christians. Tricia chose not to question this notion, a good decision, Anne agreed. With the excuse that she couldn't stand the overcooked food – 'If they boiled the broccoli any longer it would turn into paste' – Irène stopped eating.

'Though honestly,' Tricia said, cutting the heart out of a little artichoke, 'I think she did it more to speed up the process. She was ready to go.'

'Did it work?'

'Well, she became semi-delirious. And weaker. And . . . sweet, believe it or not.' Tricia looked sheepish to admit it, and laughed. 'That's how I figured we must be close to the end. She became affectionate.'

'Did she ask to see . . . anyone?' Anne hated herself for wondering, for giving Irène even this posthumous power, but she found she had to know.

'She wanted Mitchell to come a lot. What a trooper that kid was, I was so proud of him. She didn't understand why Dad wasn't there; she was sort of insulted he didn't stop by. I couldn't bring myself to point out that he was dead.'

There was a silence for a moment, then Tricia filled it with, 'I told her you were in New York, and were trying to get to Detroit but might not be able to make it.'

Was it a lie both ways – a lie to Irène, because of course Anne could have gotten there if she had wanted to; and a lie to Anne, or a half-truth, to suggest that Irène had even asked or cared about her older daughter then?

Probably best not to ask.

Anne cleared their plates away. '*Carciofo* – that's artichoke in Italian.' Anne scraped the leaves from Tricia's plate onto her own. 'I learned the word when Jazz dragged me to a soccer match in Rome once. At some point a player missed an easy goal, and these loutish guys behind us started yelling furiously at him. Jazz collapsed with laughter and finally told me what they were screaming, to the hated player down there: *You're not a man, you're an artichoke!*'

Anne went out to the kitchen and returned with two cups of tea for them to enjoy under the low, light-polluted Venetian sky. Finally Tricia reached the end.

'I was there, with her, holding her hand, for the death rattle. That –' Tricia winced, shaking her head at the memory – 'is an eerie sound.'

'Is it a rattle, actually?'

'It is. She was looking like a corpse already, so I thought, I'm not going to know when it happens, but earlier the nurse had laid out the stages. And then you hear it and . . . there's no way not to recognize what's going on. You feel it; you hear it; then the body in front of you is suddenly . . . empty.'

Anne looked up into the night, but there were no stars there. Just a murky darkness. 'Did you touch her?' Anne asked curiously. 'If you don't mind—'

'No, no.' Tricia wiped a few tears from her eyes. 'I don't mind. Yes. I kissed her. It seemed like the right thing to do. Then I called in the nurses. They were ready, of course. So I left them to it.'

There was a silence, as the sisters had their private thoughts.

'Thank you,' Anne said, gently.

Tricia nodded, sniffed, brushed the tears off her cheek, folded her arms.

'It was *really* hard not to drink that night. Mitchell was at his dad's. I went to an AA meeting right away, straight from the hospice, then I drove all the way back across town, picked up Paul, and went to another one.' She looked at Anne with her reddened eyes. 'He was kind to me that night. That's when I knew he was a good guy.'

'I'm glad.'

'Yeah. We'd only been dating about a month or so. You know, your new girlfriend's mom dies . . . Some guys would have shrugged, or run away. Paul didn't, though.' Tricia's face was soft in the evening light, and as pretty as Anne had ever seen it: skin smooth, bitterness eased. 'He got me through it.'

Well, love did that, didn't it? Made grief bearable. Rearranged your features. Gave you light. Without that light, any face – even one commonly considered beautiful – might just as well be a photograph, or a mask.

# 30

After all the talk of the day, wearied and reconciled, the sisters said goodnight to each other. In bed, Anne tried to read, but mosquitoes bit her mind into inattention. The actual insects, whining in her ear, and bug-like thoughts that flew at her reading mind with high-pitched distraction, allowing her no peace.

What was next?

What was left?

Work, of course. Anne needed to sink her teeth into something new. She had had scraps of ideas but she needed to assemble them, put them on her desk, and then like a chef looking at the morning's basket from the farmer's market, see what could be made from it all. She had to get out her paper and pen and start. Anne had never feared the blank page; she feared hardly anything, a quality that drew other people to her, she knew. She was unflinching. For the world's many flinchers, this was attractive.

Still, there was a jumpiness in her now, a restlessness. Where was her famous, enviable calm?

The Internet doesn't always invade. Sometimes we open our arms to it, as we might to a canny seducer. Anne reached over for her laptop, and lying back on her bed, opened it so that its back lay against her lightly sweating stomach, a cold metal pet.

From: Margaret Carter
Subject: Conference Update

My dear Professor Arden. By now I trust you are living the autodidact's dream, exploring *The Encyclopedic Palace*.

You're a genius. Flannery Jansen said yes, she'll do it, and I think she has the sort of *je ne sais quoi* (read: appeal to the LGBT community) that helps jazz up our otherwise somewhat straight programme. My habits have me leaning too obviously toward women who write for *The Times*, though as Eleanor says, *Mom, didn't you know that print is dead?* Still I'm not disowning Eleanor just yet as she also gave me the bright idea of asking Catherine Li Mayer, a sexy author of a travelogue about Thailand, and she is in her TWENTIES so that does a beautiful thing to the mean age of our conference.

So now I feel we have a good range: hefty political histories! Sexy bestsellers! Award-winning poetry! TELEVISION COMEDY WRITERS! How much more diversity can anyone want? The dean will be pleased, and we all want to please the dean.

OK, I've had too much coffee, can you tell? Let's just touch base when you're back. But thanks again for the suggestion of Jansen. She hasn't written anything for a while, it seems, and her second book, a novel, was kind of a non-performer, but the Mexico memoir is still very well known, girl discovering her father, scenes of girls having sex among the cacti, etc. I ought to read it probably, as a marital aid for Lloyd and me if nothing else.

*Basta!* See you soon.

xxM

# 31

Flannery Jansen.

Anne had her own images in her night-mind, without requiring Google's help. A lovely, blonde-swept face, with the freshness of a Scandinavian complexion, her amber eyes alight with absurdity as Anne taught her lipstick shade names in front of a bathroom mirror. '*Mauve amour.*' Laughter. 'OK, it's your turn now: *Rebellious.*' The kiss, their colourful reward.

Bonnie girl. The affair's ending had a sad inevitability, with her wrong-headed appearance in New Mexico – *Don't do it*, someone should have told Flannery, but the person who was teaching her such things was exactly the person Flannery was flying to see. Before that end, though, had been the luscious, unforgettable middle: humour and raunch, flirtation and stories. There was a hunger between them and not just a sexual one; they had grabbed at each other, at some spirit each one recognized in the other. Maybe Flannery had intuitively found and known that first. Found her way in, and showed them both.

What could Google, with its literal, pixellated images, add to that truth?

All right. Flannery had aged, she had married, here she was. Flannery Jansen and Charles Marshall at a gala event in San

Francisco. An art opening. Some Silicon Valley mogul's birthday party.

The man was vast and self-satisfied, and seemed well matched to that work Anne remembered from the nineties Biennale. Handsome, if one went for a florid, Italianate, owner-of-the-vineyards sort of appearance.

And Flannery?

Recognizably the same woman. Girl, now all grown up. Anne could not suppress a smile, as if of greeting. Better groomed, twenty years on – the bestseller and its money, or marriage and her husband's status, had seemingly gotten her to pay more attention to the cut and colour of her clothes. How Anne remembered the sloppy, almost childish outfits the Californian had worn when they first met, as if she had just come off the playground; it was only when Anne ran into Flannery at that first party, wearing a sleeveless T-shirt and black leggings, that she felt the pull of an adult lust. As they became closer that spring, Flannery's fashion mutated into the half-mannish thrift-store aesthetic favoured among her peers. If their relationship had lasted longer, Anne might have taught the younger woman a thing or two about ways to enhance her lovely shape. How to look after herself. How to know she was beautiful. Someone else must have done that in the interim. At the age of – what would she be now? Thirty-eight, thirty-nine? – Flannery had grown into a kind of grace. To judge from the two dimensions of her on the screen.

Yet you could still see in the facial expressions a lack of desire for attention. The husband did not have that. It was clear from Marshall's self-regarding grin that he knew about being photographed, and was all for it. In the images that surfaced before Anne, on her laptop, in her bed, Flannery Jansen (she was still

*Jansen*, thank God) half-ducked her blonde head, eyes dipped down, pretty mouth smiling, but sideways, somehow.

Anne knew that look.

She also remembered what that gorgeous person looked like, stripped of her shyness; not physically stripped, that is (though Anne had those scenes too, in a file at the back of her memory), but shedding her layers of self-protection to gaze directly at Anne, and even allow herself, sometimes, to be gazed upon, admired, the same way.

So long ago, those hot afternoons and steamed-up nights. Anne had not expected to unlock those memories again.

Anne's fingers hovered over the keyboard, her head back on the pillow. She knew it was important not to succumb to a hurried correspondence one might later regret. Late nights were hazardous that way, even without alcohol to loosen inhibitions.

Dear Flannery,

– she began.

A gondolier sang, rather badly, out in the night.

Tourist chatter, English, floated up to her.

The cursor blinked. Indifferent to her actions, its pulse awaited her decision, like a butler.

*Don't write to her. What would you say? You will see each other soon enough. You can discover in October whether there is still any connection between you. No doubt Flannery has seen the names of those attending the conference. Who knows? Maybe she is hoping to see you, too.*

Anne closed her laptop. She placed it on the table beside the bed, turned out the light. Her dreams would, she supposed, be busy with outsized kestrels, a rain of coins, a strange wooden time machine.

*Serenissima*. Tomorrow was their last day there, then she would journey back to New York, Trish to Detroit. *You're right*, Anne reassured herself. *Yes.*

*You can wait.*

# PART THREE

## October

# 1

'Red eye' did not begin to cover it.

Yes, Flannery's eyes were red, and her skin grey, and her hair deadened by six hours of desiccating aeroplane air, but as she shuffled in the dawn's early light to the baggage claim area she was hardly aware of her appearance. Mostly she was nauseous and scratchy-throated, and had a new dread that after all the trouble caused by this short trip she would end up condemned to her hotel room, fighting pneumonia. The dread coexisted with Flannery's rocklike, throwback conviction that that was all she deserved, for leaving her little girl behind.

She should not, the throwback voice chided, in one of those sing-song tones from fifties movies, that went along with floral printed dresses and buns in the oven, have left Willa alone with the child's father (haphazard; erratic attention to detail) and grandmother (anxious, and vague about habits or schedules). Yet – the modern voice protested – surely she, Flannery, should be able to attend a short professional conference *once* in a year. She was a woman with a job and she needed to do it. Charles travelled all the time for his work without even blinking! It was only fair. It was her turn. Finally, in the middle of those two registers, the unaligned, purely maternal voice within Flannery, with no politics, only the animal drive to ensure her daughter's well-being, stated, with the slightest tremor: Willa would be fine. Why shouldn't the kid learn the different ways of Dad and Grandma? It would not kill her. Probably. And, as Nietzsche said first and self-help gurus had been repeating ever since: that which doesn't kill us, makes us stronger.

Sure. Maybe Willa would be stronger by the time Flannery returned; maybe Flannery herself would be.

She couldn't, certainly, be in much worse shape than when, outside the airport, she boarded the grandly misnamed 'limo', a soulless van whose reek, of some industrial chemist's idea of pine, nearly made her retch. She recalled the similar vehicle twenty years earlier: as imagined from California, the *limo* was surely going to be a fancy town car that would whisk Flannery from New York's John F. Kennedy to Yale. In the event, she was disoriented by the shabby bustle of the airport, disappointed by the dented shuttle bus into which she had folded her long-limbed seventeen-year-old self for that first, epic journey – and surprised by urban, grey New Haven. At least by now, Flannery had few expectations, so she found a seat, leaned her head against a salt-and-grit-spattered window and, like a child, fell back to sleep the instant the wheels reached the highway and a steady speed.

She dreamed scarcely and fitfully, snatches like the blurry home movies shown in art films to denote a more innocent past. (A noisy party; a train trip; a holiday gathering where she knew no one.) Flannery awoke with a start as the van was nosing up a street where once she had bought books and bagels. Discreetly, with her adult hand (thirty-eight, for heaven's sake), she wiped nap drool from her mouth, then looked out the window purposefully, as if she knew precisely where she was going and why she was here.

The leaves. The colours. They were nearly over, and fallen,

but some of their fire still clung to a few brave branches. At the sight of them Flannery's spirits rose, and she felt the stir of pleasure this season had always inspired in her, a vibration that had nearly the same pitch to it as love.

# 2

The van stopped at a couple of the residential colleges first. There were twelve of them, scattered across the dense Connecticut blocks; as freshmen you were assigned one on arrival and then were expected to remain loyal to it forever after. It had been, in Flannery's experience, like being at a table with strangers at a large wedding – you just made conversation with your neighbours as well as you could. The van's brief tour included the modernist outlier, a polygonal concrete creation that hardly featured in Flannery's history; the green-shuttered Georgian revival that must have comforted old boys with dreams of plantation ownership, and where a sporty girl resided with whom Flannery had a jaunty, Diet Coke-fuelled affair; and her own gothic-styled college, faux-Oxford and double-courtyarded, from which she had fled early on, playing out her loves and studies off campus. When the van pulled up at the familiar dark, heavy gates, a pretty mixed-raced Asian woman – *hapa*, Susan Kim would call her – made her way to the sliding door. As she crab-walked by, she touched Flannery's shoulder.

'Flannery Jansen, right?'

Oh, God. Had this woman seen Flannery drool? She wore immaculate crimson lipstick and a sleek black jacket. Flannery recognized her too, now that she was something more like awake. The author of the Thai sex adventure novel.

'Yes, hi. Are you Catherine Li Mayer?'

'Cathy.'

'Good to meet you.'

They shook hands, awkwardly, while the anoraked woman driver waited on the sidewalk with Li Mayer's bag.

'I'm so glad you're part of the conference. I loved your book, I'd really like to talk to you about it.'

Flannery felt, in relation to the crimson-lipped twenty-something, a grizzled elder statesman, dribbling food down her tie.

'Oh, I am too,' she smiled, wiping the invisible crumbs off her chest. 'Glad, I mean. About the conference.'

'You're not staying here – at the college?' the young woman pressed, as if perhaps Flannery were too addled to have noticed they had arrived.

'No, no. I opted for a hotel.'

'I'm sure that's smart.' Which Flannery took to mean *how middle-aged of you*, but then it seemed that this whole exchange was either some coded competitive session, which Flannery suspected she was losing, or it was simply a straightforward, friendly greeting, and what Flannery really needed was a strong cup of coffee, as soon as possible. 'I got the note suggesting dorm accommodation and part of me shuddered, like, Oh my God, total PTSD! But I'm so cheap, I can never resist something offered for free. I'll probably regret it.'

Flannery grinned, unable to think of a witty reply. She hoped her expression was friendly rather than grotesque.

'Well, I'll see you later. You're going to the lunch?'

'Definitely.' Flannery had hoped to avoid it. The first item on the agenda had, she recalled, been described as optional. 'I'll see you there!' Flannery gave a little wave, as she realized with dismay that she now would have to go to the lunch, actually. She had thought she might just hole up in her hotel, and sleep. Or fret. Or daydream.

Failing to control her hours and her days: well, Flannery had, of course, brought her problems with her. No number of air miles would change the person she was.

'You're staying at The Den?' the driver asked in brusque Connecticutish, referring to the hotel. Flannery nodded.

'Last stop,' the driver said, superfluously, as Flannery was now the only passenger left in the pine-wracked van.

# 3

Hotels had many meanings.

For some the word was simply synonymous with sex. Romance, or adultery. Or both.

For people with children, as Flannery had learned first in New York, hotels were not havens so much as a set of obstacles to be navigated. When Willa was a bit older, a toddler, Flannery spent an easier weekend with her cousin at a 'family-friendly' inn in southern California, but they had ventured there without Charles, for whom staying in such a place would have seemed an admission of defeat. Charles never intended to let fatherhood dumb him down or expose him to environments he considered tasteless. The parent of Willa's who would clock hours at the primary-coloured playground, or a frantically loud plastic hell-chamber where kids had bouncy birthday parties – that was always going to be Flannery.

The very fact of a hotel's unfamiliarity usually made Willa uneasy. What Willa most wanted from more or less the minute their front door closed behind them was to get back home to her own bed, and the bath and toys that she knew. In spite, or perhaps because of, the uncertain currents in the air at home, Willa did not feel altogether safe leaving it.

When Flannery travelled with Willa, feeling a close kinship

with the girl's emotional rhythms, she understood her child's suspicion of unknown accommodations. By herself now, though, with her beloved daughter thousands of miles away, as Flannery stood at a reception desk, being treated with warm deference by a slender, smooth-faced young man eager to make her comfortable, she was reminded of something she had not experienced in years. A meaning hotels had for the solo traveller. Not romance. Not obstacles.

*Escape.*

'Thank you, Diego. That's really kind.'

The remarkably agreeable honey-eyed young man helping her had given Flannery the plastic key card to her room early, several hours before she had expected it.

'Sure, Miss Jansen. It's not a problem – I'm guessing you might like to relax after the long flight.' *Miss Jansen!*

'I am a little tired, it's true.'

'I bet.' Diego's smile was either suggestive or concerned, and when Flannery realized she could not tell which, she knew that an hour or two by herself was essential. That and more coffee. Flannery dispensed herself a large cup from a ready supply in the lobby, then rolled herself and her bag upstairs.

The relief that greeted her at the door – a white, clean, spare, handsome, association-free room, comfortable, ample, and empty – was as pure as a tall glass of water after a hike through the desert. The click of the door shutting behind Flannery had such sweetness she nearly wept. She walked around the bed, giddy with joy, slipped off her travel sneakers and lay down, gently, on the pristine coverings. How could such pleasure be possible? Flannery exhaled a sigh of disbelief, and inhaled air that had no food or fight or family in it. Through the broad, generous windows Yale gave Flannery its modest skyline: the white, gold-dipped tower of the nearby college, the traceried masonry of the monolith from which the bells famously rang, the blunt gymnasium in the distance.

She breathed.

# 4

Flannery had taken her own small piece away from here when she left, the way people ran off with mortar fragments after the Berlin Wall fell – that desire to keep a piece of the edifice that shaped your life, even if you were ambivalent about it. No one in Flannery's family had any connection to the university, or considered it anything other than a place you heard about. A nonplussed 'Oh, my!' had been her mother's response to the news of Flannery's admission, as if Flannery had just announced her intention to learn sky-diving, or travel to Mombasa.

Attending Yale had changed what was possible for Flannery. When younger, Flannery might have denied this, perhaps out of her own anxiety of influence. The place had not been directly responsible for her job in publishing, or for her trip to Mexico, or her ability to turn that tumultuous emotional adventure into an engaging narrative, a book that combusted into success. The university governed no part of Flannery's life, and she was sceptical about its alumni campaigns and reunions. This *bastion of power and privilege*, as she had enjoyed calling it in her protesting young days, perpetuated structures of elitism and exclusion. Well, of course it did.

Yet here was Flannery, returned, to match her own stone fragment with the buildings still standing, to understand how her piece fit into those storied structures, and what precisely she had taken away with her when she left. At thirty-eight, she was finally willing to acknowledge a debt to the place (distinct from the financial one, which Charles had discreetly helped her with, his other great generosity to Flannery, after Willa). These monuments, with their exhortations and expectations, had given Flannery, a raw, soft-skinned Westerner, the confidence and education to move out into her life.

Why else had she come back now, but to avow publicly this gratitude to her alma mater?

Oh, one other reason: because this university, across its streets and classrooms and library upon remarkable library, had changed her in one other profound way.

It had given her Anne.

# 5

Anne tried to play that morning, but couldn't.

None of the pieces felt right, her fingers missed and fidgeted, and sitting still, something she normally managed so well, was not coming easily to her. She had to pace. It was not yet time for her train.

When Anne was young, she had been driven to play the piano for hours by a vicariously ambitious grandfather, who succeeded in drumming the joy out of her playing, and much of the feeling, though he demanded Chopin from her, and got it. When she quit in high school her mother berated her, of course; but in New York, encouraged by Jasper, Anne had reclaimed her pleasure in the instrument, taking lessons from a lively Polish woman with bleached hair. On the occasions she and Jazz had argued, playing was often Anne's route to self-calming, and from there to reconciliation with him.

In reorganizing the apartment after Jasper left, Anne thought to move the piano from the living room to Jasper's former study, to create a small music room. Together, she and the Polish teacher had rolled the upright in there, a satisfying exercise that proved to Anne that even significant physical tasks could be accomplished without him; but gradually Anne discovered that this only served to emphasize how solitary and closeted her playing was now, which lessened the consolation.

She closed the lid over the keys.

The study's built-in shelves had been cleared of his French history, the *Robert* dictionary, framed photographs of Anne and Jasper, as well as the more recent shots of Jazz's sister, and his niece and nephew. Anne had swiftly repopulated the bare shelves with objects of her own, to counter the yawning reminder that he had gone.

She looked at the display she had made. Photographs: well, you had to have them. Otherwise your life looked hollow and lonely. She kept a few Jazz had taken of her, several cityscapes, Mitchell's school snap from a few years earlier, and a recent one from Venice of Tricia out on that tiny balcony. Stones from beaches Anne had gone to, a few ash-coloured pieces of sinuous driftwood. Sea glass, in a hexagonal porcelain dish. Then a new addition, an aesthetic anomaly but it lit something within Anne to see it: a shot glass with a grinning alligator and the word *Everglades* on it. From the hot, fraught trip she took there with Flannery. It was astonishing that this random object had survived twenty years of shifts and relocations. When she had found the kitsch piece in a box with some old photos she had been sorting through at the end of the summer, she rescued it and put it out on display.

The two women had fought in Florida, smoked there, talked there, made love there. Gotten sandy and salty and sunburned and sulky there. Anne had never been back to that state, even in the years she had lived in Atlanta, and somehow she doubted she ever would, though the place had a kind of untamed heat in it, in Anne's memories.

Flannery had given the shot glass to Anne as a present, before they left on the train to go back to New Haven. 'I thought about getting you one that said, "*You're either a gator – or you're gator bait!*"' she told Anne during a mock solemn presentation at the Amtrak station. 'But that seemed a little loaded.'

# 6

Now that she was all the way here, Flannery felt a strange shyness, and near reluctance, to see Anne. Need she go out after all? Couldn't she just call in sick and hide out for three days in this heavenly room? She doubted that the women conferees really required her insights or anecdotes. It seemed to Flannery as though Cathy Li Mayer would be more than capable of speaking on her behalf. She was younger, chic-er, and certainly had superior lipstick.

*But what if Anne thought so, too?*

All right. Enough of that, Jansen. Pull yourself together.

Flannery sat up on the absurdly comfortable bed and pulled out two poorly folded sheaves of paper from her backpack. She sighed.

**Schedule for Events October 19th–21st**

THURSDAY

| | |
|---|---|
| 12.30 p.m. | Informal lunch, Regent Dining Hall,<br>Regent College |
| 7 p.m. | Readings at Hunter Hall: Ellen Kessler,<br>Melissa Green, Andi Chatterjee<br>Reception after, Greenwich Bar & Grill |

FRIDAY

| | |
|---|---|
| 11 a.m.–12.30 p.m. | |
| | Gender and Writing: Panel discussion, moderated by Professor Anne Arden, Adams Auditorium, Art Centre |
| 2–5 p.m. | Workshops led by participants, Peverill-Cooper Hall |
| 7 p.m. | Dean's Dinner, Sillitoe College |

SATURDAY

| | |
|---|---|
| 10 a.m.–12 noon | |
| | Gender and Genre: Round table discussion and student Q & A, Adams Auditorium |
| 7 p.m. | Remarks by Professor Arden, introducing readings by: Catherine Li Mayer, Lisa Sahel Jefferson, and Flannery Jansen |

It was an awful lot of reading, discussing, remarking. Flannery anticipated a collective attempt to establish *cred*, however defined – book sales, prizes won, TV appearances made – while also reaching a hand out to the students. That was why they were here, after all, to pull the kids up and along, too.

Flannery felt a wave of exhaustion. She did plenty of helping along of a younger person back at home, and suddenly felt she had not an hour of energy left in her to encourage anyone else. Having secured leave, at last, from family life in order to work, Flannery found that what she wanted above all was to kick back and read, without interruption, without any obligation. An essay on bees. A short story by a dead Russian. Even the goddamned *newspaper*.

However, her reading was not her own. It was an essential politeness to know the work of the other speakers going in; she knew how disconcerting it was to meet a fellow author at an event who clearly had no idea of who you were or what you had written. Flannery had the Li Mayer book in her bag, and had YouTubed her way into familiarity with Chatterjee's comedy.

Kessler she recalled as a curly-haired precocious classmate, editor of one of the university's elite journals, who had matured into a sought-after commentator on Soviet injustices. Jefferson would always be associated with the recital of her poem at the presidential inauguration. (A wind tunnel of a day, but her delivery was forceful, and dignified – Flannery had watched a clip of that, too.) A few women on the original list had not come, and Flannery tried not to feel she had wasted time reading them, too.

The work she knew best, as it happened, was *The Awakening of Influence*. Flannery had first read it just after she returned from Mexico, her mind still full of that adventure and the sounds of Spanish. Adele judged Anne Arden's work to be show-offy and unintelligible, but Flannery, though not confident she understood every argument, scanned the book for genius and hidden messages, and believed she found both. It was a study of the ways American women writers influenced one another, a book in dialogue with, if not in defiance of, Harold Bloom. Flannery appreciated Anne's unearthing of the 'codes of communication' between Cather and Chopin, Dickinson and Bishop; but what she felt above all was a wistful sensation that she was Anne's eager student again, noting the authors Anne revered and her interpretations of their work. That Flannery felt some reflected glory in the book's importance, a faint proprietary link to its brilliance, was, of course, absurd, and she never confessed those feelings to anyone. Still, it was no wonder Addie hated *The Awakening of Influence.*

Flannery had already at that time begun to pen her own narrative, the story of Don Lennart, and through all that fevered writing – the pages just poured out of her, which gave them the momentum and intensity people responded to – she had one particular reader in mind. Flannery dedicated the memoir to her mother, who 'gave me so much'. But her own coded communication was to Anne. *I wrote this, hoping to get your attention.* When Anne's postcard duly came, those simple few lines in her slant hand, Flannery held the object close to her like a talisman, well aware of her foolish sentimentality but again feeling that, unspoken, it need do no harm.

A low golden light, late autumn morning, came through the hotel's plane glass window and hit Flannery's bleary eyes. She really ought to read the Li Mayer book right now. Or Jefferson's latest volume of verse. Or take on the history of the gulag. The gulag, for God's sake.

But wasn't this hour hers?

Wasn't she a free agent?

Flannery lay back on the beautiful white bed and reread Anne Arden instead.

# 7

Anne came into the living room, where the river glittered beyond the windows. There was a stillness that felt – she knew this was fanciful – like a calm before the storm.

One more check of her appearance before she left. Anne stood in the garish light of her bathroom, assessing her face while thinking of the particular hazel eyes that would be on it. A short sharp line divided the space between her fine brows, a punctuation mark of concentration or concern (not all who knew Anne knew how she worried) and, at times, exasperation. Anne believed patience was overrated, as a virtue. Wasn't it better to get things done, be efficient, state your point? Why was waiting for other people to make up their mind and come around so much better? That forehead line was no doubt darker, deeper than it had been twenty years earlier. Jasper's leaving, her mother's death; and a furrow brought on by thought, too. The Adriatic voyage had sparked ideas for a new work.

Anne was packed and ready. She fastened her satchel with the books and papers she needed, but as she did so, one of the titles in the leather pouch caught her eye.

Checking the kitchen clock, Anne could see she was right on the edge now of timing, between an earlier train or the one after. If she took the second train, she would not arrive until the afternoon.

The lunch was optional. Margaret had written to say so.

> All attendees are created equal, but some are more equal than others. Don't worry if you don't want to come to the first meet and greet over sandwiches and germ-sprayed dining hall salad. You can just come in for the readings. If I don't see you at lunch, why not come to my office around 4.30/5? The good news is I got you the sumptuous guest suite at Guilford. It's the Ritz of college accommodations. You're welcome!

The meet and greet.

Anne and Margaret had corresponded a few times about the conference. As one or two writers dropped out, Anne kept an eye out for one West Coast participant, who was still planning to attend.

The clock's hands moved, and Anne's bag waited by the door, reticent but, pointedly, ready to go. The earlier train would leave without her from Grand Central if she sat down to read. She turned over the volume in her hand. 'Raunchy, moving, unforgettable,' said the *New York Times*, and Anne thought, *I remember her that way, too.* She sat down on the couch, and started reading.

It was very good. Swift, funny, observant. Vibrant. Not perfect: Flannery's youngness shone through, like skin through a gauzy blouse, at points of staged toughness or bravado. You could tell that a brittleness underlay the surface. This was clearer now, some years on. Making comedy out of your abandoning dad was an old trick; it worked well for the story but in the margins you could find tracings of Flannery's distinctive sadness. The tequila tales masked it some, but only to a reader too casual to wonder why the tequila flowed so fast and so amusingly. As for the steamy scenes – they were strange for Anne to read, of course, bringing a flush to her thighs, a rapidness to her pulse. She had an unsettling recollection of Jasper, in their Atlanta home, holding the hardback and commenting dryly to Anne, 'She writes well about sex, your former paramour.'

Anne had rolled her eyes at the word *paramour*, but was gratified that Jasper had taken time to read the book.

'The title's a play on Sybille Bedford's travel book about Mexico,' she told him. '*A Visit to Don Otavio.* The whole memoir is in part a riff on Bedford.'

'She's one of your pets, isn't she?'

Anne frowned. 'Flannery? Certainly not. She and I—'

He laughed. 'Sybille Bedford. Isn't she one of your projects? Rescuing her?'

Anne bristled at 'rescue', it sounded like something you would do for an abused chihuahua, but it was true that Bedford was a writer Anne had written about, and valued, and had tried to bring into the light.

Since dissertation days, in fact. If Sybille Bedford was in Flannery's book, as a kind of guiding spirit, that was not such a mystery. Anne had been the one to introduce them in the first place, one frost-bitten February afternoon, when she and Flannery had lounged together on the couch in Anne's overheated off-campus apartment, and Anne had read aloud to her lover from Bedford's book. She could remember the feeling of Flannery's solid head in her lap, and her own fingers playing idly with Flannery's fair hair as she read.

# 8

Some traits you are born with; no one asks you ahead of time if they are to your taste, and only a surgeon's or a chemist's hand can change them. Tufts of infant down will turn a Scandinavian fair and eventually fade to ash. The tiny nub of a nose will grow straight and long. (That was what happened with Flannery, anyway – with her daughter, at six, the nose was too soon to call.)

Other elements, Flannery reflected as she began to get ready to face the world, were within your control. Your honesty, with others but as crucially with yourself; your willingness at intervals to scrub off the limescale of self-deception before it caked so thick you could not see who you had become. Your capacity to stay calm and not flail in emergencies real (a direly ill friend) and imagined (was my child just snatched from the supermarket?). Your ability to amuse and forgive yourself.

Flannery was aware that she could be, even now, awkward or ridiculous. It was hard to miss. She could share a cookie with Willa, and after brushing clean her daughter's dinosaur T-shirt discover that her own was coated with crumbs. She once gave a decent sales pitch to a pompous bow-tied gentleman at one of Charles's openings, only to realize from the man's smirking response that he was one of the gallery's co-owners. When teaching, Flannery had learned that however thirsty she got, it was a bad idea to have any kind of drink with her, as she was likely to send it flying, spilling over someone's manuscript pages as she gestured to make a point.

Luckily, these misadventures tended to make Flannery laugh now. Charles's patience was strained by his wife's clumsiness – 'Maybe keep your hands in your pockets, Beauty?' he breathed with slight threat into her ear when they visited a painter friend's cluttered studio – but Flannery saw no point in hating herself for this quality any more. She had tried that for years, and it hadn't gotten her anywhere.

Before Flannery left The Den for what she thought of as 'the wretched lunch' she tried to eliminate any rogue sources of embarrassment: she was freshly showered and her teeth were clean; her button-down blouse was blemishless and dark enough to shrink the risk of dismaying sweat stains. Her brown leather purse, if in no way chic, was at least not bursting visibly with tampons or snack packs of cheddar bunnies. She looked, in her room's mirror, like an adult, a competent one. She resembled a writer. She might even still be considered pretty, she thought charitably, if the light did not catch the fret lines about her eyes too harshly. Maybe the other assembled women authors would take her seriously, and have no suspicions about the indignities or crushed confidence she had fled.

'Oh, who am I kidding?' Flannery muttered aloud, as she strode up the broad street toward Regent College, where the lunchers were to gather. She knew perfectly well, as did her silent audience, who she was trying to impress. One person above all. It wasn't a secret. Not from herself, it wasn't.

'Whom,' Flannery corrected herself. '*Whom* am I kidding . . . is that it?' That didn't sound right either, she thought as she stepped through the gateway of the Georgian college and toward the dining room. Unfortunately as she stepped Flannery failed to notice the two-inch wooden frame jutting up into the open doorway, caught it with the toe of her boot, staggered, skidded forward – and fell lengthways along the abrasive flag-stoned ground.

It was hard to laugh initially, as Flannery had an animal sense that she had been watched as she fell, and besides, she had hurt herself, a bit. Her purse flew into a muddy flower bed, her wrist took the brunt of her weight, and the knee of her trousers was scuffed.

'God. What an idiot!' She looked up, embarrassed, sure of what she would see. Those unforgettable green eyes gazing at her, under a bemused raised eyebrow, as Flannery reenacted an exaggerated, literal performance of their first encounter. *I fell for you, Anne. Get it?*

But instead it was a solid, pioneer-built woman with pewter-shaded hair and a friendly face who reached her. 'Do you need a hand?' This was Margaret Carter, Flannery knew. 'They're hellishly slippery, these stones . . . Are you Flannery?'

'Hi. Yes.' Could there be any doubt? Would any other Woman Writer make such an entrance? 'It was that ledge in the doorway.' Flannery tried at once to pick up her purse, straighten her jacket, and pull the trouser leg back down over her boots. 'I'm sorry for the slapstick routine. Glad to meet you.' She brushed off her grit-embedded wrist to shake her host's hand, thanking God, silently, that Margaret Carter wasn't Anne.

'Not at all!' Margaret said. 'We're so pleased you're part of our conference. It's a long way for you to come.'

She meant it literally, of course. Margaret Carter could not have known just how far Flannery had travelled to arrive here – counting internal as well as external miles. The two women kept on that logistical level, as Margaret led Flannery toward the dining hall. They chatted about the Faustian bargain of taking the red eye ('Yes, you get an extra day, but you lose your soul in transit,' Margaret noted) and the drugged wooze of jet lag – but the real ground covered was their immediate mutual respect and liking. Margaret Carter, who might have been a literature scholar sceptical about someone who had written a 'memoir' at twenty-six, or a cartoonish character wielding old-fashioned gender politics like a seventies hairband, was neither. She was a bright, energetic bespectacled woman with a warm, inclusive humour, and no need to show off. She wore a loose linen jacket and jeans, which put Flannery at her ease, and her pleasure in Flannery's arrival appeared sincere. Part of Flannery's fog lifted.

'I gather,' Margaret mentioned as they approached the hall, 'that you were a student of Anne Arden's, as an undergrad?'

'Oh!' Flannery put her hand to her mouth, as if to stop any compromising words from getting out. 'Well, not her student exactly, but . . . right, when I was a freshman, she TA'ed for Professor Bradley's class, and I took that class. But not in her section.' Flannery heard herself covering up again, after all these years. Burying the dangerous information about Anne and her, like an unfired pistol, deep in the sand.

'Martin Bradley!' Margaret exclaimed. It was a great detail to land on. 'What a character. He was just winding down, after the better part of four decades, when I first started teaching here. His were the glory days of the department.' She gave a deprecating laugh. 'Foucault coming to read, Derrida guest-lecturing. The golden era.'

As they approached two black-painted swing doors, a couple of hoodied undergraduates exited, on a wave of familiar dining hall aroma: melted cheese and build your own burrito ingredients, murky soup and toasted bagels, all over a stringent undernote of bleach.

'Glory days,' Flannery echoed. 'I remember.'

# 9

'Anne's a good friend of mine,' Margaret continued.

'Really? How . . . how is she? I haven't . . .'

But they had arrived at a broad, chipped, heavily varnished table, that bore its burden of a thousand undergraduate plates as a weary mule does its sacks of corn – around which a cluster of recognizable women ate and talked. Andi Chatterjee, her face colourful and camera-ready, spoke with the comfortable volume of someone who might later repeat her best lines to her million followers on social media. Beside Chatterjee sat Ellen Kessler, scarcely aged and carrying the weight of her achievements lightly, along with a tidy string of pearls and a silk scoop-necked top. There was Li Mayer, laughing confidently – the woman had nothing but confidence – as she tried to jolly the thin, almond-skinned woman beside her (Jefferson), who was a self-contained elegance next to Li Mayer's burst and bubble. Flannery looked at the four women avidly, but could not see . . .

'We're not all here yet,' Margaret Carter said, den-motherishly. 'Anne's coming later today, and Melissa Green too. The New Yorkers are the last to show, of course. Let me introduce you. This is Flannery Jansen . . .'

Flannery helloed and smiled, her disappointment simultaneous with a hot flush of relief. *I don't have to look or sound good for her just yet. I still have time to pull myself together.* Yet the news that this was for the moment an Anneless event also instantly drained what energy Flannery had summoned. It was as though she had expended all her social coin on the amiable Margaret Carter, and now, broke, she was faced with this phalanx of famous names.

However, she was here now. She had apparently walked in 'just as we were beginning to play the autumn guessing game about who'll get the Nobel this year, in literature,' Kessler said. The phrase 'guessing game' made Flannery think of Willa, and she had a sudden, sharp pain of daughter-missing, a quick blade in her side. The names of a Japanese novelist, a German one, and an American were tossed in the air like balls by a juggler. The drastic gender imbalance in the list of past prizewinners was noted. Doris Lessing's award was fondly recalled, and Chatterjee did a note-perfect rendition of Lessing's receiving the news, filmed as she climbed out of a London taxi: 'Oh, *Christ*,' with genuine exasperation, followed a minute later by a wry facing of the journalist: 'Right. I'm sure you'd like some uplifting remarks of some kind.'

Flannery had the wit to use this as a segue to talking with Lisa Jefferson, next to her, about the need for a Poet Laureate to be 'uplifting' ('It must be quite a weight?') and thereby avoid talking about herself. When everyone stood for coffees she felt she could, without blame, make a break for it. The Women Writers nodded their farewells, and Margaret stood and embraced her, confirming Flannery's sense that they might become friends. On her way out of the college, not that anyone was watching now, Flannery goose-stepped over the ledge with exaggerated clearance and exited into the mercifully writerless street.

# 10

Grand Central station was, in its way, a church. It was hard not to respond to its Beaux Arts majesty, the sloped celestial ceiling, and shafts of light pouring through the great high windows as if from God. Santa Maria would have felt at home here, too, Anne guessed. If there had been a few angels around the place, instead of outsized crystal chandeliers.

There was always a coming down from that soul-expanding hall into the drab reality of the commuter train. Ticketing and waiting areas often do that, Anne thought: promise so much light and air, though the planes or trains usually lack both. Once settled in a blue vinyl seat, she was resigned to a couple of unlovely hours, and thought of the difference of this multi-stop journey. *From the carriage, after travelling through vibrant, historic Harlem, watch as New York City changes to its sprawling outlying suburbs and then transforms into wealthy Connecticut. At our first stop, sleek Stamford, you may disembark if you like for a stroll around this bustling bedroom community, and sample local delicacies such as peanut butter pie . . .*

Anne gazed out the window at the moving landscape. She was nervous. This was why she was playing uncharacteristic games with herself. Why ignore the source? Face it down. That was what Anne was known for doing. In her work, and in her life.

She pulled *A Visit to Don Lennart* from her satchel, and flipped it over to look at the postage stamp-sized author photograph. A small black and white face with a bright, deflecting smile – Flannery had always had a warm Californian beam, though Anne came to appreciate the beauty in her when she was serious, too, and not trying so hard to please, to be nice.

This author had waited for Anne in a train station, once. At dawn. The one Anne was on her way to right now. New Haven. The two women scarcely knew each other, had gone out for a drink just once, though the girl wore her adoration like a hapless puppy. She was smitten. You couldn't miss it.

New Haven's station had grand heights by then, too. When Anne first visited the campus, the train station had been a maze of cramped underground tunnels, to one side of the original abandoned building. It was the time in the eighties when up and down the East Coast the great cities, Baltimore, Philadelphia, Washington, and even New Haven, were restoring stations to their former old-world elegance. One after the other they emerged from their dire seventies shells – something like the way a person might shed her restrictive Midwestern skin and discover her more cosmopolitan self.

Anne remembered catching sight of the tousled sleeping figure on one of the polished-wood benches in the station. Did she know that hapless student? She shook off the question in order to reach her train to New York on time, but once on board she heard her name called out. A wild-haired girl was on the platform with something for Anne. Pale in the November morning light, and slight in proportion to the station's dimensions, yet with a passion that was great, and bold, written on strips of paper in her yearning poem, and hidden like clues in the pages of a book she had brought Anne for her journey.

Anne had sat on a train much like this one then, heading the other way, wondering what she had done to inspire this old soul. 'Being a muse,' she later joked to Flannery, 'is a big responsibility.' She had spoken this, no doubt, with a kiss, or a fondling, the playfulness of mutual infatuation. As Anne's work intensified, though, along with the intensifying adoration of the eager freshman, the line became less of a joke. Anne could not be as much for Flannery as Flannery wanted her to be. *I can't hold everything, babe. I may contain multitudes, but only my own. Not all of yours, too.*

Anne never regretted leaving Flannery. There had been no other course. She was deeply in love with Jasper, the man of her life. But as Anne moved toward a gathering of people being encouraged to write the world, she thought of that distant girl, that dawn, that poem.

There was no reason to be nervous.

# 11

Flannery was no longer used to the bite in the air, though it helped her shake off her sleepiness to feel it again. She walked by the marbled incandescent lightbox of the manuscript library, along the wide grassy walkways beside high-ceilinged classrooms where as a kid she had first ingested Kierkegaard and Hegel, Auden and Rich. Flannery's present still pressed in close, but as she ambled, she felt her past wash over her like a brief spring shower. She had found adulthood here. (How was Willa? Charles had gotten her to school, she knew that much, surely a good holding place for the next six or seven hours.) That feisty, rebellious self she had been in her thrift shop blazers and drainpipe jeans, a look she took back home to California on vacations, with mixed response from her mother and cousins. (She thought of Charles's irritable text message about her mother's 'interference': 'Is she really staying here every night?') Flannery knew that young woman she'd been the way you know a character in an old familiar children's book, but the river of experience between them now, broad and loud as freeway traffic, made it difficult for the two to communicate. (A short voicemail from the school to say that Willa had arrived without a lunch but they would provide her with one, no problem.) Their voices got lost in the sounds of the current. She thought of those dinner table games – what would you tell your earlier self if you could? *You're going to become more confident, you will go far, you'll have success. OK? And then you'll turn a corner, your life will change, there will be the miracle of a new person. Not all of it's good, but I don't want to wreck it for you.*

And the younger self? What would she say forward in reply? *Cool. Just don't go so far out there you disappear.*

Her cell phone rang; she took it from her pocket, saw Charles's number and answered it, teeth clenched, then her husband was with her and the younger ghost Flannery evanesced.

'Hi. How are things going?' It was best, she knew, not to mention her mother, or the message from the school, anything that might set him off.

'I'm just trying to park. This fucking city. I wish all these tech brats would just *go home*. Or move to Palo Alto. Fine. You want to build computers, or establish start-ups or a billion-dollar social media empire? That's fine. Go ahead. Just go and do it in fucking *Mountain View*, please, and leave us alone.'

Flannery held the phone some distance from her ear as he continued for another paragraph or two. When there was a pause, she brought the phone closer again. 'How's Willa? I loved the breakfast pictures.'

'Oh.' Charles allowed himself to be redirected. 'She's great. We're having a fantastic time together. We made breakfast sculptures this morning.'

'Yeah, you sent pictures. They were very sweet.'

'The kid's meticulous. I mean, she has an engineer's mind. I made us waffles' – meaning toasted, from the freezer – 'and put out a bowl of berries, and so she takes blueberries and places them neatly inside waffle-squares, then balances the waffles on four support frets of strawberries. On her request, I gave a decorative spritz of whipped cream on the top, and then she drizzled maple syrup over the whole thing.'

'It looked delicious.' Flannery suddenly had a surge of hunger.

'It was. The kid's a genius.'

'She's got to be.' Charles might not hear the irony in Flannery's voice, but it didn't matter. He had always enjoyed the reflected glory aspect of parenthood. 'Well,' Flannery said. 'I've met some of the people. The first real event is later, though.'

'Oh, thank Christ!'

'You found a parking spot?'

'Yeah. Come on, Mrs McGillicuddy, you and your Buick can move along now. Listen, I gotta go, Flan. Love you. Have a great time.'

And he hung up, leaving a spacious silence in his wake.

Flannery had to eat. The hunger now was unignorable.

# 12

Anne stepped out to the curved sidewalk outside the station and slid into a lime-green cab. She could have told the taxi driver to take her to the college where she was staying, but she realized she had skipped lunch, and so gave him instead the name of a sloping side street, where there was one of those classic dives. It was a place with decades of names carved into its dark booth tables, perennially dim lighting, and the never-broken promise of warming, easy-to-eat food along with beer and coffee to fuel generations of gods and men (and eventually women) as they acquired their light and truth and valuable, sterling degrees. Anne never used to frequent the place much, preferring a lighter, jaunty spot patriotically called The Yankee Doodle, but the latter had long since closed.

It was the odd, dead time of day, three o'clock, a nether hour when the people who lingered were either time-muddled students working off the undergraduate jet lag of a late night, or paper writers sitting over a glowing laptop, backs hunched, eyes flitting back and forth across the screen, pausing just to sip the coffee.

But there was someone at a booth who did not belong in any of those categories.

An adult, not a student, and not a graduate student, you

could tell from her lack of books. Nor, from her distracted air, a professor. Professors tended to look wary at popular food joints, as if every person in there was planning to sidle up to them to ask for an extension, or query a grade. This woman – blonde, pretty, troubled, a coffee cup to one side of her – had a deep, abstracted gaze as she stared at the bench back opposite her, picking out some unseeable reality. Her left hand was holding and rubbing the wrist of her right, a fretful gesture. Anne responded to the contemplative expression. She knew that mouth, had once known it very well.

She had been Anne's girl, for a spell, a long while ago. And she had always enjoyed long, quiet periods when she neither read nor wrote, but simply thought. Anne remembered that.

The solitary figure looked up, feeling eyes on her, and there was a silent, immeasurable piece of time during which the two women saw one another, not smiling and not breathing, stopped by the same sensation.

Recognition.

# 13

The moment of stillness passed.

Anne walked carefully, as if not to scare away a wild or imaginary creature, to the poorly lit table. As she drew near, though, she saw that Flannery was laughing, shaking her head. When her smile was genuine, her face had always become illuminated, like a saint's. All that old worry, her rigid eagerness to please, softened in the warmer climate of her amusement.

'Here?' the all-grown-up Flannery said, raising her eyebrows, and she stood, taller than Anne remembered, to embrace Anne in greeting, kissing her on one cheek. She had a fruit scent of shampoo on her, and, underneath, the pulse of something else.

'It had to be somewhere,' Anne answered, and she held Flannery's shoulder under her palm a moment. 'Besides, the light in this place is flattering. You look wonderful, Flannery. And well.'

And the bonnie girl blushed at that, just as she would have in the past. She gestured to the bench across from her.

'So do you, Professor Arden. You look great.' She winced slightly, as if wishing she had found a better word.

'Are you working? I don't want to interrupt . . .'

'No! Just hiding in my lair. Please. Make yourself at home.'

'I'd like nothing better, but I've got to get some food in me. This conference will require strength.'

'It already has.'

'You went to the lunch? It was—'

'Optional. I know. I should have opted out. The dining hall food was nausea-inducing, I couldn't eat it. The minute I left I ended up coming here.'

'Good call. But you met your fellows? Your fellow women, that is?'

'Some. I wasn't feeling that full of . . . fellowship, to be honest.' Perhaps fearing she had said too much, Flannery added shyly, 'But I like your friend.'

'Margaret Carter?'

'Yes. Though her name keeps making me think of the Magna Carta.'

'Margaret's a good thing.'

'I thought so right away. I made a kind of disastrous entrance, but she made it seem . . .'

'Unimportant.'

'Right.'

'Margaret is someone with a great ability to get to what's important. She leaves all the chaff behind, instantly. She knows if someone is worth her while.'

They paused, and watched each other.

'It's very good to see you,' Anne said.

'Yes. Same.' Flannery smiled again, but this time a Nordic sadness lay under her expression. It was hard to be sure in the gloom, but Anne thought there might be tears at the corners of Flannery's hazel eyes. The younger woman seemed beyond speaking for a moment, but reached out and touched Anne's arm. 'Go get something to eat,' she said, trying to collect herself. 'My lair and I will stay right here, and wait.'

*

She had cleaned her mood away like an emptied plate by the time Anne returned. It may have taken some will: the light on Flannery's face had just a shade of the artificial on it now, like an actor's in a scene shot with spotlights, when the glow on the skin is cooler than that cast by daylight.

'They've changed the name of this place,' Flannery noted. 'It used to be called Naples.'

'Maybe they wanted something that sounded more American. Wall Street: that's a sign of the times, I suppose.'

'Well, they serve gluten-free pizza now, too. That doesn't seem very Neapolitan.'

'I was in that part of the world this summer,' Anne ventured. 'I had a dish called *spaghetti alle vongole fujute* – with escaped clams. The sauce had cherry tomatoes, garlic, parsley – but no clams. They had escaped, it seems.'

'I like that. So you're just supposed to think of the clams, wistfully.'

'Right. The dish tastes better for imagining them there.'

There was a beat between them.

'You were in Italy?' Flannery asked politely.

'And Croatia. And on the sea between the two.' Anne described her journey aboard the *Stella Maris*, highlighting moments she thought might amuse Flannery. The glint-eyed Swedish captain and his taste for aquavit ('Or,' Flannery suggested slyly, 'for what aquavit might permit'), severe Austrian Greta whose face melted into sentiment at the mention of her dachshund at home. Watching at a factory in Murano as ordinary-looking men, who might in another place be the cable guy or the trainer at the gym, shaped candy-coloured delicacies from the molten glass. Swans, vases, globes of light.

Two decades before, Flannery would have hung on such stories, as on the promise of a life she wanted but feared she might never lead. Anne was the Experienced One, with Paris or New Orleans in her pocket, and Flannery was desperate to catch up, a yearning that gave Anne's lighter tellings a weight they could not bear. Anne learned in their short time together to pare back her travelogues. She found the hunger on the girl's face sometimes heartbreaking, sometimes simply irksome. Flannery's unvarnished envy put Anne off her narrative stride.

Now, though, Flannery had clearly gotten to see the world for herself, or enough of it that she could listen to the stories as Anne intended them – not as showcases of a glamorous life but as character sketches, landscape studies. Verbal postcards. She had written only once to Flannery, over the years. Now that seemed an oversight; she could have been writing to her all along.

'Did you go to the Biennale?' Flannery looked down as she asked.

'Yes, with my sister. It was remarkable – it covered so much ground. That is, acres, but also aesthetically, a mass of ideas and content.'

'Kind of like an encyclopedia?' Flannery asked, with a wry smile.

'You could say that.' Anne mirrored Flannery's expression. 'Yes.'

'I've heard about the show.' A decision seemed to flutter across Flannery's face, and she chose not to continue with wherever that line of thought might lead. To Marshall, probably. 'Still, not a bad junket for you. Nice work, if you can get it.'

'It's true. The Biennale was just vacation, but the cruise before it, though cruisey, was work. I had to give a few lectures.'

'You had to sing for your supper,' Flannery said.

'For my gnocchi, yes. And my runaway clams.'

'There's more of that in this business than I used to realize. We have to perform, though as a reward we do get to visit glamorous conference rooms, or –' Flannery gestured around the dark wooden booths – 'famous Italianate eating establishments.'

'Or lunches in dining halls.'

'Exactly. That was my treat earlier – well, I already told you. Make your own burritos, and tableside speculation about this year's Nobel prize.'

Anne shook her head. 'It was good of you to go.'

'Well, I only showed up for one reason.'

The seventeen-year-old Flannery might have spoken this suggestion indirectly, or at an angle. This one gazed right into Anne's eyes as she spoke, and it was Anne, actually, warmed by the words, who found she had to look away.

# 14

Walking back collegewards they fell into a comfortable stride together.

'I did have a nice talk with Lisa Jefferson at lunch,' Flannery said, 'about being Poet Laureate. What that even means, here.'

'In Britain they have to turn out lyrics for royal weddings, or the birth of the young prince.'

'Right, but what are the great American events, you know?' Flannery laughed. 'The Superbowl? The election?'

'That could be an excellent new genre: Superbowl sonnets. Though she did write that poem for the inauguration.'

They talked about the presidential race for a few minutes, and the country's alarming rightward tilt. 'Actually,' Flannery admitted, 'I'm worried about having to talk politics with Melissa Green – she wrote a column a while ago in favour of Homeland Security surveillance that I found somewhat fascistic. I'm going to try not to say so.'

Flannery was aware that this aspect of herself, a smart newspaper reader with opinions, probably postdated the time she and Anne had known each other. Flannery had been embryonic then, or more to the point, so infatuated with Anne that political realities seemed distant and unimportant to her that winter and spring. It was after they split up that Flannery had become a rally-goer and a protest marcher with her college friends, tramping up the National Mall to make a case to an unlistening Congress about one injustice or another. She wondered if she was trying to signal this difference to Anne; if she was performing, to a degree, the role of *more mature and sophisticated now than you might have expected*. Couldn't Flannery simply relax around Anne, not try to prove anything? They were both, she suspected, finding their feet. Two pairs of boots clipped along the stone paths, gradually falling in to a complementary rhythm.

Flannery's phone buzzed. Her internal clock, set not just to California time but to the schedule of her daughter's day, registered that Willa was still in school, so the message would not be her first dread (*No one is here to collect your child*), though there were always the other deeper ones (*Willa fell off the monkey bars!*). Apologizing to Anne, she removed the device to take a look.

Charles.

> What are arrangements today – yr mom picking W up? Have to go to South SF to pick up slate, will take a few hrs.

'Everything all right?' Anne looked sideways, sensing some shift.

'Pretty much.' It was too soon for Flannery to want to mention, or describe, Charles to Anne, though avoiding talking about him was difficult too, like driving a large detour around an awkward roadblock. 'It's just . . . a message about my daughter.'

Anne abruptly stopped. They had reached the top of the steps that connected the two libraries – the buried undergraduate cave, and the great, cathedraled Sterling, home of ten thousand volumes. The two women stood near Lin's elegant circular fountain, whose moving waters murmured assent – or question.

Anne faced Flannery. Her startling celadon eyes still made Flannery gasp.

'You have a child?' she asked, in a low voice that caught at Flannery.

'I do, yes.' Somehow Flannery had thought Anne might have known.

'Sit down,' Anne commanded her, gesturing to the graphite-coloured stone around the fountain. 'And tell me.'

# 15

So Flannery talked about Willa. Apprehensive, as she had never forgotten about Anne's lack of interest in or desire for children; but also having wanted, since her daughter's birth, one day to tell Anne of Willa's existence.

She did not get very far. Immediately, at the name, Anne stopped her.

'*Willa*? You called your child Willa?'

'Yes.' Flannery could not know whether Anne's thoughts were moving over the same memory as hers – of Anne, at twenty-eight, bare-legged in her overheated apartment, lying on her back across a bed that had seen their recent entwinings, reading aloud a few paragraphs from *The Song of the Lark*. Flannery hardly knew who Willa Cather was – her high school English classes had failed to mention her – and understood that she must add the great Nebraskan's pioneer novels to the stack of Books She Had to Read, not least because she was at the heart of Anne Arden's dissertation, her future book. It was a good thing they broke up, Flannery used to kid herself, once the fissure in her pride had healed, so she could get started on all that reading. How otherwise would she have found the time?

'Is it a family tradition?' Anne asked, her centre frown line deepened in bemused disbelief. 'Naming children after American writers with odd prenames?'

'Now it is, I guess. Two generations. My mother started it.'

'You couldn't have chosen Edith, or Kate, or . . . Emily?'

'It had to be Willa.' Flannery hesitated. 'Honestly, it was the only name Charles and I could agree on. Otherwise she might have had to be Iris, after his aunt. And though I respect her, I wouldn't have wanted Iris Murdoch on anyone's mind.'

The fountain issued its watery purr into the pause between them.

'And –' Anne dipped her hand into the stream, tracing the numbers carved there with two cooled fingers – 'what is she like – your Willa?'

Flannery reached instinctively for the phone in her pocket. That was how you shared information now, through the photo album you carried with you. Anne put a moistened hand onto Flannery's arm – gently. 'Show me pictures later. *Tell* me something, would you?'

'Oh. OK.' So, shyly, Flannery tried to locate one or two of her best anecdotes, words that might illustrate and animate Willa, transform the girl in Anne's mind from whatever generic went along with the word 'kid' to a picture of an actual person. People who were uncomfortable around children, in Flannery's experience, tended to think of them as a cluster of characteristics, generally inconvenient ones – noise, demands, messiness – rather than as human characters. Flannery had taken an ethics class in college that tackled the question of when personhood began – before birth, as anti-abortion advocates claimed? Or at birth? Or later? In her thirties, with a tiny self that grew and moved within her, Flannery had seen new depth in the question. A day after giving birth Flannery could, to her own astonishment, see a person there, a small Willa, in that loud bundle.

It was a curious experience, to describe one of your essential loves to the other – the two people for whom you would give up everything, if it would do them any good. You wanted them to feel close, even though you suspected they might never meet. Perhaps this was how travellers felt in a previous era, holding a lock of their cherished one's hair as they told their host in a remote rainforest nation about their intended, left behind. Odysseus sharing his yarns about Penelope, while she stayed home and wove. And unwove.

Anne asked no questions, and her expression was hard for Flannery to read. She was listening. She did not grin at the cute stuff – the improbable names Willa came up with for her vast collection of small stuffed animals (a giraffe called Mrs Huffenstuff, a unicorn named Bruce), or the girl picking up, at three, a copy of *A Visit to Don Lennart* and exclaiming at the picture on the back, 'Mommy, that lady looks like you!' But she nodded when told about the Lego constructions, and the characters Willa invented who went with them. Finally Anne said with a small, almost melancholy smile, 'All right. Show me one or two of your pictures.'

Easy. Flannery removed her phone again, found one of Willa laughing at the park, the background a blur of green and grey, the main focus that spark-bright heart-shaped face.

Anne held the phone, and read the image closely, as if it were a map, before handing it back to Flannery.

'She has your hair,' she said softly, in a tone as though she had said something quite different. With the lightest hand, a hummingbird wing, she touched a strand of Flannery's blonde; then said, without affect, 'I think it's time to get back to the college.'

# 16

They reached Guilford in silence, though not an unfriendly one, and said an ambiguous goodbye, knowing they would meet again a few hours later in the overlit marketplace of the evening's readings. Flannery felt as she did when she climbed out of the pool, after swimming: suddenly exposed, in a public place, shivering at the cold air on her skin.

Had something else altered the atmosphere between them? Their anxiety in each other's presence had subsided quickly into charged pleasure at the restaurant, but in the past minutes a balance had been lost. That sweet girl Willa was somehow between them; or Charles, a buried reference; or Jasper, the man unmentioned. Anne must have someone else beside her these days – but how could Flannery ask? And how could Anne tell her?

'I'm not staying here,' Flannery blurted, at the college gate. 'I decided to stay in one of the hotels. The Den.'

Anne nodded, scarcely registering interest. 'Sensible, probably.'

'It's kind of the opposite of how it used to be, isn't it?' Flannery continued, in some unstoppable gush reminiscent of adolescence. 'Back then I was the lowly freshman in the dorm, and you were the grown-up living off campus.'

There was nothing to do but hate herself the instant she had uttered this inanity. It reminded them both of the teenager Flannery had been: goofy, awkward, overeager. Flannery was so appalled that all she could do was give Anne an equally awkward pat on the shoulder and say, 'Anyway, I'll see you later . . . It's great to see you . . .' before turning her back on her former idol, so that Flannery need not witness the pity or irritation that might be playing across that familiar face, the pursed wide lips, the emerald assessing eyes. *Whom am I kidding?* Flannery wanted to say to herself, and would, perhaps, when she was a safe block or two away. *I'm the same idiot I ever was.*

'Good to see you, too,' Anne said, or so it sounded, as Flannery put her hand up in a gesture of joint farewell and retreat. She returned to her Den, blind to the streets and students, thoughts and regrets crowding out her vision. She thought of installing herself in that quiet, solitary room and filling it with the sound of calls to Charles and her mother and whoever else was required to make Willa's pickup arrangements work from this distance. No, her mother was not signed up for that particular day, as a week earlier Charles had confidently – in fact, almost indignantly – assured Flannery he would do it, there was no need for his mother-in-law.

So for this afternoon, the hotel room would no longer be an escape. It would simply become the place where Flannery went about the mundane and necessary task of finding someone to take care of her child. Something about her conversation with Anne made this feel like an activity she had to do alone, in secret, as if the rest of the professional world should never have to know.

# 17

Uneasy.

Something was making Anne uneasy. For the first time in a long while she wished she had a cigarette. Flannery's casual comparison of their accommodations gave Anne the unnerving sense that in returning to the college now, she was somehow moving backwards. The idea upset her.

She found Margaret, who helped settle Anne in the suite – 'It was good enough for Toni Morrison, so I don't want to hear any complaints' – and then they walked together back to Margaret's own second-floor office. The expansive, lead-windowed chamber overlooked one of the courtyards and had much the character of Margaret herself: warm, interesting and untidy. Lined with erudition. Bookshelves stretched floor to ceiling, with some of the unlikelier inhabitants (Julian of Norwich; William Hazlitt) half obscured by photographs of Margaret's children, mugs with pens and scissors in them, scattered cables or chargers, and ceramic dishes collecting paperclips, cough drops, stamps, or coins. To Anne, for whom neatness was as essential as eating or sleeping, such a workspace was anathema, but she sank into the generous leather armchair with relief.

'This chair is obscenely comfortable,' she said to her friend. 'All right, it's official: you have better digs than I do.'

Margaret poured them two shot glasses of Aperol taken from a bronze tray perched at a slightly drunken angle on top of a few volumes of the *OED*. They sat together for an hour, trading talk about work (Margaret was finishing an interpretive biographical work on Poe, and the ideas poured out of her), family (they sat and told sad stories of the death of parents), and colleagues (the gossip circulating about the chair of Margaret's department, whose messy tangle involved a young Mandarin instructor and his betrayed wife's exposure of a sordid email correspondence).

'When will people learn not to write things down?' Margaret tsked.

'That's a rhetorical question, isn't it? We know the answer is never.' Anne eased deeper into the armchair's forgiving embrace. 'As long as human beings fall in love, or lust, they won't be able to keep themselves from putting the sentiment into print.'

'There's my cue! So, Professor Arden, what love notes have you been penning lately?'

Anne was thrown off balance by the question, and had a brief disorienting moment of wondering if Margaret had seen Anne walking with Flannery; or if she had somehow intuited lines Anne might have thought of writing.

'What do you mean?' she asked, almost sharply.

'Relax!' Margaret laughed and leaned forward. 'OK, let me put it more bluntly: what did you think of Steven?'

'Marovic?'

'Yes, dear.' Margaret tilted her head. 'Your cruise mate.'

'Oh.' Anne stared back, keeping her own bright eyes wide open. 'He was good company.'

'Yes. He found you good company too. I have to tell you, I

think he was smitten.' Margaret looked satisfied, as though she had engineered this result.

'He's . . .' Anne looked down at the pooled crystal liquor in her glass. How to express her reaction to the man? 'Bald,' she said succinctly.

'Oh! Bald.' Margaret waved a hand. Her own husband Lloyd's hair was thinning. 'That doesn't matter. Come on. Bald is the new . . . um . . .'

'I don't want to know how that sentence ends,' Anne interrupted, though she was laughing now too. 'All right, how about this? Steven Marovic is married.'

'Divorced. They're getting divorced.'

'*Getting* divorced.' Anne's gaze wandered over to the bookshelves. Always something so pleasantly distracting in another person's library. Harriet Beecher Stowe. George Eliot. Darwin! *The Voyage of the Beagle.* With effort, Anne returned to the subject. 'People can be *getting* divorced for years, Margaret. It goes on and on. It's a gerundive state.'

'Sometimes. In Steven's case, it's reaching its conclusion.'

'All right.' Anne kept her face neutral.

'He thought that you might draw him out about it.'

'Well, I didn't.'

'No. I gathered that.' Margaret knew not to push Anne; she respected the invisible hand held up, urging her to pause. 'But another time,' Margaret concluded lightly, 'you might.' Margaret stood, collected their glasses, and returned them to the tipsy tray. 'And now,' she said, gesturing ruefully to her comfortable jeans and easy flats, 'I had better change into a more imperious outfit, so I can open the literary games in style.'

# 18

Anne considered Margaret's metaphor as she dressed for the evening.

Was tonight, she wondered, more Greek or Roman? An ennobling competition like the Olympics, or an arena full of gladiators and a fight to the death? Anne had built her academic career on questioning the notion that writers had to figuratively kill each other to be heard. Freud, and Bloom after him, were certain that destroying your antecedents was necessary in the creation of self, and Anne had believed this to be wrong, or at least distorted.

'You're a literary pacifist,' Jasper had told her once. 'You don't believe in the validity of battle.'

Anne closed the door of her suite and stood out in the musty corridor, and had a sharp awareness, like a cramp, of being alone. She closed her eyes, held on to the door handle a moment, made herself breathe. It came over her suddenly sometimes, a physical sensation. For the most part, Anne was past feeling self-conscious about being single rather than partnered at such events. Most would have left their Others behind, anyway, and Jasper had never been essential to Anne's social self: they were too independent, and also too deeply connected, for that to be an issue. Nonetheless, having Jasper's strong arm to hold on to when she went out into the world had provided a years-long comfort, and the lack of it sometimes still left Anne feeling strangely unsteady.

She straightened, opened her eyes, resolved to be all right; then set off to the auditorium on the old campus where the readings were to take place. The side street had a film set artificiality to it with the lamplights, the dampness of the flagstones, the unnatural quiet. It seemed possible that Gene Kelly or Lauren Bacall might step out of the shadows and start singing, or at least smoking, but the tall figure who approached from under the stone crossbridge, shoulders curved in a thoughtful, inward posture, wearing a canvas coat that Anne could see was not adequate to the autumn chill, was more in the line of Claire Danes, or Cate Blanchett.

The woman looked up. Before she could remember their previous awkwardness, recognition lit her hazel eyes, and she lifted her delicate chin with a shy smile.

'Flannery!' Anne's muscles untensed. 'Thank God it's you.'

A speechless pleasure broke over Flannery's lovely face, and Anne felt much better, abruptly, about the evening ahead.

'Ditto.' Flannery brushed the hair unnecessarily away from her face. That familiar gesture – she had it at seventeen too, a constant, unconscious grooming, that doubled as a way to occupy her hands. 'Hi.'

'I was thinking about something a little earlier, about tonight,' Anne said chattily, as though picking up a conversation the two women had just left off. 'Let's walk. You'll have an opinion on this, I'm sure.'

They fell into step together.

'I might,' Flannery said. 'Try me.'

'A group of women writers,' Anne began, keeping her voice low, as she wasn't eager for her facetiousness to be overheard.

'Are they going to be vying for position as they show off their talents for the audience?'

'Competitive, you mean?'

'Yes. Or will it be convivial, mutually supportive? More like a dinner party.'

'Like Judy Chicago.' Flannery considered. 'Frida Kahlo sitting next to Virginia Woolf? Georgia O'Keeffe chatting with Rosa Parks?'

'Right. Though that makes the scenario seem a fusty seventies remnant. Old-school feminism.'

They walked together across the chiaroscuro lawns. 'There's this famous scholar . . .' Flannery's voice had a confident music Anne suddenly recalled: you met her as a ducking, mumbling person who could hardly be heard, or understood; but, when she came to know you, and let her mind take flight, her voice was suddenly beautifully clear. As a bell. 'She wrote a whole amazing book about women writers not trying to, you know, slaughter each other, but instead to work off each other. I'm just a lowly novelist, but I did read it once.' She coughed. 'Possibly twice.'

'Hmm.' Anne wrinkled her face. 'Did the scholar ever expand on, develop the idea – move it past that initial, somewhat pat thesis?'

'It wasn't pat!' Flannery held Anne's arm for emphasis. Anne felt the touch through her layers. 'It wasn't some hackneyed battle cry, it wasn't a sally in the culture wars, and it wasn't about victimization. It opened up a *conversation*. It cast light on writers who had been more in the shadows.' She was sincere, this woman; Anne could not pretend otherwise. 'Anyway,' Flannery said in a lighter tone, 'she did develop the arguments further in her second book. So there.' The fluorescence of a campus security post caught the lines on the younger woman's face: the smile-etch around her mouth, the worry furrow across her eyes. Anne was oddly affected to see the signs of Flannery's ageing. She was not, then, Dorian Gray.

'All right,' Anne conceded. 'Though I believe the follow-up work isn't as widely read as the first.'

'Tell me about it,' Flannery said, with a rueful laugh.

In the distance Anne could see Catherine Li Mayer and Lisa Jefferson emerging from one of the other gateways. Soon, this happily private moment would be over.

'On the subject of influence, though, Ms Jansen, if I may . . . It seemed to me that Sybille Bedford gave you more than just a title to riff off of. That your path paralleled hers, geographically. Is that right?'

'You always were a close reader,' Flannery said, adding softly, 'I was hoping you'd notice.'

Was that sincere, too – the suggestion that Flannery had written with Anne's reading it in mind? Or merely flirtatious? Anne was left wondering, as Flannery then opened the weighty door for Anne, and the two women entered, together, the arena.

# 19

It was like surfacing from the depths of a thick, murky pond. It was like coming out of a dark, close cave and inhaling fresh, oxygenated air. It was like having held your breath for several years, and finally letting it go at the point when you were nearly faint and asphyxiated.

All of the analogies that crowded Flannery's excited mind had to do with breathing. She was breathing again.

Listening to the writers read from and talk about their books, Flannery felt an expansion around her heart and lungs. The jolting alert of her intellect, as of some spell-pricked princess who had been slumbering in a castle tower, was every bit as multicoloured and wonderful as in a Disney movie, the kind she would watch with Willa.

Margaret Carter, who had cleaned up nicely in an elegant aubergine dress, gave a generous, well-judged introduction to the conference and the evening, carrying her politics lightly and with humour, and had the audience eager for Ellen Kessler, the first speaker.

Kessler discussed the world, and this reminded Flannery that she cared about the world – yes, beyond her self-involved San Francisco square of it. Kessler's delivery, without notes, of an impassioned disquisition on the nature of totalitarianism, along with a poignant example from a family she had interviewed in Belarus, jolted Flannery. From Kessler it required a slight shift in one's seat to absorb Green's tales about being a *Times* columnist: the pressing need to be original on a weekly basis, taking in each day's headlines as potential material. Green did not, like Flannery and a million others, spend most of her time following up links sent by her friends; it was her pieces that others forwarded around. She was more clicked upon than clicking.

Finally Andi Chatterjee, who was as sharply funny as could be expected of someone who contributed significantly to the nation's comedy diet. 'Shamelessly promoting' her first book, *Chatterjockey*, she was a starry crowd-pleaser, and Margaret Carter had been savvy to close with her. She read a section on the perils of not being thin in Los Angeles, introduced with the line, 'Hi, my name is Andi Chatterjee and I am not an anorexic,' which earned a cheer.

The hour and a half ended on a buzz of excitement, students and faculty afterwards seeking signatures in books and a word with the authors. Every sentence had made Flannery think. She had almost forgotten how much she loved to think.

Next to her, throughout, sat Anne. They laughed and applauded together. There was not a moment when Flannery had been unaware of Anne beside her.

Afterwards, there was a collective walk in the dark to a spirited reception, where Flannery lost Anne, for a time. An eagle-nosed, pepper-haired man was determined to monopolize Professor Arden's company while behind him, like parishioners waiting to make confession, others stood, wanting their turn. Flannery drifted off, wondering who to talk to – she might be oxygenated, but she still had not found her voice in this noisy group. She made her way to the bar, having till now forgotten this institution's dedication to liquoring up its alumni; an image came to her mind of those late May afternoons when the campus was awash with blazered drunkards bonding under canvas tents. Waiting to catch the bartender's eye, Flannery was jostled into by the ebullient Chatterjee, who immediately turned the collision into a self-deprecating anecdote and insisted on getting Flannery a martini to apologize. Before long the two were drinking and swapping clumsiness anecdotes, engaging in an intense competition over whose were more embarrassing. Flannery felt younger, and alive. 'I really want to *win*,' she told Andi. 'I think I've got this.' And she related the spill on her way into the college earlier that day, showing off her bruised wrist as evidence. Chatterjee one-upped her with an account of a television awards dinner she had attended in a turquoise dress at which she suddenly, without warning, got her period ('a week early, in my defence; just one of those little menstrual jokes God likes to play') which meant she had to stay pinned to her padded chair for the evening so the red blot would not show.

'I thought of telling that story tonight,' Andi confided, 'but I didn't want to make the boys squirm.'

They chatted until someone came to escort the comedienne to an adoring cluster of undergraduates. She excused herself with the line, 'But now I have to go talk to people who aren't a whole foot taller than me. You've been giving me a complex,' and gave Flannery a practised Hollywood kiss before flying away.

Still animated by the martini, Flannery appreciatively greeted Ellen Kessler, who was good enough to feign remembering Flannery and to say artfully, with information possibly gleaned from the conference programme, how wonderful it was that Flannery's memoir had been such a success a decade earlier.

(Did she slightly emphasize the word *decade*?) Flannery's hunch was that Kessler was more gladiator than Olympian.

Abruptly, Flannery was exhausted. Jet lag snuck up on her like the premonition of a hangover. She was not, herself, a fighter or a competitor of any kind, and it was not even clear that she was someone you would want at your dinner party. Maybe she should go back to the murky pond, the airless, idea-free cave she was used to; suddenly she had little to say about that old Mexico book of hers, or the scarcely read novel that had followed it, and only the sketchiest of answers to the inevitable question, 'What are you working on now?' (Why hadn't she scripted a response to that ahead of time, on the red-eyed plane?) She managed one coherent political note to Kessler about Belarus, then excused herself and made her way to the door. She retrieved her too-thin coat and was for an instant synonymous with the seventeen-year-old who had arrived in this state ill-prepared for the cut of the icy air or the way the cold seeped through your flimsy layers of protection, or how clever, energetic and ambitious everyone was. The way they never let up.

'You're not leaving, are you?' A hand on her arm, the face she had always wanted alight by her side. Flannery had not pictured, nor had the Internet accurately told her, how Anne's face would age, but it was a change, not a diminishing. If anything, Anne's beauty had grown starker, more defined.

'I think I should,' Flannery heard herself say over the shouting and drunkenness, as oily fingers plucked snacklets from belatedly offered trays around them. 'I'm being empanelled in the morning, you know, and I want to be able to speak complete sentences for that.'

'Right. I'm the moderator.' As if Flannery would need

reminding! Anne gave her a suggestive look. 'I'll try to wield an even hand.'

'I remember that hand.' Swiftly, Flannery took Anne's and kissed it, a semi-ironic gesture of gallantry, then said a garbled goodnight to the bewildered, rose-cheeked woman she had flown all this distance, finally, to see.

# 20

Back in her white, clean, association-free room. No bills, no dishes, no stuffed animals. No one else. No one asking her or telling her. She need not be anyone in particular: novelist, memoirist, soldier, spy.

Flannery showered again. It felt ritualistic, a cleansing; and as she stood in the stream of water, Flannery wondered what she was washing off. The room full of smart peers and students, talking, joshing, trading notes on their work? Or that familial self she was at home, the woman tied by law and kinship to Charles Marshall and her beloved evolving Willa?

Or might she even be rinsing away some slick of emotion she felt, being around Anne?

*What are you most frightened of?* she asked herself. Flannery had always been her own sternest interrogator, exposing her internal contradictions a step ahead of anyone else who might question her. *How can you be this and then say that? Why would you pretend over here, then deny over there?*

Now she pressed herself:

*What do you fear more: being home, or being away from home?*

*What are you escaping from – and what do you imagine escaping to?*

*Is either place safe?*

This hotel room was, for the moment, still a haven. In the important ways, it was empty: containing of Flannery's only a laptop, a few nice clothes, a short pile of books. As she had noted with a cautionary relief when she came back in, no one else was here with her.

The room would only remain safe, however, if it stayed a place of solitude.

*Are you really imagining Anne might come back here with you? (How could she not?)*

*What would happen if she did?*

It was behind a blank door in her mind, the answer to that question. Shuttered, dusty. A closed-up shop that went out of business a long time ago.

Flannery turned off the shower. With brusque motions she towelled herself off, her pale skin pinkened at the stomach and thighs from the heat of the water. She did not look at herself in the mirror but left the bathroom, slapped moisturizer on herself with the haste of a harried Slavic masseuse at some low-end spa, then put on her heather cotton pyjamas and climbed into the soft, white, laundered sheets. Flannery reached for the telephone, sent a brief affectionate message to Charles including a line for Willa, who should by now be asleep, and set to work getting into that same state herself.

*What would happen if she did?*

Flannery had always been proud of her imagination, its flexibility and stamina, travelling to surprising places, but right now it was tethered, a tamed bird, unable to reach the higher air.

By the bed was Li Mayer's book, but Flannery was not in the mood to read about sex acts in Thailand. She reached for Jefferson's difficult, diamond-edge poetry instead, hoping its lyrical obscurities might act as a soporific.

*Ridiculous. Why torment yourself? One, it would never happen; two . . . it would never happen.*

*And you would not want that wound reopened.*

*Besides,* she answered herself irritably. Silently. *I don't have to want Anne to touch me. It is not about that. It would be enough, more than enough, just to . . . sit across from her, and talk.*

# 21

Her dreams said otherwise.

That was the problem with dreams. They were like toddlers, wandering off without your permission to areas you'd rather they not go. They stumbled with uncanny accuracy into your private effects. Why even have deep, cluttered storage areas if you couldn't stash things there that were not meant to be found? Flannery had learned over the years that Charles, in spite of being generally self-involved, had moments of unselfconscious intrusiveness, making a sudden unapologetic dive into Flannery's files or notebooks if he was hit by a bolt of jealousy. The safest place for Flannery to keep anything she wanted secret was in her own head.

But dreams could make their way there, finding what was hidden.

There was kissing; there was an embrace; there was, inevitably, a bed. Flannery tossed in hers, alone, on The Den's fourth floor, writhing in the stiff sheets as her night mind took her to places she had not agreed or planned to go.

There was a vibration beside her. A repetitive pulsing. It did not build; there was no climax; it simply continued, monotonous.

It was Flannery's phone.

'Hello? Yes?' she slurred into it, not yet awake, confused about where she was.

'Beauty!' sounded a hearty voice in her ear, like some character from a children's film. The goofy bear, or the friendly ogre. 'Were you sleeping?'

'Hi,' Flannery responded weakly, her head falling back down on the forgiving pillow. 'Yeah, I was. It's . . .' She pulled the phone away from her face and squinted in the darkness. 'It's one thirty here.'

'Of course. Fuck. Sorry.' Charles paused politely. 'Listen. I just got the most insane email from Gregory. You've got to hear this.'

'Really?'

And her husband proceeded to read aloud, from California, an email exchange between himself and one of the dealers at his gallery about the progress of the piece for Detroit. Issues had come up over the payment for the piece because of the city's bankruptcy proceedings, and the fact that the Institute was a publicly funded museum. Charles canvased these complex issues with a combination of insight, self-righteousness and his distinctive sarcasm, and Flannery could do nothing but close her eyes and let his humorous irritation and caustic protest sluice into her tired ears. She considered wordlessly how Charles's urge was a libido, of a kind: the unstoppable spilling of one's story, whether or not the listener was ready for it. For Charles it was at times simply the telling that was important, rather than any response.

'Crazy, right?' he said, at a stopping point. 'Can you believe this shit?'

'It *is* crazy,' Flannery agreed. 'I can't quite believe it, no. God.' She allowed an ambiguity she knew would go unnoticed on what she found unbelievable exactly: Charles's story, or

Charles himself. 'Listen, hon, I am kind of exhausted here, and I have to do this thing in the morning, I should probably go back to sleep.'

'Sure. Absolutely. Get some rest. You have a big day tomorrow.' Sometimes he spoke to Flannery just as he spoke to Willa. She wondered whether in some way a women writers' conference at an Ivy League university and a first-grade field trip to the aquarium seemed pretty much equivalent to her husband.

'I just wanted to catch you up on what was happening.'

'OK. Thanks.' Flannery yawned.

'Goodnight, Beauty. Sleep well.'

'You too. I love you guys.'

She placed the phone back beneath the bedside lamp, and tried to rediscover her interrupted dream. But the landscape had changed now; she was in a different city altogether; and whoever was beside her, in this episode, it was no longer Anne.

# 22

She knew now that she *wanted.*

The word went both ways: a want was a hollow that you hoped would be filled, and a desire, a pushing out toward the object of your affection.

Anne wanted Flannery. She had lacked her all this time, without realizing it; and now hoped to find her again, hoping the want was mutual.

Together the following morning they shared a stage, and a fluid group discussion. Anne hosted, or *moderated*, as though the job were a question of tamping down spirits if they ran too high, acting as a conversational thermostat. It was something she could do in her sleep and nearly had to, given the rough, wide-eyed night she had spent, tossed on squalls of uneasy revelation. It was complicated to want again. Thinking of Flannery next to her during the readings, near her for a few minutes at the bar after, where Anne had hoped she would stay longer. Back and forth Anne turned, between the hollow and the push, the emptiness and the hope to quench it. Sleep would have helped her accept this, but sleep was hard to find.

The panel went well, with challenge and argument, good-natured sparrings and playful riffs. There were a few good lines, one or two from Flannery, and afterwards there was the necessary milling about. A woman with a pink streak in her dark hair cornered Anne, in order to tell her enthusiastically, 'You're such a rock star!' She was a former student, now teaching.

Anne tried to deflect her excessive praise. 'Oh! Hardly.' She gestured at the women around her. 'These are the stars. I'm just . . . management. Or the roadie.'

The woman laughed, then pressed on with a story about teaching *The Awakening of Influence*, until Anne felt she had to stem the flow. 'Thanks, Alice. It's good to see you. Excuse me, though, I have to find . . .' She looked around, through the unimportant others, till she located her.

*Flannery.*

She stood still and graceful, a modest birch, her fair hair falling in a benign rain about her shoulders. Flannery had grown into her appearance and her shape. The structured navy jacket she wore complemented her slender height, her jeans enjoyed the lean length of her legs, and her crisp white shirt suited her fair skin. (Anne's skin turned grey and dull in white whereas Flannery shone.) Yet her discomfort at being looked at endured. She had the instinct to shelter her face, as though it were some vulnerable crop that might be blighted by the bad weather of an unwanted gaze, and so her hand swept frequently across her eyes, shielding them, in the guise of brushing phantom strands of hair away. She seemed distracted, staring at some unseen dust-miced corner of the lecture hall – just thinking to herself, even here, even with all the noise about her – but when she caught sight of Anne her eyes focused and widened. They locked with hers in relief.

'Hi! You were great,' Flannery said, moving closer to ward off interruptions. 'And you had, as promised, an even hand.'

'Thanks. You had some good lines. I liked what you said about chick lit.'

'The gum joke? Yeah, it's not new, but it makes people laugh.'

'It did.'

'You've got some serious fans,' Flannery noted. 'The lady with pink hair, for instance.'

'I feel for her. She's an adjunct here – underpaid, overworked, no job security.' Anne winced. 'She told me I was a *rock star.*'

'You always hated all that, I remember.' Flannery, the former fawner, was speaking levelly – eye to eye. Anne liked this. 'You didn't want groupies, even though you had them. My roommate Susan Kim would have taken a bullet for you. Plenty of people would've.'

They were standing so near each other that Anne felt Flannery's heat. Something deep in her loosened, though it was too soon to start swooning.

'Well, some fans,' Anne spoke softly, 'were more persistent than others.'

'Oh, I know.' Delicately, so as hardly to be seen, Flannery's fingers slid along Anne's lower arm, a caress that lit places in Anne she had forgotten how to name. 'Some fans' – Flannery's voice had both hint and humour in it – 'just won't *quit.*'

For a moment Anne could only utter a low guttural syllable of surprise. 'Yes,' she managed, with the small amount of breath she found.

'You've got to watch out for those ones.' Margaret Carter was edging toward them from across the room, and Flannery millimetred away from Anne, back to a more proper distance. 'Listen,' she said, in a voice almost empty of insinuation. 'I hope we'll get a chance to see each other more during the conference. It would be good to, you know . . .'

She let the sentence dangle, and as Anne collected herself,

she wondered, like one professional admiring another, or an old hand enjoying the new slant of the former protégé: when had Flannery learned such arts? She had had a couple of decades, of course, but still, here she was, keeping a person guessing, on the edge of her seat. Changing the pattern of Anne's breaths. Touching her in the right spot.

'To talk. Together,' Flannery finished, then in the same smooth movement turned to Margaret, who was smiling and congratulating them both on the morning, and Anne could only, catching herself, follow the younger woman's lead.

# 23

The writers were slated to spend the afternoon running workshops with students, but Anne was 'At Leisure', in *Stella Maris* parlance. As Flannery, unleisured, was led away; she cast a mock-longing look at Anne and put her wrists together in a gesture of shackling, shuffling her feet behind the other members of the authorial chain gang.

And suddenly in the emptied auditorium, here was Steven Marovic, not quite meeting Anne's gaze as he invited her to join him for a coffee.

'Steven!' Anne exclaimed, displaced for a moment. 'I hardly recognize you, without a Balkan sun overhead, or a deckchair at your elbow.'

He smiled, but the fact was the professor did look different to her here in New Haven; or perhaps it was now, these months later. It might have been having Margaret's overeager urgings in her mind. Or, more likely, it was that something within herself had, like a hand, or a page, turned over.

'Coffee!' Anne said with collegial enthusiasm. 'That is an excellent idea. It's my drug of choice, during a conference.'

Marovic smiled again with more confidence. Anne felt something in him relax. He seemed to have heard the timbre of her voice; so many messages between people were on an animal level. Wordless. Somatic. *We will not be lovers. You can stop worrying about that.*

At the nearby bookstore cafe, over espressos ('They were better in Dubrovnik,' Anne noted) Marovic popped his question.

'So. Anne. You're a reader of Rebecca West?'

She laughed, happily surprised by this opening gambit. 'Of course.'

'I thought so. You quoted her once, on our journey.' He coloured slightly. 'I am preparing a trip for the alumni group to the former Yugoslav countries – Croatia, Serbia, Montenegro, Macedonia – organized along the lines of West's itinerary in *Black Lamb and Grey Falcon*.'

'That's a brilliant book.'

'Precisely. I feel the same way.' He gave a small, formal nod. 'Might you be willing to lecture on it?'

'Oh! I see. Provide readings to go along with the tour? As on our cruise?'

'That's it.'

Anne leaned forward over the small circular table. 'You know, an idea came to me a few years ago. I wanted to think about West alongside another English writer, Sybille Bedford. They fascinate me: two women writers, English – adopted English, in Bedford's case – who wrote fiction as well as non-fiction, and who both wrote keenly and with total confidence about realms often considered masculine. The law. War. European history.'

Marovic looked pleased. 'There you are.' He brushed a hand over his hairless, contoured head, a phrenologist's fantasy. 'You already have the lecture started.'

'I do. I could begin writing it after this conference.' She closed her eyes a moment as an unrelated image, of a fellow conference-goer, fluttered across her mind. She recovered. 'Tell me, when would this be?'

'Summer 2015,' he answered. 'They must plan far in advance.'

'Of course. That sounds fine.' By then, Anne would be even more experienced inking them in, her holidays, her summers. 'But, Steven,' Anne exclaimed, with mock horror. 'This will be on land! No *Stella Maris* then.'

'No.' He shook his head ruefully. 'Trains, it will be. And hotels. Not quite the Orient Express, but. More like that.'

Anne gazed out the large plate-glass windows of the cafe to the New Haven sidewalk, where students walked, head down, buttoned up against the afternoon chill. 'Tell me,' Anne asked. 'Do the faculty on these trips sometimes bring . . . someone with them? A guest?'

Steven Marovic blinked his dark, spectacle-magnified eyes. 'Of course,' he replied suavely. He was a sensitive man; she had seen that on the *Stella Maris*. He had dignity, and Anne appreciated that. He knew what she was asking. 'It can be arranged.'

'I just wondered.' Anne returned her face to him, relaxed, as though the question had been idle, almost insignificant. 'I simply wondered.'

# 24

The metaphors flowed, vivid or pallid, the characters spoke in voices supple or wooden, the pastiches worked, or they didn't. A marijuana farmer struggled to adjust his attitude after the passing of permissive new laws; a teenage girl kept an exaggerated sex diary that was discovered by her brother.

Whose idea was it that writers should want to do this, sit around a formica table with a piece of fiction under discussion, like an anaesthetized body about to be opened up, probed, and rearranged? Flannery was the chief surgeon here, the one with authority to order the removal of a spleen or the draining of an abscess, but she was surrounded by second-guessers looking on during the operation, each offering an opinion on which words should end up in the biohazard bin of cuttings, and which ones might remain.

She had performed such procedures plenty of times; it was a job that hitched itself to the real work of writing the way an ugly trailer containing all the gear is hitched to a sleeker vacation vehicle, slowing the leader down, and changing its momentum. Across the nation, writing workshops had been proliferating along with global coffee chains, and probably by this point in the century every fourth American either knew how to make a skinny no-foam cappuccino, or had critiqued a fellow student's character sketch, one or the other.

On this afternoon, however, Flannery was finding it hard to concentrate. The students, she could not fail to notice, were strong – their work, if self-conscious, nonetheless sophisticated. There was some vying for position, as you'd expect, but they were a good set, easily corralled and hardworking, like obedient horses at some dude ranch resort, familiar with their tasks and capable of performing them.

A line from the sex diary story floated into the classroom air.

'*When they slept together again, it felt like refracturing a broken ankle that had just almost healed, and Kira felt weak.*' The author, a caramel-skinned woman with a pierced nose, stopped there.

'That's interesting,' Flannery said sleepily to her students. 'Do you think that works, as an analogy? Maceo, what do you think?'

A rough-edged young man, who looked like a singer in an indie band, offered, after some hesitation, his opinion. Flannery made a good effort to listen, or thought she did, only to realize after he concluded that she had missed most of his point and so could only nod sagely, ambiguously, without either agreeing with or challenging what he said. Flannery felt badly about this, as she aimed to do her work well, and to respond to the stories the students had brought to her, whatever cannabis field or suburban bedroom they were set in, however many taboos were broken.

*Go back to your rooms, everyone*, was really what she wanted to say to this group of people. *I think you're all very talented. You show great promise, honestly. Almost all of you. And I'm sorry to have to send you out early, but* – the apology would have been genuine, she would just have to hope they understood – *all I can think about is when I'll see her again.*

# 25

Later, Flannery was preparing herself for the dinner.

One love was drawing Flannery forward, accelerating her pulse, making her second guess every one of her own perceptions and intentions; but the other love troubled her mind too, waves of parental remorse breaking over her. She had left her daughter behind! She was three thousand miles away! This was another reason Flannery had avoided escape before: not all could be pinned on difficulties with Charles, some had been apprehension about her own internal scold.

Flannery called home, and reached her mother.

'Hi, honey!' Laura greeted her cheerfully. 'How are you?'

Her ear was filled with maternal warmth, and even from a little cell phone it was a restorative, calming substance. Sometimes you didn't have to dish it out; sometimes you could take it.

'Hi, Mom. Good, things are good. How are you guys?'

'We're just fine! You've caught us eating ice cream. It's *hot*. High eighties, even in the city! We stopped on the way back from school.'

'Really?' Flannery was so steeped in Connecticut, it was a challenge to conceive of California.

'Yes! We were just about to play a game of . . . Here, Willerby, it's your mom. Watch out honey, don't let it drip.'

And suddenly Flannery's mother's voice became instead her daughter's, saying, 'I got peanut butter *pretzel.*'

'You did? What is that – a flavour?'

'Yes!' Willa giggled in anticipation. They had a running joke about the crazy taste combinations concocted by the fancy ice cream place in their neighbourhood.

'Did they have my favourite?' Flannery asked. 'Salmon caramel?'

'No!' Laughter.

'How about jalapeño and coconut?'

'*No!*' More.

'Or maple bacon? . . . Oh wait, that's a real one.' Food conversation was, Flannery realized, all you really needed to connect with your child from a distance. It was not necessary to fill in details on where you were or what you were doing. When Charles was travelling and talked to Willa on the phone, he often chatted to her about his surroundings ('Guess what I'm looking at. The Hudson River!'), but Flannery had noticed her daughter only half taking in those details. It was the self-involvement of childhood: above all, the kid needed to know that you had not forgotten them. And that you cared still that they were getting fed. 'OK, so after the peanut butter pretzel ice cream, what game are you and Grandma going to play?'

'Rat-a-tat Cat.'

'That's a good one. I hope you win—'

'Do you have a message for Charles, honey?'

The switch back to Laura was unannounced.

'Oh, no. That's OK, I can try him direct on his phone.'

'He hasn't been here much today. He was out late last night . . .' She paused. 'I think he's working hard.'

Flannery heard the slight suggestion in her mother's hesitation, and chose to ignore it. 'But things are OK with all of you guys?'

'Really, fine!'

It was, Flannery accepted, the other reality. Things could actually be fine, without you. That was a whipsaw of motherhood: *Oh my God, they need me so much* flipping in a bereft instant to *Hey, everyone, don't you need me?*

'That's great, Mom. Thank you so much for everything you're doing. I'm glad it's working out.'

'Of course, honey. I just hope you're having fun there, talking about your books, seeing old friends.'

Flannery felt a deep plunge of gratitude.

'I am, Mom. Thanks.' She tilted her head back so that her eyes were on the white plaster ceiling. She breathed deeply, so she wouldn't cry. 'I am.'

# 26

At the Dean's Dinner, Margaret, or the god of seating charts, contrived to place Anne and Flannery adjacent at a long, rectangular table in a golden-lit oak panelled room that was every stereotype of Ivy League opulence. A mustachioed white man in a coal-dark suit gazed out sternly from a Reynolds-like portrait on one wall; across from him, a couple of racehorses, perhaps his, took the course at Saratoga Springs with grey oil smears for riders, each capped with a bright daub of colour, money green or social register blue. Alongside the table a broad ornate fireplace, last used decades before, suggested warm fireside conversations about the next senatorial race, or the nascent CIA, amidst gravel-voiced quotations from Caesar, or H.L. Mencken. *A bastion of power and privilege*: that undergraduate placard-rattling protest came to Flannery's mind again. Well, here it was. This was what a bastion looked like, up close.

'He reminds me of someone,' Flannery said softly, nodding at the off-black coated gentleman. Anne tilted her head.

'Really? Who?'

'I don't know. Murphy, maybe?' Flannery risked a joke that stretched back to the night their affair began, in the apartment of one of Anne's New York friends and eventually across the Murphy bed they folded down so that they could . . . spread out. After that first raucous night, 'Murphy' became a comic character in their romantic banter: sometimes a voyeur, sometimes an instigator, occasionally a figure of propriety or disapprobation. The face of the outside world, looking in at the illicit lovers. It had been a time before marriage equality, when caution was still the norm.

'I see what you mean.' Anne's gaze fixed on the painting, as if absorbing a provocative point of art history. 'He does bear a resemblance.'

First courses of fishcakes were delivered, hardworking Margaret gave another short speech (Flannery had to admire her reworking the material, like a glib stand-up), and then the dean himself stood, a tall, craggy figure with exaggeratedly large ears and nose, like a cubist sculpture. He opened with a charming anecdote illustrating his collegiate daughter's precocity and made a smooth, eloquent transition to the vital contributions made by so many women to the university, and his own and others' consistent efforts to bring more women onto the faculty, a delivery that sounded both rote and earnest. By the time they were on their pucks of peppercorned beef with dauphin potatoes, Flannery, while still punchy, could feel the social exhaustion that always waited just behind her rare moments of extroversion. At the table's other end Andi Chatterjee went into her famous imitation of Hillary Clinton, and the table gratefully stilled to enjoy it.

'That's very good. Very good,' the dean approved, shaking his head, chuckling, then told a story masquerading as a joke against himself which required him to describe the time he was invited to the White House to meet the then president.

White uniformed work-study students came back and forth to the table with cake and coffee. 'I did that job for a year,' Flannery told Anne. 'My senior year. Helping cater big dinners for guests, alumni, faculty. By this point in the evening I always just wished they would skip the damned coffee and retire.'

'Let's.' Anne leaned in. 'I'd rather walk, anyway. Wouldn't you?'

Wouldn't she?

*Wouldn't she?*

Flannery *ahemmed* into her water glass, which triggered a genuine coughing fit that eventually prompted her to say in a strangled voice to Margaret, 'I'm so sorry – I'm fine, I'm just going to step outside,' and then head out and down the steps into a blissfully quiet courtyard.

She coughed, recovered, waited.

Five minutes later Anne appeared, holding two coats. 'I made excuses,' she said, 'for both of us.' She held Flannery's coat, and as Flannery stepped into it, Flannery felt she was giving herself over to Anne, ready to follow her anywhere. Together the two women left behind the bastion and its privileges, and entered the city's sleek, black October streets side by side.

# 27

It was important, implicitly, for the walk to have no destination, so the two ambled around in gothic shadowed squares in the damp air trying not to know where they were going. They meandered up a quiet side street, along a busy, shower-slicked thoroughfare, then turned to walk along the top of the town's church-studded green.

In Flannery's circumscribed undergraduate years this area had marked the edge of Known Territory, beyond which the alarmist campus police warned freshmen not to go. When Flannery fell into her passionate days and nights with Anne, this green was one of many lines she crossed, as Anne's apartment lay on the far side of it, nestled in a student-free part of town.

'Your place was across there,' Flannery indicated, as if Anne might have forgotten. 'I knew this path so well.' She intended her tone to be jaunty, not maudlin, but feared it may have wavered.

'I used to worry occasionally that you'd get lost or stray, trying to find me.'

'I was pretty clueless, wasn't I?' Flannery was amused. 'You were worried you might have to come and find me in the pound.'

'You were adorable.' Anne stopped just beyond the rays of light cast by a park lamp. 'As I believe I told you, once or twice.'

'You did.' Flannery's hands were deep in her pockets. She shivered.

'*Flannery.*'

It was a statement, not a question. Anne's eyes were a fired emerald, her cheeks pale coral with the chill, and her lips pursed, as if she were about to speak. Or perhaps . . . not to speak. Anne took a step closer to her. She reached a hand out to hold Flannery's arm. And looked at her, and waited.

Then she kissed her.

There, on the green, in the dark, Flannery was met again by that perfect persimmon mouth. She had not known, had not anywhere suspected, how deeply she had missed it. A low moan moved through Flannery as she opened her own mouth, and self, to the kiss.

Borders dissolved. Passion blossomed, and heat took hold. Flannery forgot words and meanings. Her heart darted, a hummingbird. She took her hands out of her pockets and laced them low around Anne's back.

Flannery had forgotten this. The sensation that the base had just fallen right out of you, hollowing you out, leaving nothing but hunger within you and only this one person who could satisfy it. Your palms starting to press and fold. Remembering; and wanting to be reminded.

'Don't you have a room somewhere?' Anne asked, at a vibration so low she was almost inaudible. She grasped the lapels of Flannery's inadequate coat.

'I do,' Flannery replied, her voice hoarse. 'Let me take you to my Den.'

'So primitive sounding,' Anne said. 'I like it.'

# 28

Primitive or sophisticated; first lover or tenth; a Murphy bed or the rug in the living room or a luxurious hotel mattress with starched white sheets. It made no difference, finally. When two people came together who were meant to, the night and the meeting were elemental, and the trappings ceased to exist.

All that mattered were the bodies. And the selves.

It had been years since either Flannery or Anne had made love to another woman. They both discovered that it was not something you forgot. Their hands knew; their fingers found; their skins kissed too, along with their mouths, and everything became slick with this kissing. All that wetness, which seemed to have retreated into locked closets of grief or disappointment, was released again as they rediscovered one another. The first fondlings, whispers and hesitations turned over in the darkness into quickening breaths, heated holds, and that urgent mutual clutch. *Don't let me go. Don't stop.*

*I won't stop.*

Neither tried to turn on the lights. Neither was inclined to ask, or comment. They mostly communicated in the wordless calls of that kind of night encounter, though now and then they murmured each other's names in passion. And gratitude. And frankly . . . shock.

It had been a while since Flannery had stayed in the room while making love. Had it been years, sadly? Was she that far gone? She had gotten into the bad but hard to shake habit of being elsewhere while her body moved and manoeuvred with Charles's. It was not an evasion she was proud of, and she knew that a sense of obligation was not a great erotic motivation, but sex had seemed necessary to keep some level of domestic peace.

She was present with Anne, and this was the first shuddering revelation in touching her after all this time – that Flannery herself was there to do it. Wide-eyed, even in the dark, opening Anne adeptly, drawing on her younger self's confidence and that old, adoring knowledge she had long ago acquired. She was stunned that she still could be that person. Her hands befriended Anne's curved muscled shoulders, caressed those legs that could take on miles.

For Anne there was necessarily the shyness of being older than Flannery, a comparative whose former advantage had become – there was no way to ignore this – a liability. Where she had been proud of her body, she now had a nascent bashfulness, but the want she felt was intense and Flannery, this miracle girl, was not going to let age or ceremony stand in her way. Flannery was going to take her, and did, and Anne would lose her voice and her propriety in the orange light that came through the unshaded windows, sanctioning this union, forgiving them both their altered forms.

'It's still you,' Anne said, after a lush hour. She lay on her side, facing Flannery, her fingers resting on Flannery's arm. Flannery kept a palm close to Anne's breast.

Flannery closed her eyes, hid her face in Anne's shoulder, breathed the familiar scent of her.

'You're beautiful,' Anne added, speaking down into the tousled hair that fell over Flannery's ear.

Flannery lifted her head to look up at Anne's face. 'That's funny,' she said. 'You took the words right out of my mouth.' She brushed the folded back of her index finger along Anne's smooth cheek. 'I was going to say the same about you.' She touched her thumb below each of Anne's luminous green eyes, then gently kissed those loved eyelids.

'The words out of your mouth?' Anne was remorseful. 'Let me fix that. Here. Why don't you take them back.'

Anne found Flannery's mouth again, to make up for the loss.

They kissed, and kept kissing.

Kissing had always been the heart of it.

# 29

Later, Flannery could try to avoid clichés. There would be plenty of time for that afterwards: the reassembling of language and order. For these disorienting, reveried instants, her head could flood with tritenesses, and no one need ever know.

*It felt like it did the first time. It was as though they had never been apart, not for an hour.* This was not exactly true. Anne's body was certainly older and different to the touch, and Flannery's too, with a low scar across her belly from the caesarean, and the pouched slack of gymless days. But her sentimental heart willed it to be true, tried to make the years fold in like an accordion, as if the intervening history had taken place in a parallel universe, while in this one it was just the previous week that Flannery had slept with Anne in Albuquerque for what she had feared would be the last time, ever.

'My mind is filled with terrible songs,' Flannery confessed. 'I don't even want to tell you which ones.'

'No. Don't. It would ruin the moment, probably.'

'I worry about that too.'

The women embraced, their legs entangling, their breaths pooling and waterfalling together, purposeful rapids. Fingers in blonde or russet hair, lips on lean neck, palm along thigh, or pressed against a concave lower back.

There was a pause. 'It is true, though,' Anne said again, eventually, 'that in moments of strong feeling –' she brushed her lips just below Flannery's eye – 'it's hard to find words that are original.'

'All the sap rises. The sappy lyrics.' Flannery bit, very gently, Anne's shoulder. It was so sweet. 'You can't ever get past them to say something new.'

'"I love you is always a quotation."'

'Winterson!' Flannery exclaimed. 'That is a great line. Also, you know, she writes very well about ravishing redheads, with brilliant green eyes.'

'And Venice,' Anne diverted her. 'The need for webbed feet there.'

'How *are* your feet?' Flannery slid down along the bed to hold one, an overdue reunion.

'Mmm. Didn't you once promise something about "bringing me, unshod, to bliss"? Speaking of quotations?'

Flannery winced. 'I can't believe you remember that.'

'Oh, I could recite the entire poem if you like.' Anne raised her voice slightly. '"I'd like to pay your palms / the same favour that you pay these pages . . ."'

'Stop. Stop!' Flannery cried, placing her palm half over her lover's mouth to block the words. 'I was a kid! It was a love poem! You can't quote it back to me. Have pity. For God's sake.'

'"Searching them for grooves and images / and the secret signs of hunger . . ."'

'Seriously. *Stop.*'

'Just a minute ago, in the dark –' Anne's laugh was low, and contagious – 'you *didn't* want me to stop. Which is it? Make up your mind.'

'Oh, I've made it up already, sweetheart.' Flannery's answer came with her own laughter, which caught slightly on the emotion in the back of her throat. 'When I say *stop*, I only mean with the bad poetry. Otherwise' – she felt the heat rise within her again – 'please keep going.'

Time passed. *The earth moved.* That was another thing they said. All those people, the ones who had already said everything.

Eventually, after all that rush of pleasure, the women's songs of praise in midnight voices, they both felt the need to regain balance. They talked to each other in ordinary tones, as if they were friends, after all. Languid after-chat.

'I enjoyed Venice,' Anne said. 'But it was just . . . a city, in the end. It didn't seem the place of all those fantasies, and fictions. Maybe because of the heat, and the crowds. Or because I was there with my sister.'

'Patricia?'

'Yes.' Anne was impressed. 'I can't believe you remember her name.'

Flannery considered telling Anne that though other details fled from her mind – the name of the characters in *Middlemarch*, where she had put the car's registration renewal form, the date of Willa's school's benefit auction – a locked, safe file in Flannery's memory was labelled *Anne Arden*, and it had an extensive array of contents. That, and the one containing Willa's pronouncements and caretaking arrangements, were secure in Flannery's mind and incorruptible, barring a complete meltdown of the system. The fact was Flannery could still have given back to Anne a travelogue from a journey Anne took to Berlin in her twenties; an unpleasant tale about her mother's slapping Anne's cheek in fury at her backchat; or, a happier option, if for Flannery bittersweet, a story about jazz discoveries in New Orleans or a long walk in southern France

Anne had long ago enjoyed with Jasper. No doubt that golden couple had carried on travelling after Flannery and Anne had parted ways.

'Jasper and I went to Venice together, once. So it took some effort not to be swallowed by a wave of nostalgia.'

She startled at the way Anne had replied to her unspoken question. It used to happen years before, too, that kind of mind-reading.

'It's been two years,' Anne added, answering the next thought as well. 'Since we split.'

Flannery wondered how to respond. It would have felt coy to pretend she had not known or guessed about this. She wanted to seem sympathetic without being prurient, tactful but not feigning indifference.

'You didn't have to . . . erase him, I hope? Overwrite him?'

Anne paused. 'No. I wouldn't have wanted to. I thought of him, and missed him, but . . . it was all right.' She looked directly at Flannery as she said this, and even in the dim light Flannery could see the willed trust, the open gaze. Also, that in speaking the sentence Anne was trying to make it true. It gave Flannery a sharp feeling, something like pain.

'It's as we were saying before,' Anne continued. 'Grief is difficult to talk about too, in anything but the most tired phrases. It's all been said.'

Flannery kept her calm hands on Anne's arm. She considered asking more; but what was there to ask, really? Whether he left her, or she left him? Flannery could not see how it would help her to know, or help Anne to tell her. The openmouthed Internet had already blurted out the basics.

'He has children now . . . ?' Flannery's voice was tentative, and she avoided the clause that might have followed – *and you never wanted that.*

'Twins. Yes. With his French wife.' Anne regarded her fingernails, performed a small gathered moment of grooming. Her first nervous gesture.

They lay in silence. Anne's body shifted, she exhaled, and she grasped Flannery once, as if in conclusion to her story. However much more there was – and pages' worth, there must be – she would not speak more of it here, now.

Flannery held her lover, and held her tongue.

# 30

'I could do right now,' Anne said, yawning languidly, 'with a cigarette.'

'You still smoke?'

'No. I stopped. But I still smoke about once a year, and if I had one with me, this would be the night.'

Flannery had quit smoking right after college; it was like short hair, something that looked better on others than it ever had on her. Anne, for instance, had been brilliant with a cigarette, a sultry Marlene Dietrich, and over the years the scent of cigarettes had caused an occasional erotic flutter within Flannery, arousing as it did her sense memories of Anne.

'I wonder if college kids still smoke a lot.'

'In New York they do. Or they vape. But it's on the street now, of course, which takes most of the joy out of it. Standing outside in thirty-four degrees, with an icy wind – you have to be committed.'

'Not like lighting up over drinks at the Anchor Bar.'

'No.'

'Drinking the coolest drink – white Russians . . .'

Anne stroked Flannery's hair, as if she were a child. 'It was a cute choice. As if we were on a date getting ice cream sundaes or something.'

They were thinking of their first awkward drink together: Flannery stuttering and self-conscious, Anne's eyebrow raised perpetually in irony. Anne had sipped a cinematic martini, looking very sexy as she smoked, while Flannery made a haphazard stab at adulthood, ordering a sweet, heavily iced drink that would mask the taste of the vodka, so she might not gag.

Anne regarded Flannery now, narrowed her eyes, and took a drag from an imaginary cigarette, reenacting her seductress role. Flannery brushed a few fingers through Anne's deep auburn hair, then reached out to borrow a puff from it herself.

'I completely shocked Willa once,' she said, after faux-exhaling, 'by telling her, in passing, that I had smoked in college. You should have seen her face. It was like I told her I had robbed a bank.'

'Capital offence?'

'Definitely a blot on my reputation.' Flannery shook her head. 'You know. If she sees you throwing a yogurt pot into the trash instead of the recycling, she's going to call you on it. *The environment, Mom.*'

'She has standards.'

'Right.'

'But that's a good thing?'

'Well, it is, yeah. She's . . .' Flannery laughed, bashfully. She was not sure whether to continue. Was Anne curious about Flannery's child, really? Or did she view her as an impediment, a dull conversational detour?

'Go on.' Anne rapped her knuckles lightly on Flannery's arm, for encouragement. Flannery looked steadily into the lovely olive eyes, and didn't blink. 'Really?'

'Yes.' Anne nodded. 'You've told me a few stories about Willa, but I would have to meet the girl myself, to know her.' (Flannery's ears strained to hear whether Anne's conditional contained intention, or not.) 'So tell me about you. How becoming a parent changed *you*.'

Flannery wondered if she understood the question's undertow: what might have happened to Jasper, with his twins? She decided to be honest.

'I don't know. It improves you,' Flannery said. 'Willa's improved me, anyway. Not, Oh, I'm this better, selfless person now, just . . . becoming a mother strips out a layer of bullshit, of self-indulgence. I had too much of both. You can't really afford it, when there's a little person counting on you. She keeps me on my toes.'

Anne was attentive.

'And hypocrisies. We all have them – well, most of us.' Flannery made a face, to acknowledge that her former heroine might still be more perfect than the rest of the world. 'Willa checks me on mine. She's funny about it, but she catches me out. And because it's her, I don't mind. I check her on hers, too, of course. *No, you can't go to Esmé's fun ice skating party and then a month later not invite her to your birthday. Even if you're mad at her*. It's like we're in this project together: getting older, and learning, and trying to be decent people. Obviously, in years I have a head start on her. But not always in instincts.'

'Your voice is different, Flannery.' Anne's was suffused with affection – no jealousy, or sourness. She returned the gesture, brushing wisps of blonde out of Flannery's eyes. 'When you speak about Willa. You're louder.'

'Am I?'

'You sound more like yourself.'

How remarkable it was to be noticed. Flannery was not used to it. She was right, Flannery thought, yet how could Anne, not having seen her all this time, still know Flannery enough to see that in her?

'Thank you.' It was the only thing she could think of to say. Then she kissed Anne's eyes, one after the other, for the gift of seeing her. She drew Anne closer to her again, and slowly, surely, covered her, wordlessly, with the love that was flooding through all of Flannery.

All of her.

# 31

This lifeblood, lust.

Here it was again. The hunger to have this girl, Flannery Jansen, in her hands – thirty-eight! Yet still a girl – and that mouth on her own. Anne was stunned by the strength of it. This was why she had been so nervous, of course, the previous morning at home in her apartment, walking across Grand Central station, and on the train. She had not been sure if she was ready for this return.

It was startling to relocate her appetite. Anne had thought she might have lost it. Not that she had mourned its disappearance. Other desires – for stories, for a well-cooked dish, for a particular strain of music – remained, and if her libido had receded, as it was scripted to do at the age Anne had reached, where was the harm?

When she missed Jasper, as she did often, if with less intensity than in the first year after their split, it was not usually their lovemaking Anne yearned for. She felt keenly the lack of his conversation, his company, the way he held her as they slept, as though he was keeping them both from falling off the edge. His humour; their jokes. The couple knew each other's rhythms and preferences the way you know the route you take to work every day. That was the metaphor of long-term partnership –

the well-trod path. Their history was half her life. Jasper reliably gave her pleasure (usually first, he was ever the gentleman), and she fully enjoyed returning the favour, savouring his body as it aged and changed. Anne had retreated internally as Jasper moved ahead into his new life, and the few affairs she had had, while distracting, only confirmed her doubt that she would really know again that lifeblood, which had coursed so thickly between the two of them in their years together.

Questions about dating irritated Anne because the word was so anaemic, describing an activity that had mostly to do with assuaging your ego, filling the calendar so you would feel less alone. It did not seem related to the intensity of this midnight venture, the urgency Anne felt to find and touch every part of her former lover, and to open herself up to her in turn. A phrase of Cather's, *That breathless, brilliant heat*, came to Anne's mind, and if Cather meant it about the land and not a body, it was perhaps only because the Nebraskan had not known Flannery.

At seventeen, Flannery had been a pretty, tall, lissom young woman. (On a current campus, she would have been called *hot.*) She had not known her beauty, or even her own body, then. Drawn to her, Anne had unwittingly taken on the role of her deflowerer. A different person might have relished that naivety in Flannery, but Anne had not asked for the responsibility, nor understood she was assuming it until afterwards, when Flannery revealed that the fold-down Murphy had been her first sexual bed. The news dismayed Anne, and eventually became an element that distanced her from her desire. It was too much to be everything for this young woman: the first, the most, the older, the wiser. The teacher. Anne acquired surprising truths from Flannery too, as they both acknowledged, but ultimately the relational authority tipped in Anne's direction and the thing simply could not stay balanced.

Twenty years on, Flannery was calmer and surer, aligned with her own personality, rather than standing a foot away from it, willing it to be different. She had made peace with her intelligence, having less need to prove it, and had let herself be aware that she was pretty. She knew her humour, her extant moments of awkwardness, her imagination, and even her capacity for pain – both absorbing it and possibly inflicting it. Anne thought this might be one of the sources of her melancholy.

Anne could feel this woman's comfort with the contours of her character. There was no longer the air of striving and eagerness about Flannery, as though what was most important might be around the very next corner, and she had better just check; which had been charming, turning wearisome. At seventeen, eighteen, she had wanted so much, felt she had so far to go, and in her young passionate certainty had determined that Anne was the one to take her there. It was clear to Anne that Flannery had long since gone to many elsewheres on her own, and with others.

The years had, to Anne's eye, only enhanced Flannery's loveliness. Far now from that age of innocence, Flannery was marked with the blemishes of experience, which deepened rather than lessened her grace.

# 32

They lay in the referred urban light amidst a disarray of sheets and the half-leavings of clothes. Flannery was as modest as she had always been – her lean legs were tucked beneath the quilt cover, for propriety – but Anne, boldened, lay half-naked on the bed. She brushed a soft thumb along Flannery's jaw.

'You know, I'm not as much older than you as I was before.'

Flannery smiled at an angle. 'I'm catching up with you,' she agreed. 'I think that's a math thing.'

'Is it?'

'Yeah.' She moved her curved hand along Anne's thigh. 'It's all about proportion, right? How much of your life you've lived.'

'We can't know that. How long we have. Unless you've acquired other powers since we last saw each other.'

'No. But, you know . . . if you and I meet up again in another twenty years, I'll be nearly sixty and you'll be pushing seventy, and we'll be practically the same age.'

'Seventy! I don't plan to be around till then.' Anne shook her head. The thought appalled her. 'Besides, do we really have to wait that long?'

'You'll be great at seventy.' Anne heard Flannery sidestep the question. 'I'll be the one all wrinkled and worn out.'

'Ah, I think you're wrong there, babe. Age cannot wither you.'

'Sure it can. It already has.'

'Nor custom stale your infinite variety.'

Flannery tilted her head. 'It's nice of you to say so. Though you may be thinking of Cleopatra. Different lady.'

With a serious expression, Anne traced over the two grooves etched upright into Flannery's brow. Anxiety, or anger? Or anger caused by anxiety?

The younger woman made a rueful face. '*Exactly.* There will be a lot more of those. They'll be even deeper by then.'

'Cares of the world?'

'I've had a few. Then again, too few to mention.'

The worry lines gave Flannery's face a sorrow that had been absent years earlier, which added to her attraction, though it was hard for Anne to explain why. 'They're a sign of character,' she offered. 'Though I wish you had fewer of those cares. Dear girl.'

The phrase made Flannery look away, out the window, in the direction of something she had not yet described.

'Thanks,' she said, then concealed her face in the act of giving Anne an embrace, in the centre of which Anne's hearing picked out a brief muffled cry. Not, this time, of pleasure. Anne stroked Flannery's head for a moment.

'Another cigarette?' she pretend-offered, with sympathy.

'No, thanks,' Flannery demurred. 'I'm trying to quit.' She lay on her back, her hands clasped over her chest like a saint's, and stared up at the midnight ceiling. Anne lay next to her, companionably, gazing at the same hotel room sky.

'Charles is an artist,' Flannery said after a while, as if Anne did not know that already, and as if it explained a great deal. 'He can be difficult.' Her shoulders moved in a shrug against the pillow.

'He's done very well.'

'He has. Actually, he did one of the pavilions at the Biennale once. A long time ago, before I knew him.'

'Yes, I saw it. The year I was in Venice, with Jasper.'

'Really?' Flannery made a comic grimace. '*War and Peace.* I guess that piece divided people. Some loved it, some hated it.'

'Jasper rated it. I found it . . . loud.'

'Oh, did it have audio? I didn't realize that. I thought—'

'No, not actually loud, just loud, in making its point.'

'Oh.' Flannery laughed. 'Yeah, that sounds right. Charles is loud, and he does like to make his point.' She sighed, and Anne could see that one of the complicated emotions travelling across Flannery's face was, actually, pride. And why not? Marshall was successful, and his work was interesting (more so, in her view, than giant balloon animal sculptures, or divided shark tanks). 'He's finishing a piece right now for the Detroit Institute of Arts. Your old city.'

'Yes. I know.' They were bound to reach this point eventually. Anne braced herself. 'My sister works there.'

'In Detroit?'

'At the DIA.'

'Patricia – your sister – works at the DIA? You're kidding, right?'

'I'm not. She does.'

'Jesus. Patricia Arden?'

'Hanes. Her married name.'

'Patricia Hanes is your *sister*? Jesus Christ. I can't believe it.'

Anne gave her lover's shoulders a light shake. 'It's all right, Flannery. Don't panic.'

'It isn't all right. They're having . . . issues with each other, aren't they? Fuck.' She exhaled, a sharp snort of disbelief. 'I bet you've heard some stories about Charles.'

'I have,' Anne admitted. 'Occasionally, in the past month or two.'

'*Christ.*'

Anne lay on her side, and turned Flannery's head toward her; then held Flannery's cheeks in her own cupped hands. '*Flannery.* There's no point in invoking the deity. He has nothing to do with it.' Flannery's eyes were burning into Anne's with some kind of fear, or embarrassment – or perhaps guilt. 'Why does it matter?'

'He just . . .' Flannery was agitated. 'Charles manages to be everywhere. Even here! Even with you. There's no getting away from him.'

'I don't think he's actually here.' Anne made a jokey show of looking under the covers. 'Unless he's being very, very quiet.'

'You understand what I mean.'

'OK. All right. But he's part of you. Of course he's here.' Anne moved her fingers along Flannery's lean arm. To calm her – and to feel her, too. There was strength there. She was reminding them both.

'I didn't come all this way to talk about Charles,' Flannery said, though she seemed to hear the petulant note in her own voice. She allowed the calming to work; her face softened. 'I came out here, sweetheart . . . to see *you*.' Flannery moved to pull Anne closer again, but Anne, for a moment, resisted. She felt certain that this attempt at hiding was not one to indulge.

'Flannery, love.' For a moment Anne felt older again. The shower-how. The longer-travelled. 'Both are possible. You may have come all this way to see me.' She kissed that bonnie girl on either fair cheek, three times, as the Dutch do, in greeting or farewell. 'But you may also have to talk about your husband.'

# 33

Flannery had thought of Charles. Of course. If you had a husband, however unlikely or unimagined he might be, however often you argued, with whatever lack of recovery after, you did not forget him, just because you were thousands of miles away and in the arms of a woman you had always, impossibly, loved.

Flannery had turned her phone off so there would be no vibrating news or queries from California, but she knew that a reckoning lay ahead. Inside, and out. Even before the horrific coincidence of Anne's sister knowing Charles, Flannery had the sense of his being there in New Haven, with her. They were tied together. She realized that her sulky child-like blurt – *There's no getting away from him* – was not only true, but was supposed to be true. It would be wrong to fault Charles for that.

'Marriage.' Flannery stated the word, as though she could just deploy it and it would do all the work for her: of explanation, excuse, illustration. Celebration. Disappointment. 'Well . . . you know.'

'I don't.'

'No, I just mean . . .' Flannery winced, feeling the familiar potential for tactlessness. 'With Jasper, I'm guessing, you—'

'We never married.'

*Oh.*

'Oh.' That stopped her. 'OK. I guess I thought . . .'

Anne had never been one to fill up empty conversational spaces, even, or especially, awkward ones. Flannery had to make the effort. Find the words. Complete her own sentence.

'Well. That makes sense to me, actually.' Flannery resolved not to recede into one of her mumbling apologies. Not tonight. 'Maybe marriage is only for people who need the paperwork. The documents. Whereas you and Jasper' – this was risky, no question – 'didn't.'

Anne declined to respond to this speculation, asking instead, 'Is that why you and Charles married?'

It was one way to tell the story – *I got married because I was pregnant* – and because familiar, it was an easy narrative to hear, but a fuller truth was that Flannery herself had wanted documents, paperwork, binding. She could try to explain this, but Anne had never previously been very interested in Flannery's personal history, and Flannery's instinct at this late hour was that the evening, with all it already carried, could not additionally bear the weight of her exploring the way her parents' marriageless state might have led by a winding route to her own possibly reckless adoption of that legal status, that resolution, for herself.

It would be best to keep it simple.

'Yes,' Flannery said. 'Because of Willa.'

Anne found the scar low on Flannery's belly and moved her index finger along it, without commentary. This was where Flannery had been opened for Willa to emerge into the world, on the long night of Willa's birth. Charles had carried the infant first, as Flannery lay weakly on the operating table. Exhausted. And joyful.

Until now, Charles had been the only soul to know this altered body of Flannery's: at thirty-eight, having given birth to Willa, breastfed the baby for a year, worn herself out for several sleepless years over her care. Softer in places than she had been, more worn than she had been, more whole than she had been.

'Charles changed me,' Flannery acknowledged. Tears came to her eyes. 'And I did love him, too. Of course. Getting married wasn't just a . . . transaction.'

Anne nodded. 'You still do.'

Flannery pursed her lips, and almost laughed. 'All right, professor,' she sniffed, brushing the salt from her eyes. 'Yes. I do. He can be awful. He can be charming. I don't need to tell you all the details . . . But yes. Charles is under my skin. We share flesh and blood. It's . . . I don't know. *Biology*, for God's sake. Oh, you don't want me mentioning God. OK, then. It's life. We made a life together.'

'Right.' Anne had the expression of someone who has led the student to the anticipated endpoint. But her face was in shadow, and that could only be cast by her grief for Jasper.

Flannery moved impulsively toward Anne and embraced her. She held her very close in this quiet room, where they had already explored so much together; and this press now was not a sexual one but simply the seize of love she felt toward Anne, knowing that she was in pain, or had been. It was not, Flannery knew, a pain that she could heal, or solve.

'He and I . . . we're so different from you and Jasper.' How to put her thoughts into words? Flannery and Charles had touched each other, yes, but they did not reach each other. Anne and Jasper had always had a deeper connection. Hearts and minds aligned.

'How can you be so sure?' Anne's voice was low. 'You didn't know Jasper, or us together.'

'I met him once or twice. In Albuquerque, let's not forget.'

Flannery grimaced. 'But more than that – through you I knew him. It was as though he was always with you. I felt it.' Flannery knew she was walking a high wire here.

A silence stretched between them, and Flannery feared mightily that she had overreached, trod heavily on her idol's beloved toes. She knew better now than to try to amplify or fix what she had already said. She was capable of keeping quiet, too. At last, Anne spoke.

'Don't idealize, Flannery. It's a bad habit for a writer. Jasper and I . . . we were just a couple. Like anyone.' Anne took a breath, held it, then exhaled slowly. 'It was a beautiful system that we had, together. Then –' she opened her hands, as if releasing a bird, or to reveal a vanishing – 'it stopped.'

Flannery didn't answer. Was that all Anne and Jasper had been? There was no way to explain to Anne the grief this would cause Flannery, to lose the image she had held in her own darkness with Charles, of Anne and Jasper having created something uniquely pure and enduring. A different love. A truer one.

What picture would keep Flannery company now?

# 34

'I'm going to leave in a little while,' Anne said.

'You are? I'm sorry . . .' Flannery was bereft and distraught, until she felt the tender press of Anne's kiss. Their lips together spoke so much. Named this. Whatever it might be. Flannery was stirred again, and could imagine diving back in, but Anne pulled back slightly, brushed her fingers over Flannery's mouth.

'Don't be sorry,' she hushed. 'It's not the scandal it was, but I still think it best that I not be seen stepping out of the hotel with you in the morning.'

'Oh, I agree.'

'Besides –' Anne raised a suggestive brow – 'I have to introduce you.'

'To whom?' Flannery asked sleepily. Fatigue was sneaking up on her.

'To the *world*, babe. The one you're writing. Tomorrow evening. Remember?'

'Oh, that.' Flannery brought her hand to her forehead. 'Them.'

'I'm not even sure where to start.' Anne sized Flannery up. 'What are you – a memoirist, or a novelist?'

Flannery shrugged in mock apology. 'I guess I'm . . . undeclared.'

Anne issued a short laugh. It was an old joke between them, from the days of Flannery's undergraduate quandaries over her major. The two women had from the start enjoyed seeing many sides of any given word.

'Actually, I'm precisely nothing right now. I haven't been writing at all. It's –' Flannery tried to chuckle, as if to undercut what she said next – 'incredibly depressing. I don't even know what I'm going to read from, believe it or not. I don't have anything new.'

'Nothing? Really?'

'Just scraps. Ideas. Hardly anything written down. I don't have the time . . . or, you know, the heart.' The last word was all but inaudible.

'Well, tell me one or two of your ideas,' Anne said. 'Talk.' And, propped up on her elbows, she kept her gaze steadily on Flannery, until Flannery submitted.

'At some point I thought about writing for kids. Because of Willa, obviously.' She shrugged sheepishly. 'You probably think that's a stupid idea.'

'Listen – it's not as though I think of children as some lesser form of being, you know.' Anne's voice was tart, her manner feisty. 'They're people. They read. I once knew a child who liked to be read to from *How to Cook a Wolf*.'

'Really?' What was Flannery questioning, though – that there was such a child, who appreciated M. F. K. Fisher; or that Anne might know her, or him?

'Yes. He kept hoping, I think, that the book would turn into a horror story, or possibly an adventure, rather than a book about food. Carry on. What else?'

'Um. A couple of years ago I started writing this surreal, bitter story about a woman trapped in a royal family, in some unnamed European country.'

'That's unexpected.'

'Yeah. It turns out I couldn't pull it off. It ran out of steam.'

'There's no shame in that.'

'No, but there's no manuscript in it either.' Flannery hesitated. 'All right, last one.' She took a breath. 'Something in the marital comedy line.'

'Hmm.' Anne's scepticism was unmistakable.

'But dark,' Flannery clarified. 'Edgy. Otherwise, it will just be whining.'

'Dark how?'

'Murder!' Flannery exclaimed with delight. 'It involves murder.' She was sounding more confident now. 'I have a title.'

'Yes?'

'*Reader, I Murdered Him.*'

Anne did laugh. Flannery had forgotten how thrilling it was to make her laugh.

'Here's how it works. The narrator confesses to the murder in the first chapter, but then it turns out that so many people want to kill the guy – his studio assistant, his dealer at the gallery – that slowly doubt is planted in your mind as to who really did the deed.'

'So the victim is, as it happens, an artist?'

There was a pause, in the air of the small hours. 'Well,' Flannery conceded. 'I might end up changing that.' Her voice had humour in it. 'Anyway, all of this is in my head. None of it is on paper. I have nothing new on paper.'

'So read something old.'

'I'll have to. I'll probably just read from *Don Lennart*. I can practically recite passages in my sleep. It's a crowd-pleaser, leaves 'em laughing, which is good.'

'The novel you wrote is better.'

Flannery propped herself up with sudden alertness. Someone

– a smart person and an incomparably sharp reader, who loved Flannery (yes, these few hours had convinced her of that) – was speaking about her work.

'Do you think so?' Flannery asked.

'Oh, Flannery. Of course it is. You know that. It's sad and strange and gorgeous. *Don Lennart* is very good; but the novel is better.'

'The publishers didn't think so. It didn't sell half as many copies. They weren't pleased.'

'Willa Cather won the Pulitzer Prize for *One of Ours*, which became a national bestseller. It's one of her worst novels.' Anne shook her head. 'Don't make me start giving a Cather lecture in the middle of the night! There is an outer reality and an inner reality, and you know the difference.'

What calmness you felt within, when someone named a truth about yourself, one that you had scarcely admitted.

'Lately, I haven't always known,' Flannery said softly. 'But when you say that, I know you're right.'

'Don't forget that. Don't lose that compass,' Anne instructed her sternly. 'I mean it: *don't*. If you do, you're lost.'

'You're right,' Flannery said, wondering as she said it if it were already too late for her to make her way back.

# 35

A fitful dream about hands and mouths in an orange light. Her body being touched. That shattering relief.

A snowfall in a memory-blurred landscape; it might have been Michigan. Notes cascading diagonally across contrasting keys.

The half-awake jolt of a reminder, from the business department of Anne's brain, that she must send in a recommendation for one of her students seeking a fellowship. A recollection of Steven Marovic's Yugoslav invitation, and the seeding of a new bed of ideas. Such were the workings of Anne's predawn mind, after her dark walk back to her solitary suite, and a brief patch of sleep.

And the sensation of sore muscles, a salty aftertaste in her mouth, and a deep new vibration within her, or possibly the quieting of an old one. The body's bashful admission that it has changed, in being seen and held again by someone who loves you.

Someone you love.

It went both ways. Anne knew this now.

She loved Flannery. The heat of her humour, the salt of her intelligence, that golden fall of her hair; the life in her eyes and smile and how they riffed off one another. Her gentle voice, speaking softly and calling loudly, that mad paradox that was and always had been Flannery, timid and bold, apologetic and self-deprecating yet also knowing better than anyone what she truly had to offer a person about whom she was passionate. The ballad of Flannery's beautiful body, the deep breathless lyric of herself inside, that wet, untranslatable centre of her.

Anne loved her.

Yet the revelation need not disrupt any existing order. It was a discovery of something previously concealed, like one of Kepler's geometric harmonies, an aesthetically pleasing arrangement of the constellations. It had always been there. It served no cosmic purpose, was simply a good in itself.

The love between these two women did not refer to anything outside itself. Anne believed this: that the connection between her and Flannery had no bearing on Anne's relationship with Jasper. It never had. She did not fall in love with Flannery out of reaction against him, nor return to Jasper out of weariness with this very dear, and then very young, girl. If Anne loved Flannery now and still, it was not out of missing the Jasper who had left her, a man changed from the one she loved for twenty years. This love, here, came from Anne stepping forward into a future, finally. Stepping into this river, which was never the same twice. Jasper had for years shaped Anne's days, her travels, her work, her home. But Flannery also, Anne knew, having seen and held her again; Flannery was in her bones.

When would they see each other again? Five o'clock that morning had no answer to that question, though even sleep deprived, Anne knew this hunger within her would not just be forgotten, or stashed on a far-off shelf. Another twenty years must not pass. Not five, not two. The two women would have to braid their paths together more often. Anne planned to know Flannery in her forties, as her daughter grew older and became more of a companion to her, and the younger woman made whatever peace she needed to with her marital situation. When next they met, Flannery would be bolder, less beaten down. Might Charles Marshall learn about the women's university tryst? Anne had the sense the information would not prove integral to whatever decision Flannery and Charles reached.

Also, Anne wanted an encounter after Flannery had produced another book from her depths, not the shallows. She would do it. Anne could feel Flannery's heart fluttering, eager to escape – Anne had almost held it, it seemed, beating there in her palms as she and Flannery opened up one another. Once that heart was freed, Flannery would find her way back to her nimble, expressive fingers and the mind that animated them. All that was stored in her would be let loose on the page, and if that happened, she could not fail. Anne hoped to be able to embrace Flannery when that happened; to lie alongside her, go to those dark, wet places with her, celebrate her midnight self.

Their story must continue. The certainty seized Anne. That pattern would be there overhead, to be noticed and highlighted on however many starred alignments the two women were given to spend together, enfolded in one another.

And now, this October, for one more night, at least – Anne had the thought clearly, before subsiding again into a short, auroral catnap – for one more late, hourless night, they would touch.

# 36

'Hi, sweetheart.'

'Hi.' That dear far-off voice; she sang her 'Hi' in two syllables, a small songbird. Love bloomed, a colourful bouquet, in Flannery's chest.

'How are you, Willerby?'

'Fine.'

'Are you getting ready to go to school?'

'It's Saturday.'

'Of course, gosh!' How quickly Flannery had lost track. 'Well . . . Are you getting ready to *not* go to school?'

Willa half laughed.

'You've got soccer practice, I guess.'

'Mmhmm. Then Dad says we have to go to the lumber yard.'

'Oh. Well, that could be fun.'

There was a young yawn.

'You sound sleepy.'

'Yeah.'

Flannery cast around for something to say, finding it oddly difficult. She knew this little girl as well as her own hand – which she turned over to look at, as if for inspiration. 'So, sweetie, it's my last day at the conference. I'm doing a reading tonight, then I'll get on a plane back to San Francisco in the morning. I'll see you tomorrow! I can't wait.'

'Me too.' The girl slurped something. Cereal, probably. She sounded intent on eating. 'You want to talk to Dad?'

'Sure, sweetheart. You guys having fun together, you and Dad?'

'Uh-huh.'

Well. What did a telephone ever tell you? Charles kept suggesting a video call, but Flannery was sheltering behind her exaggerated technophobia to fend it off. In fact, she simply baulked at having to be seen, had an atavistic shunning of any lens; and perhaps feared the pang she'd feel, watching Willa at a distance. Wasn't that half the point of going away, anyway – to be out of sight? Was that advantage of travel really over now, in these years?

'Yeah, why don't you put Dad on. Have a good practice, honey. I love you.'

'I love you too.'

A short clattering, then: 'It would be easier if we just FaceTimed. Then we could all talk at the same time.'

'Hi.'

He grunted. 'So. Tell me: why can't soccer start at noon? What is the point of getting all these six-year-olds on the field so goddamned *early*?'

'It's a pitch, in soccer. A soccer pitch.'

'OK, but my point stands.'

'They schedule it to maximally exhaust the parents. It's a conspiracy.'

'That's what I thought.' She heard Charles tearing into a pastry like a bear. He chewed into the mouthpiece. 'So, how's it going?'

'Well. It's been going really well.'

'Terrific.'

'I've been talking with some people here, meeting old friends . . .'

'Excellent.' He swallowed. 'Listen, before we get Messi out the door here, I wanted to tell you. It turns out I have to fly to Detroit myself. Otherwise they're just going to fuck the whole thing up.'

'Is Willa right there listening?'

'She can't hear me.' Audibly Charles moved to a different part of the room. 'Anyway. I knew I'd have to go later, but I've got to make sure they get things right at this stage. Now.'

'It's not something Baer could do?'

'It really isn't. It has to be me. So I've booked a flight for tomorrow.'

'*Tomorrow?*'

'Yeah. It leaves around noon from SFO.'

'That's more or less when I get in.'

'Perfect! Maybe we can have a quick coffee at the airport before I board.'

'But who'll be watching Willa?'

'Couldn't your mom?'

Flannery closed her eyes. 'I'll ask.'

'You would not believe these people. Total amateurs. They haven't prepped the courtyard in the right way, so the installation is going to be a nightmare, and then they keep turning all the problems around on *me*, like they're my fault. This woman Patricia Hanes is such a fucking *schoolmarm*—'

'Charles. Can you please try not to let Willa hear you?'

'I don't mind if she hears me. She can know what these people are like.'

'Don't you guys need to go pretty soon?'

Her husband sighed, a deep, pastry-fed sigh of virtue and of duty. 'We do. Otherwise, you know, she'll get dropped from the starting line-up.'

'Just be grateful we're not the snack family this week. You'd have to be at the market buying nut-free granola bars and fruit roll-ups.'

'I just hope all this sporting frenzy is worth it. It better be Willa's ticket for getting into college, or I'm going to be really pissed off about the loss of sleep.'

Flannery sighed. 'OK. Look, I'll call Mom, and see what we can figure out. I'm reading tonight, by the way. I'm the headliner, supposedly.'

'Are you? Great.'

Was there more? Did Flannery want there to be more?

'Willa, Muffin,' Charles called in his stage voice, performing fatherhood. 'Have you got your stuff ready? Do you want to say bye to your mom? See you, Beauty. Knock 'em dead tonight.'

'I'll try.' Flannery said. There was a sentence formulating in Flannery's mind – *There's a friend of mine I saw again here, honey. I hope you'll meet her sometime. She's . . .* – but in the event, Flannery did not yet have to find the right adjective for Anne, as Willa was too busy looking for her pair of cleats to come back to the phone, so Flannery hung up and left them to it.

# 37

The quiet in her room after the call was so . . . quiet.

Flannery had a scratchy throat and tired eyes, though also a foreign warmth within her, and the sweet soak of memories of the night before. Indulgently, she called for room service. She was not ready to face a restaurant full of people.

Maybe, Flannery considered, Charles's need to travel to Detroit was a positive. Returning to San Francisco and enjoying a few days alone with Willa might be easier for Flannery than a simultaneous reunion with her husband. She might find a way, at some point, to speak that not yet uttered sentence to her daughter, about her rediscovered friend. Mother and daughter could play, lounge around at home, eat easy food. When Willa was occupied, Flannery could work. The prospect felt newly promising, somehow, to Flannery. Maternal loneliness did exist – people wrote and spoke about it more than they used to – but Flannery had a source of solace now, and it was not simply playing fictional reels in her mind of the life and love of a part-imaginary couple. The comfort would come from the woman herself. The solace was Anne.

At the door of her Den, Flannery gratefully received a silvered pot of coffee from a friendly, uniformed man, along with a basket full of carbohydrates. She poured herself a cup, then looked out at the morning campus through her window: spires and halls and geniuses. The university's buildings, ever improved and added to, were the recognizable elements of the institution, but, of course, it was the hearts and minds that made the place what it was. She drank, and thought. Flannery had always thought well here.

Flannery did not feel she was turning her back on Charles, even as she looked ahead with mute excitement to another night of recollecting Anne. This old, first love was part of the fabric of her self too, whether her husband had paid attention to the weave or not. Her wakeful hours that long night had brought Flannery back a piece of herself, replenishing some essence. (Physics again: adding substance to the beaker of her character, while taking no element out of it.) If Charles loved her – however he loved her – would he not want that for Flannery? Would he want her to be whole?

She replayed the amiable conversation they had just had on the phone, hearing Charles's assertive baritone in her inner ear. The relationship between herself and the man was more layered and resilient than she sometimes admitted. Did the marriage tie explain this? Flannery, a native sceptic on the subject, doubted it was the promises she and Charles had made at City Hall that united them; people broke those vows all the time without thinking much of it. Hadn't he? Hadn't she? In twenty-first-century San Francisco such promises turned rapidly into yet another set of ephemeral messages, like texts or emails – one more collection of overwriteable words stored in the boundless cloud.

If it wasn't the vows, was Willa the unseverable link between her and Charles? No doubt. From her life with Charles Flannery had learned for the first time that a child can actually connect two people. What a thought! Fatherless as she had been, growing up, Flannery had not been schooled in this obvious life lesson. As a girl, she had not been that bridge between Laura and Len – not, at least, until she wrote her book, which finally created a relationship, on the page and in the reading world, between her distant and estranged parents.

Flannery's coffee-warmed fingers twitched slightly.

She got out her notebook, sat at the broad desk with its university view, and started to move her blue pen across the green, lined field open before her.

*Why write these pages when she'll never read them?*

She looked at the sentence. Didn't everything reduce to grief, finally? It was first and last and security, that familiar deposit. I love you, I miss you – weren't those always the essentials?

She scribbled notes to herself, the start of an authorial conversation. She might not use them, but they got her mind working again.

> *You did not find the love you expected, your beloved never became your beloved, your husband and you spoke different languages, the texture of your affections was complex and surprising, sometimes even to yourself. Especially to yourself. You were heartbroken when she died, and you said so.*
>
> *You lost people.*
>
> *You found people.*
>
> *One person in particular was there all along, though you had not allowed yourself to know it.*

Anne had for all these years been in Flannery's melancholy meandering mind, but mostly as a character. Flannery had not expected her to become real. With a wit she had not known she still possessed after some wearying and tumultuous years,

Flannery had nonetheless engineered this passionate reunion, come here, to this important place, to find her Anne. And having found her, she did not intend to lose her again.

Flannery had the morning free, and she got to work.

# 38

*Coda.*

Late that evening, they were entwined again. They were going to give each other one more night entire. Anne ceased to worry whether she would be seen emerging from The Den, and Flannery, knowing she was already going to be flying home exhausted and exhilarated, figured the two states would cancel each other out so let go of worrying about what shape she would be in on her return. While she was alive, she would live.

They came together, then slid apart, they lay in lamplight and moved in darkness, they were silent and inarticulate or they were wild and vociferous, and then relaxed together afterwards, talking like friends. There was a miniature infinity of emotional shades to enjoy on this last night, so they followed the rhythms of one another's comedy or solemnity, chattiness or quiet. They were wet and hungry, then sticky and sated. Their breaths sped, then slowed. There were tears once – Flannery's. She didn't want to talk about it, so they didn't.

'What made you write that piece?' Anne asked Flannery at last, during a conversational stretch. 'It did not sound like *Reader, I Murdered Him.*' Anne moved her fingers through Flannery's thick blonde hair.

'No. Well spotted.' Flannery tilted her head back, savouring her lover's hold.

'I respect the mystery of the creative process, and all that,' Anne clarified. 'I just wondered. It wasn't one of the ideas you mentioned before.'

'No. It's new,' Flannery said simply. 'It happened to someone I know. Losing someone she loved, a great deal. That's all. People cover the death of husbands and wives and parents and children; but there's not so much written on the death of friends. I don't know . . . the lines just arrived in my mind.' She answered the hair gesture with a lick of Anne's neck.

'Inspiration.' Anne inhaled. 'Like a train emerging out of the mists.'

'Just like that. A train. A feather falling. The muse. Who knows how it works exactly?'

Flannery looked at this woman with the wildly green eyes, whose beauty she had known since she was old enough to board an aeroplane alone, and set off thousands of miles to break new ground. Flannery touched Anne's arm lightly, a small, familiar gesture – a wordless reference to the fact that they would, somehow, keep alive this warmth between them.

'The muse,' Flannery repeated. 'That's you.' She cupped that elbow, the tenderest intimacy, in her palm.

Anne flushed. 'I don't mind being a muse,' she said. 'In fact, I'm flattered by the idea. But . . . I want you to promise me something.'

'Anything. The moon. The stars. Name it.'

'I'm serious.'

'OK. I'm serious too. What?'

'Don't,' Anne asked, from a place deep within her, 'don't turn us into a story. All right?'

'Not another erotic memoir?' Flannery kissed Anne's shoulder.

'Not another erotic memoir. Not a *roman à clef*, wherein clever readers can guess the real players. And not a long, confessional poem published in some obscure literary journal. None of that.'

Flannery considered this.

'You don't want us on the page at all?'

'I don't.'

'You want this kept just between us?'

'Just between us.'

Flannery thought of a story she could tell, or choose not to tell. She thought of the book she was next going to write. She thought of the years-long love she had had for this person lying next to her, and the importance of agreeing to her request.

The pact was sealed, as was so much between them, with a kiss.

# 39

## PAGES FOR HER

Why write these pages when she'll never read them?

Still.

I had to try, at least, at last: after the dust to dust had settled, the ashes gone back to being ashes. Language, the now voyager; it's the only traveller that makes it across that border, as she of all people knew. Pushing its dark boat back and forth between worlds like Charon in the legend. She dealt in words, they were the stuff she handled, and that's what her friends have left to offer her, apart from the occasional fistful of pretty flowers.

The Serbs eat food by the headstones of their dead. They picnic there, for companionship. The Japanese leave food or drink for their ancestors, so they might have a bite when everyone else has gone home but the foxes, who sneak across from hell to uproot evergreens planted on the grave by the deceased's beloved. Some mourners build pyramids. Others launch funeral ships, laden with goods. Jewels can be placed in hollowed eyes to burn undimmed, though without the humour those eyes had in life, as they caught the world's jokes or pretensions. Children are given supermarket bouquets to leave as a mark of respect; the buds may wilt but the plastic wrapping will endure, immortal. A writer's fans deposit pencils in a cemetery cup. Visitors place a button or a tiny toy atop a headstone.

It's our shared urge to try to fill the fearful new emptiness with substance or with sound. The symbolic lyric of a flower. The power of the dirge. A voice crying, or murmuring:

I miss you.

I love you, and I miss you.

I don't speak to my dead, and my dead don't speak back. I've never had the art. They stack up, inevitably. It's the order of things. One person dies, then another, and on it goes. The lost parent's lost parent; the college lover, felled by a vicious illness; the doomed and moody cousin. I always meant to talk to her more, and now it's too late. All I can do is turn half sideways, no longer facing them, and fill my notebook.

Take a setting, seize it. Find a piece of her spirit later, elsewhere; cherish it.

There are lions and there are lionesses. She knew this, too; it was her territory. The lion is admired, he is the figurehead, it is his profile drawn and reproduced by artists and designers and it is his roar we hear across the bush, or the overcrowded wilds of civilization. The lions are superb. They are tawny and brilliant. You need not search for royalty references to make sense of these creatures, as our tinsel human kings are so small next to those dramatic animals, but if it comforts you to do it then, yes, certainly, call them kings.

Just don't ignore the lionesses.

The lioness is better practised at camouflage than her mate. Knows more about hiding. You might mistake her relative slightness, or the green stillness in her eyes, and it's possible that you won't at first sense her lean and muscled strength because she's quieter with it. Her feline beauty, inevitably, will distract you. Don't let it. Know that even as she paces the city streets she has that veld in her veins and fierce heat in her bones; she's never lost her sense of scale or her feel for the night's thorough darkness, or the hunger that goes along with both. She knows that the cooling dead are only ever a moment's open-jawed pounce away from the hungry living. She can be ravenous, and she can run for miles. Don't think you'll catch her. Be satisfied if you can breathe beside her for a while, unharmed.

Flannery read for a while. She was on a stage, not a place she had been for a few years, and was unused to the squint-inducing lights and the adrenalined alarm of seeing faces arrayed below her. Before she had gone up she had had an acute hit of nausea, and pressed her left hand to her stomach to quell it. She thought of trying to locate a particular face in the crowd, but knew she had to do this without reference to anyone else. She was on her own.

Yet once she began, her voice strengthened and Flannery let go of everything else: anxiety, pride, doubt, ambition. It was the start of a narrative, just the start. A woman had a friend she loved, who died. She had been taken cruelly, and too early. Other loves and loyalties would come into the plot as the tale unfolded. It was too early to say where they would lead. The words had begun, she was hewing the story out from the rough rock of the blank page, and Flannery intended to watch them, use them, to see what form finally emerged.

She did not leave the crowd laughing. She read the just-finished passages aloud for her allotted half hour (a little less, to be modest), and left the audience serious and alert, themselves a little ravenous, wanting more. The people who listened to

Flannery, mindful of their own griefs as she read, wanted to know from her story – this is what people come to fiction for, after all – what to expect from their own lives. How would it work out? Where would they find comfort? When would they recover?

Flannery knew when she looked up afterwards, coming back into the world around her again from her dream, that this was where she would live for the next while, in her imagination. That landscape, that voice. Those people. That book.

She would go back home to California and write it.

# Acknowledgements

I was younger then.

I am lucky in my friends. They're brilliant.

I'm grateful to my wonderful family.

I miss the people I've lost.

My agent and editor have shown great faith in this story, and with their astute readings and suggestions have helped me make it a better book.

The faults are mine.

My kids give me heart. Also, they laugh – if not necessarily at my jokes, at other people's jokes, and that keeps everything going.

Love is the best thing.

Thanks.

**Now you've read *Pages for Her*, why not go back to the beginning to *Pages for You*, the story of Flannery and Anne's first, long-ago love affair . . .**

# Pages for you

When Flannery Jansen arrives at university, she is totally unprepared for an encounter that will rock her existence. But when she comes across Anne Arden in a local diner, Flannery falls dramatically and desperately in love. Flannery is quickly embarrassed in the face of the older woman's poise and sophistication, and under the gaze of those impossible green eyes, but slowly their paths intertwine, and soon Flannery becomes Anne's eager student in life and love.

'A love letter written for a lost lover . . . mesmerizing'
Helen Dunmore, *The Times*

'Candid, fresh and vivid'
*Sunday Telegraph*